LIVING A LIE

RACHEL SAN
ORLY KRAUSS-WEINER

Literary adaptation: **Orly Krauss-Weiner**
Literary editing: **Amnon Jackont**
Proofreading: **Nitsan Ben Avraham**
Translation and linguistic editing: **Yron Regev**
layout: **Marzel A.S. — Jerusalem**

**Printed, digital and English versions of this book
can be purchased online at the book's website:**
www.living-a-lie.com
**As well as in bookstores around the country,
and as advertised on the book's website.**

**You can also find us
on the "Living a Lie" Facebook page.**

Contents

Chapter 1

"Itay!"

I emerged from the depths of the swimming pool like the Loch Ness Monster. I grabbed the ball, threw it as far as I could and shouted, "Catch!" Surprised, Itay burst into laughter and waded his way to the ball using his floaters. And all this happened just a few moments after the tears had come unannounced, just like that, on a sunny Saturday morning, as I was sitting by the children's pool trying to relax after all the ball games had exhausted my energies. What else could explain the sudden tightness in my throat as I watched my son jumping up and down, having fun in the water? But whatever the reason, I knew it was only a matter of seconds before the errant tears would come flooding out.

They were coming at the worst possible moment, threatening to ruin my son's happiness on this lovely day. In the past, it would only have taken a brief moment of silent brooding for Itay to notice my mood, wrap his little arms around me and ask, "Why are you sad, Mommy?" How could I tell him? How could I not be sad when our little family had broken apart when Itay was only three-years old?

When he was born, I was convinced I would give him brothers and sisters in just a few years, and together, we'd be a warm, happy family, just like the one I had spent my own childhood in. Back then, I could never have imagined that my son's father, the supportive, appreciative man I had married with so much love between us, would change so completely. Sometimes I think a woman can see the true face of the man beside her only after marrying him, but by then, it's too late.

I couldn't possibly tell Itay all that. So, I always smiled and said, "I'm not sad at all, Sweetie. I was just thinking about how much I love you. More than anything in the world." Then Itay would press his small body very close to me and say, "I love you more than anything in the world too, Mommy." And when he wrapped me in his childish hugs, the happiness in my heart made me smile. He had always been able to delight me with that magical innocence of his.

Either way, crying had never been an option for me. Not during all the months of child custody discussions, mutual allegations, and nervous discussions with the lawyer. And not during all those months leading up to the official separation. I had never, not even once, considered the option of crying, not even when I had been alone in my bed. I believed crying wouldn't solve anything, all it would do was make me feel weak — and that, I simply couldn't afford.

But I should have known that nothing in this life conforms to the plans you carefully make. Not even the damned tears that decided to well up in my eyes and the lump that choked my throat with the worst possible timing — in a swimming pool, right in front of my son's cheerful eyes. The only thing I could do to prevent the tears from bursting out was to slip into the water and swim towards Itay. That way, if the worst came to the worst, I could always blame the chlorinated water for giving me such red eyes.

"Excuse me," I suddenly heard a masculine voice. "Are you the mother or the babysitter?"

Turning, I saw a man with European features and a baby face. He was tall and muscled, his brown eyes engulfed me in a kind of heat I couldn't explain. I liked his swimsuit too, light-blue boxers that brought out his tan. I forgave him for the lame pick-up line and answered, "Of course I'm his mother."

"Please forgive me if my question seemed a little inappropriate," he apologized quickly. "It's just that you look way too young to be a mother."

"All right," I allowed myself a smile. "You're forgiven." I looked around. "And where are your children, may I ask?"

"Over there," he pointed at a water slide packed with children. "They wore me out, so I sent them to play by themselves a little. I'm Razi Zonenberg, by the way." He extended his hand.

"Pleased to meet you. Nicole," I replied and shook his large, warm hand.

"A lovely name." His smile broadened. "Were you born here in Israel?"

"Of course," I replied.

"You live here in the neighborhood?"

"Yes." I pointed at the row of buildings towering over the Country Club's fence. "Right over there."

"And what do you do in life?" He seemed determined to find out a lot about me in the shortest possible time. "A fitness instructor perhaps?"

"I wish, but not even close," I laughed. "I'm in television."

"Like a broadcaster?" he said.

"No! Not even close again, I'm a CFO. I spend most of my days in an office. No time for fitness, I'm afraid."

"Well, I couldn't tell," he replied running his brown eyes up and down my exposed body, which was barely covered by a leopard-print bikini. "You look amazing, and the energy you have for your son, playing with him like that, well, it's just awe-inspiring."

"Thank you," I muttered. I was embarrassed by his words. I turned to look for Itay, who, at that moment, ran up to me, his face full of laughter and smiles.

"Did you see that, Mommy? I swam the whole length of the pool with the ball in my hands!"

"That is just amazing, sweetheart." I leaned towards him and held him in my arms. "You're the champ, you know that?"

"So, can the champ have some ice cream?" he asked enthusiastically.

"Of course he can, but only after lunch," I said patting his head. After my divorce, and despite the unavoidable guilty feelings, I had made a firm decision not to spoil my child too much.

"Oh no!" Itay looked deeply disappointed. "Does that mean we have to go home now?"

"No, peanut. I brought you some sandwiches and cut vegetables," I told him, smiling.

"There's a restaurant here." Razi, who had, until then just been standing behind me, listening quietly, suddenly decided to interfere. "Why don't we all go and have lunch together with my children?"

"Who's he?" asked Itay suspiciously.

"I'm Razi," he smiled at Itay. "And who are you?"

"Itay," he replied, a little less hostile, but still reserved.

"So, what do you say, Itay? How about some chicken fingers and fries instead of a sandwich and cut vegetables?"

I gave Razi an angry look. My previously positive impression of him was starting to wear off. Who did he think he was to interfere so bluntly with my son's diet, offering him fat-saturated and non-nutritious foods like chicken fingers and fries? As a father of small children, I'd have expected him to know that just wasn't right, especially after he'd heard me refusing Itay's request for ice cream before lunch.

"Yeah!" Itay cheered happily, and before I could utter a word of objection, Razi's little son and daughter showed up next to us. They were much less enthusiastic about the idea of going to the restaurant.

"I'm not hungry," the girl twisted her face into a grimace. "Come slide with me, Daddy!"

"Yes, yes, come slide with us." Razi's son joined in with his sister and started pulling him by his hand. Razi looked at me with an apologetic expression and winked. I didn't really understand what he meant by the wink and, honestly, at that moment I couldn't have cared less. I had to rescue myself, and my son, from the mess in which Razi had so irresponsibly entangled us.

"If you don't want a sandwich and cut vegetables, we can just go and have lunch at home," I suggested to Itay who looked at me, his face glum. "We brought food from Grandma's yesterday, remember? And we have Cornetto ice cream in the fridge."

"All right," Itay muttered unhappily. "But can we come back to the swimming pool after that?"

"Sure we can, sweetie," I stroked his head, knowing he'd fall asleep right after lunch, as always.

As we left the pool, I stole a quick look back at the waterslide, but couldn't see Razi there. 'It's probably better this way,' I thought to myself. 'It's a little early to be allowing another man into my life. Besides, he's got too much nerve. So what if he's charming? That doesn't give him the right to act in such a domineering way.'

By the time we got home, I had almost forgotten all about Razi Zonenberg.

*

The following day, as I was taking a short break from a board meeting, Tzipi, the CEO's secretary, told me that a man named Razi Zonenberg had been calling to speak to me. I didn't understand who she was talking about at first. When I finally remembered, I told her I didn't have time to accept any calls. I tried to hide my surprise that he knew where I worked.

"If he calls again, don't transfer the call," I said, my expression blank, and I went back to the meeting. That was the last thing I needed, calls from admirers in the middle of board meetings. Screening him would be the sensible, the right thing to do, before anything else happened.

"That Zonenberg guy's called two more times already," Tzipi announced at the end of the board meeting, as I passed by her on my way to my office. "You must have made quite an impression on him!"

"I guess so," I muttered through clenched teeth, and walked away quickly. I knew my colleagues' eyes would be drilling holes in my back. From the moment word had gotten out in the company about my divorce from Danny, all the single men had started betting, behind my back, on who would be the first to conquer me. I heard it all first-hand from the company's legal advisor, who had told me all about it in a condescending, righteous tone. But I didn't really need her to lecture me. All through my career, I had been careful to keep my personal and professional lives separate. I always wore tailored pants, buttoned shirts, and flat shoes to work, though I have to admit, I liked my heels high as much as any other woman.

I felt flattered by the fact that Razi had already called three times, but my work as the TV channel's CFO was so demanding that I had no time to think about it, or answer his calls. I was always busy solving complicated problems that constantly piled up on my desk.

At four in the afternoon, Tzipi, the secretary, called again and said rather nervously, "I'm sorry, Nicole, but that Zonenberg man is as stubborn as a mule. He insists he has something important to tell you…" I heard her take a quick breath. "… I'm putting him through."

Before I could object, I heard a cheerful, masculine voice at the other end of the line, "So, I finally managed to wear her down, huh?"

"Definitely," I answered gruffly. "What was so important that you had to talk to me in the middle of work?'

"Only that I really enjoyed meeting you yesterday at the pool." His voice bubbled with cheerful charm. "And… would you like to grab a coffee with me sometime?"

"Well, I have very little time, at least at the moment," I declared impatiently. "I have another meeting starting in a few minutes."

"How about this evening, when you have a little more time?" he insisted. "In fact, how about eight o'clock at *Café Petite* in the neighborhood?"

"All right," I replied, allowing my impatience to show in my voice. Tamar, the content manager, had walked into my office and I really didn't want her getting a whiff of the content of my brief conversation with Razi. I'd been noticing, for a while, how jealous she seemed to be of my senior position. True, I had secured it at a relatively young age, but I had worked hard to earn it, and had proven my skills in every way since, even though working so hard for such long hours had damaged my relationship with Danny, my ex.

Embarrassed by the situation, after Tamar left my office, I quickly agreed to meet Razi, just to get him off the line as quickly as possible. I sat for a moment with my hand on the phone, wondering if I had made a mistake. I realized that even if I had, I had no idea how to fix it. I barely knew the man, and from the little I did know, there was no way I could look him up in the phonebook and find him among all the other Razi Zonenbergs out there. I shrugged and put him out of my mind.

It was only when I got home at seven-thirty, tired and famished, that I remembered I had agreed to have coffee with Razi at eight. *'If only there was a way for me to call and postpone,'* I thought. *'But I don't have his number, so I guess I'll have to go.'* The thought made me feel curiously submissive — which wasn't entirely unwelcome. To be honest, there was something flattering about the energy Razi had invested in his attempts to find me. How else could I explain the fact that I found myself pleading with Itay's babysitter to stay with him for another two or three hours? I got ready with lightning speed and kissed Itay, who was already lying in bed.

"Where are you going, Mommy?" he pried.

"To a meeting, cutie." I stroked his hair. "But don't worry, it's not going to be long and I'll be home in no time."

"Who's going to tell me a story, then?" He gave me a demanding look.

"Shani." That was the babysitter's name. She was a nice, young university student studying humanities.

"But I like it better when *you* tell me my bedtime story," he insisted. He put a tiny note of wheedling into his voice. "Do you have to go to the meeting?"

"I do." I said firmly. I hugged him and felt my heart ache. I was already regretting being so rash in agreeing to this 'date' with Razi. *'Is that what it is,'* I wondered, *'a date?'* Until that day, I had always been careful to coordinate my few evening meetings so they fell on the nights when Itay slept at his father's.

"Shani is a wonderful storyteller," I said, when I sensed the resistance in his slender body. "Besides, you look like you'll be asleep in five minutes anyway."

"All right, Mommy." He released me from the hug. "But promise you'll come back quick."

"I promise, my princeling." I smiled and rose from his bed.

The café was quite full when I walked in at eight-fifteen. People were sitting in groups and couples at the carefully-spaced tables. Razi was the only one sitting by himself in one of the corners. He was watching the entrance door and, when he saw me enter, a smile lit up his eyes and his entire face beamed with pleasure. I stifled a sigh and smiled back.

Walking towards him, I could actually feel his eyes stripping me, despite the fact that I was wearing only a shabby pair of jeans and a simple white t-shirt, which constituted my usual after-hours leisure time uniform.

"Nicole, you look even more amazing than you did at the swimming pool!" he said as I reached him. He half stood and, taking my hand in his, drew it to his lips, kissing it gallantly.

"Thanks," I said, "you don't look so bad yourself."

Razi was wearing a pair of faded jeans and a black polo shirt that made him look even younger than he had at the swimming pool. I estimated him to be approaching forty, but only because of the flashes of white at his temples that added a sexy edge to his appearance.

"I'm so glad you're here." His beaming gaze engulfed me in warmth as I sat in front of him. "I was beginning to think you were going to stand me up."

"Sorry, it's just that I got home a little late, and my son wanted some extra attention."

"Well, my kids have their noses stuck in the television this time of night," he said. "They don't even notice if I'm there or not."

I subdued the sudden urge to tell him it wasn't very educational to leave your children in front of a television just so you could have some peace and quiet. Instead, and with a sense of surprise, I found myself wondering about his marital status, which seemed, somehow, important. I had assumed he was divorced, seeing as he'd invited me on this date at the neighborhood café, but I thought I'd better ask just to be on the safe side.

"So, what's your marital status?" I asked bluntly.

"Free as a bird and owing no one anything!" he

declared, and waved his hand to flag the waitress. "What would you like to drink, beautiful?"

"Actually, I wouldn't mind having a bite to eat, too," I replied. "I barely had time to nibble on the traditional donuts they always provide at board meetings."

"Of course, order whatever you like," Razi said expansively. "They have some excellent salads here. I recommend trying the salmon and cream cheese bagel."

"I'll have the Niçoise salad and a grilled cheese sandwich," I told the waitress after briefly studying the menu. "And a latte and mineral water."

"And I'll have a salmon bagel and a double espresso," Razi told her, and then to me he said, "You made me hungry again, although I had a business lunch meeting with a couple of Russian oligarchs who ordered piles of the most expensive dishes on the menu." He grunted. "And you know how it is with those guys, you can never say it's too much, because you risk insulting them. That's just the way it is with the *nouveau riche*."

"What are you hanging around with Russian oligarchs for?" I asked him in genuine bewilderment. Up to that point, he hadn't struck me as the type of man who would spend time with such vulgar characters, or so I imagined them to be from the little I had read and been told.

"I was trying to interest them in a business investment," he said offhandedly. "As a CEO, I have no choice, I have to meet with investors, even when they're not to my liking."

"CEO." I echoed. "What company are we talking about?" Despite my initial reservations about being there with him, I discovered I was interested. I realized Razi had divulged very little information about himself, and I was definitely intrigued.

"High tech," he replied curtly, and changed the subject quickly. "But why are we talking about business? Tell me about yourself, Nicole. What do you enjoy doing in your leisure time, other than rampaging round the swimming pool with your cute son?"

"Well, I don't have too much free time, as I've already told you," I smiled, "but in the little time I do have, I enjoy reading or watching movies."

"And what do you like reading?"

"Everything, from fantasy to biography, as long as it's well-written."

"Great." He was quiet for a moment, obviously thinking. The waitress returned with our food. He waited until she had gone, then he said, "Look, there's this new biopic about Steve Jobs showing at the moment. Why don't we go see it together tomorrow evening?"

I said nothing for a moment, nibbling on my salad so as not to seem over-enthusiastic. Razi was going way too quickly for my taste. Still, I couldn't avoid the thought that fate might have allowed my path to cross that of a man who was dashing and easygoing, and who seemed to share my taste in good movies to boot. And if fate was at work, why shouldn't I just go for it without over-thinking it too much?"

"Sure," I said, but only after I remembered Itay spent Monday nights sleeping at his father's.

It was only a few years later that I came to fully understand the meaning of the saying, *'Haste is of the devil'*.

Chapter 2

'*Jobs*', starring Ashton Kutcher, told the tale of the origins and establishment of Apple and the various obstacles it had to overcome before becoming one of the world's richest, most successful companies. I noticed Razi's attention wasn't exactly focused on the movie.

"Fascinating movie," he said smiling as the film ended. "Jobs was a genius."

"Yes," I said, "especially for anyone interested in the computer world."

"I suppose it's more suitable for entrepreneurs," Razi said, as we walked out of the cinema. "And for people who want to change the world."

"What are you saying?" I smiled up at him. "That CFOs can't appreciate a movie about companies that want to change the world?"

Razi burst out laughing, his eyes glinting with a devilish spark. "Why don't we discuss this over dinner? There's this really good restaurant that's not too far. We could walk there. Want to go?"

"Yes," I agreed, although I very much doubted that we would actually find an available table in any decent Tel Aviv restaurant without making reservations first. And indeed, when we entered 'Le Corton', it was packed, and there were at least ten other people sitting in armchairs waiting for the next vacant table. To my surprise, the hostess welcomed Razi respectfully and led us to the first available table in less than five minutes.

"I eat here a lot," he said, reading the unasked question in my expression. "I can always rely on this restaurant to impress potential investors."

I nodded in agreement. 'Le Corton', a French restaurant, was, indeed, very impressive. The urban-modern design, and the huge chandelier in the center of the ceiling, reminded me of luxury restaurants in Paris and Manhattan.

"Well, let's see if the food here is as good as the decor," I said and opened the menu. "What do you recommend?"

"For the first course, Coquilles Saint-Jacques, and for the main course, the lobster, of course. It's the star of the menu. Now, how about some champagne to celebrate our acquaintance?"

I hesitated, embarrassed, feeling it was a little too early for that. Still, I didn't want to ruin the mood for him, so I simply said, "All right."

"A bottle of Brut, please," Razi said to the waiter, then added, "they don't treat good champagne with the proper respect, do they?" He smiled at the waiter.

"You're right," the waiter replied. "Veuve Clicquot is my favorite."

"Mine too," Razi said laughing.

I wanted to tell him there was no need to overdo the festivities, but the waiter was back. He ceremoniously uncorked the champagne and filled our glasses.

"Cheers!" Razi beamed at me and clinked his glass against mine.

"Cheers." I smiled hesitantly and sipped at my champagne, it was cold and refreshing. *'What a difference,'* I thought to myself, *'between Yaron, my previous date — who had explained the importance of gender equality, just to make sure we would be splitting the check — and the man I'm looking at right now.'* He was a gentleman.

"You know what I liked best in the movie?" Razi asked giving me another meaningful look.

"What?"

"The fact that no one believed in him, yet he still went for all the marbles and showed everyone he was right all along."

"I agree."

Razi went silent and stared towards some distant place, perhaps wondering about what he had just said, as if he was letting the words sink in.

"So, what does your company deal with?" I asked as our first courses arrived.

"Artificial intelligence image development."

"What does that mean?"

Razi straightened in his chair and said, "As the world becomes ever more digital, the demand for higher resolution cameras is constantly increasing. The problem is, though, that lens size and information storage space are limited. Therefore, instead of storing all of the picture's information, artificial intelligence 'learns' the picture and knows, using a certain algorithm, to complete it by connecting single pixels. This makes it possible to reduce the stored information to a bare minimum. This development is going to change the world."

"Why?" I wondered aloud.

"Because the more we are able to collect data by using superior resolution photography, and refine it into valuable information, without paying for that information's storage and traffic, the wider the range of technological opportunities will be."

"Interesting," I said, but Razi cut in with a smile and said, "All right, enough talk about business, it's time we talked about you."

"Me? There's nothing much to tell. My life is simple, I don't have any dreams of changing the world."

"Which is exactly why I like you so much." He leaned towards me and looked straight into my eyes. "You have this air of matter-of-fact simplicity about you. And I'm charmed by it. Apart from the fact that you are ravishingly beautiful and intelligent."

"Thank you!" I was embarrassed by the sweeping compliment he had paid me so sincerely.

"The food's good, isn't it?" he asked, and placed a few black oysters on my plate. He had ordered them for his first course. "Why don't you try the oysters?"

I did. The oysters, cooked in butter, white wine, garlic and herbs, were spectacularly delicious.

"You were right. This is an impressive restaurant." I smiled, lifted my champagne flute to my lips and took another sip.

"I never say anything unless I'm absolutely sure I'm right." He was suddenly serious. "Here comes the lobster. Once you've tasted it, you'll ask the restaurant management if you can move in!"

This time it was my turn to erupt into stress-relieving laughter. "So how much is the rent?" I asked after I had tasted the lobster, which was, as promised, a real delicacy.

"Not something either of us could afford." He gave a mock sigh. "But we can always order another bottle of champagne to ease our frustration."

"No! Seriously, Razi," I said quickly. "I have to be up early tomorrow for another crazy day at work, and I'd better be sober-minded and focused."

"All right." He shrugged and flagged the waiter. "So, we'll just settle for some Pellegrino sparkling water?"

"By all means," I said, as I went on demolishing my lobster.

"And what about dessert?" he asked when the waiter arrived. "They do this devilishly good Pavlova and a divine chocolate mousse."

"Pavlova," I decided and smiled. "And may God forgive me."

"Does he have a choice?" He wore a look of amusement as he examined my face. "Who on Heaven or Earth could resist you?"

I was embarrassed all over again, especially because the waiter was still standing beside our table with a helpless expression on his face. "Why don't you come back down to earth and tell the waiter what you'd like for dessert?" I managed to say.

"Right," Razi smiled kindly at the waiter. "I'll take the mousse."

"Don't worry," he said quietly as the waiter drifted away. "I'll make it up to him with a big tip."

"I wasn't worried," I blurted. I found myself wondering why he was trying so hard to impress me by spending money. Perhaps I had given him the impression I was looking for a man who would take care of me financially, or maybe this was just the way he lived his life, without a care in the world.

When the desserts arrived, Razi went prattling on about his favorite movies, while I became more introverted. *Why was I being so judgmental,* I wondered. Wasn't it all right for a man to want to impress a woman? I realized that if I ever wanted to allow myself a second chance at love, I needed to stop thinking critically about every word that came out of Razi's mouth and simply let myself enjoy the evening.

When we had finished eating, he stood up and said, "I understand you're in a hurry, so let's not wait for the check." He walked across to the waiter's corner. He lingered there for a few moments then came back to me. "Come, my Cinderella, let's take you home," he said with a smile.

"Why Cinderella?" I asked suspiciously.

"Because you said you needed to get up early tomorrow morning."

"And what does that have to do with Cinderella?"

"Oh, I don't know. My mind must be working too fast," he apologized. "When you said you needed to get up early, it made me think you probably needed to get home before midnight — and the story of Cinderella came into my head. I didn't mean to insult you. It was just a bad joke."

"I'm not insulted," I said. "It's just that Cinderella isn't exactly a fairytale character I can identify with."

"I bet you're more comfortable identifying with Belle, from *Beauty and the Beast*. Especially dating me!" He smiled. "So, we're okay?"

"Of course we are," I answered, smiling myself, amused by the way he'd gotten himself out of a potentially awkward situation.

When we reached his car, Razi gallantly opened the door for me, and as I sank into the passenger seat, I felt his hand momentarily fluttering over my hip. I enjoyed the fleeting touch.

"Do you go out on a lot of dates?" he asked.

"Dating isn't exactly my favorite activity." I smiled to take any sting from my words. "How about you?"

"I don't have much time for it; working in high tech is very demanding. But when I meet a girl like you…" he said. His eyes lingered on my face. He was smiling again. "… time becomes meaningless." I smiled back. It was a charming thing to say.

He drew the car to a stop outside my building and, as he turned the engine off, I suddenly felt like a teenager again, sitting in a car with the most popular boy in high school. His look enveloped me with mesmerizing heat. Silently, he drew closer. I was ready to give in to the moment as I felt him leaning over me. He kissed me — on my forehead.

"Good night, beautiful," he said softly, and moved back to the driver's seat. He didn't ask when he could see me again.

"Good night," I answered. I heard the note of restraint in my voice. I climbed out of his car with mixed feelings. I was left with the feeling that the evening had been a little intense, but I was also a bit disappointed that Razi hadn't asked me for a second date.

Chapter 3

The vague feeling of having missed an opportunity refused to leave me all through the following morning. It intensified as the day went on and Razi didn't call. Luckily, I had an especially intense day at work, and I hardly had any time to think about him until it was over. On my way home, I suddenly felt confused and exhausted, and I struggled to understand what it was, exactly, I expected from him.

After the evening I had spent with Razi, I couldn't decide whether or not I should forget him, especially as he hadn't called. The swirl of emotions I found myself reeling from came with many question marks about the man himself and the purity of his intentions. I tried to think back over the events of the previous evening to determine if I might have said or done something that could have caused him to 'cool off'. Finding nothing, I had no choice but to come to the disappointing conclusion that Razi was looking for someone who was 'easy', and, when he had realized I wasn't, had simply given up on his passionate attempts to woo me.

"Mommy!" Itay crushed me with a sweet, excited hug as soon as I stepped into the house. "I missed you so much."

"I missed you too, peanut." I leaned down and pressed him to my heart. "Did you have fun with Daddy?"

"Yes," he replied and tightened his little hands around my neck. "He said you'd help me build my new Lego castle when you got back from work."

Shani, the babysitter, emerged from Itay's room. "Sorry." She smiled at me apologetically. "He hasn't stop playing with his Lego since we got back from the playground. I couldn't even give him a bath."

"Never mind, it's all right," I answered and turned to Itay. "It's getting really late, sweetie. You need to have your bath and go to sleep."

"But Mommy, Daddy promised you'd finish building the Lego castle with me," he said resentfully.

Danny's got some nerve, I thought to myself. He knows how my Tuesday meetings always stretch into the evening, and he's trying to make me feel guilty again. This time, at Itay's expense.

"Cutie, that was before I knew you hadn't had your bath yet." I stroked his sand-filled hair and said, "I'll come back early tomorrow and we'll finish building the Lego castle together then, all right?"

*

As I showered, my mind drifted off to thoughts of Danny, my ex-husband, the man with whom I had fallen in love when we were both studying at the Hebrew University. We had had similar family backgrounds as children. Like me, Danny grew up in a warm, loving and supportive family. His parents were kind-hearted, intelligent people, and had only been prevented from enjoying a higher education because of the circumstances of their lives. Like my parents had for me, they nurtured and encouraged him to develop, study and acquire high-paying professional qualifications in accounting. I wondered if we couldn't have bridged the rift that had come between us, and if, perhaps, I had been too quick to divorce. After all, his family had embraced me with warmth, love and appreciation, which was exactly how Danny himself had treated me throughout our years as university students. It was only after we had both graduated that the disagreements began. Danny wanted to open his own office, while I wanted to work for a large firm, having proven my capabilities and graduated at the top of my class.

Danny was obviously disappointed when he realized I wanted to carve my own career path rather than open a small accounting office with him, though he didn't seem to mind too much at first. He supported me and said he was proud when I was offered a position with a large communications company — a CFO position that carried with it a very generous monthly salary which allowed us to afford a comfortable lifestyle in a spacious apartment in north Tel Aviv. But the support and pride had lasted only until Itay was born. For some reason, my husband had then expected me to fall in love with the role of full-time mother during my maternity leave, quit my job, and stay home with our son until he was at least four-years-old.

When I explained to Danny that I had no intention of staying home, he repeated his offer to join him as a partner in his small accounting office. "You could help me from home to start with. You know, when Itay is sleeping." He explained what seemed to him to be an offer I couldn't possibly refuse. "Once he's old enough to go to kindergarten, you could start working in the office for longer hours. But gradually, of course, until he got used to you not being home for most of the day."

Danny seemed hurt when I insisted on developing my own career in a key position within a large company, and kept trying to drag me into his dream of developing one of the largest accounting firms in the country.

"It's not that I don't believe in you, but you know as well as I do, we have a baby in the house now and we can't take unnecessary risks. I just don't think it's a good idea to have both of us working in our own office." I answered his protestations in sober tones. "And don't forget we have your sister, Sivan, who's about to be discharged from the army and has agreed to help us by working as Itay's baby-sitter until she decides what career she wants to pursue." I added this to try to convince Danny to come around to my way of thinking.

But it appeared that there was another, hidden layer of frustration within Danny, concealed beneath his urbane exterior — a frustration that seethed like boiling lava. I hadn't even guessed it existed until I got a new and even better job offer from a commercial television channel.

"Danny," I said to him one day, "I want us to sit down together for a moment and try to think rationally about this new job offer. We can even write down a pros and cons checklist and decide together. What do you say?"

Danny appeared to be reconciled to the idea. We decided to have breakfast at our favorite café the following morning — the Cliff Beach in Tel Aviv. We dropped Itay off at my sister, Bat-El's place first.

We arrived at the café, sat in our usual, well-loved corner, and waited for the waiter to approach us. "Why don't we take a classic breakfast for two?" Danny suggested, and I nodded in agreement.

When the waiter moved off, I said, "The salary the new commercial channel is offering me is almost too good to be true. We could finish paying our mortgage in no time." Then I added enthusiastically, "My negotiations with them were held under strict secrecy. Neither they nor I wanted it all to go public too soon. That's why I didn't tell you anything until all the loose ends had been tied up and we'd moved closer to signing an agreement."

Nothing had prepared me for the possibility that Danny would lash out at me and go off like a nuclear bomb right there, in the café, in front of the calm, blue waters of the Mediterranean.

"Are you serious?" His voice rose. "Are you actually thinking of accepting this offer?"

"Why not?" I squirmed nervously in my chair. People sitting at the nearest tables were looking at us curiously.

"Because no one offers a salary like that without a reason." He didn't lower his voice. He was still talking loudly, aggressively. "Don't you get it? They think they can buy you, own you. You won't have a life. You'll hardly see Itay, or me, for that matter. You'll get up to go to work at the crack of dawn and come back after midnight. Not to mention being swamped by phone calls and emails on weekends and holidays. God, Nicole, I thought you wanted to give Itay a little brother or sister and spend your days with them and your nights with me, instead of spending your life in some office."

"But why?" I actually heard myself stammer under the pressure of the embarrassment and frustration that surged inside me. "Why would you even think that? Haven't I told you, more than once, that we can't have another baby before we have more financial stability? And this ... this job ... is our chance to achieve that stability. Can't you see, Danny? Three or four years from now, we could be finished paying our mortgage. And then, the sky's the limit."

Danny looked shocked for a moment. As if this was the first time he'd heard my argument.

"So that's what this is all about, eh? Money!" he growled, his anger now palpable. "Nothing else is important to you? What about our son? What about me? What's happened to you, Nicole? When did you turn into a workaholic blinded by money? It hurts me to ask you this, but where is the woman I married? I just can't see her anymore."

I was stunned. There was so much I wanted to say to him, for instance, that I had never concealed my plans from him, and that it was so unfair to be telling me now, now of all times, that I wasn't the same woman he had married. But before I could say anything, my husband rose abruptly from his chair and walked quickly out of the café.

I was agitated, confused by his attitude. I paid the check as quickly as I could and went outside to look for Danny. He wasn't anywhere in sight and I couldn't understand where he might have disappeared to. We had come to the beach with my work car, and I still had the keys, so he couldn't have driven off. I decided to look for him along the beach, thinking maybe he'd decided to take a long walk to calm down. But when I saw no trace of him, I returned, defeated and exhausted, to the car and drove home. Danny's car wasn't in the parking lot.

That reassured me a little. At least I knew he had gotten home safely; otherwise, his car would still have been there. But, deep inside, I still felt uneasy. Such dramas and impulsive behavior were very unlike my husband.

As I sat and thought about what I should do next, the idea that he might have gone to my sister's house to pick up Itay occurred to me. I didn't like to think that Danny would go to get Itay when he was in such an unstable, even hysterical, mood. So, I called Bat-El. I didn't ask her if Danny was there, just if everything was all right with Itay.

"He's more than all right, he's great," she reported. "He's been playing outside with the rest of the gang the whole day. I made lunch for them and they insisted on having a picnic out in the yard. You have nothing to worry about, Nicole."

"Thanks," I said, and finished the call, my heart aching. Bat-El would have mentioned if Danny was there. So that still left the burning question, where was he? Where could he possibly be?

I buried my head in my hands as anxiety threatened to overwhelm me. My imagination was running wild in all sorts of directions. In my mind's eye, I saw Danny driving wildly on a major highway, which would have been most unlike him. But hadn't it been just as unlikely that he would have reacted with such anger in the café, when all I wanted to do was to break some wonderful news to him? To share something I truly believed would make him happy?

The sound of the telephone startled me. It was Doron, CEO of the commercial television channel.

"Hello Nicole," he spoke with his usual authoritative voice, "Danny has just been to see us," he said without preamble, "I think we should meet at my office tomorrow morning."

"What?" The sudden relief I felt was mixed with wonder — and then with renewed anger. Danny had been to Doron! "What did Danny have to tell you?" I managed to ask.

"It's all right," Doron said reassuringly, "I understand the sensitivity of … of… this matter. Which is why a decision will be only be made once we hear your side of the story."

"All right, I'll see you at the office tomorrow." I ended the call and quickly called Danny's parents. He was there.

"Doron just called me."

"Great," he said shortly. "I hope he convinced you."

"About what?"

"About giving up this new job."

"What? Is that why you went to see him? Why did you do that?"

"I did what I had to do, for our family's sake."

I ended the call. Tears welled up in my eyes.

I sat in the wooden chair by the round table and remembered the green formica table in my childhood home, in the dining room next to the family kitchen. I had loved sitting at that table, doing my homework and watching my mom cutting vegetables to make soup. I remembered how, as she worked away with her back to me, I used to test her mathematical skills. "Mom, how much is four hundred thirty-seven multiplied by one thousand nine hundred and thirty-four?"

My mother would think for a moment, then she would turn around to face me and, her eyes glittering, answer with pride in her voice, "Eight hundred forty-five thousand one hundred fifty-eight."

I would check her answer using my calculator, and she would scold me: "You need to be making your own calculations, toys like that will rot your brain. Calculus is your security."

Deep inside, I always thought how sad it was that a woman as gifted and intelligent as my mother had been forced to give up on herself to raise her children.

*

Danny didn't come home that night. Needless to say, I was beyond stressed. The fact that my husband had spoken to my boss and involved him in our private family matters bit hard at me, and the distress I felt swelled to monstrous proportions. I couldn't understand how he had thought of such an insane idea. Right up to that point, to the moment Danny had rushed dramatically from the café, everything between us had been harmonious and perfect. If either one of us had the right to feel frustrated, it was me.

All our relatives had always spoken with admiration about my success at being both a career woman and a mother. As far as I was concerned, there was no way I'd give any of it up, especially since I also bore the burden of doing all the chores in the house on my own. On Saturdays, I would cook enough food to last us through the following week; and if anything happened to Itay in kindergarten, they would always call me, not Danny, because I was generally in the office and was easier to get hold of. And even when I was out at an appointment, my secretary always knew where I was and how to contact me.

I had done all this to make things easier for Danny, who had only just established his own, independent accounting office. I was never angry or frustrated. On the contrary, I took pleasure in being able to successfully juggle my time between the office and my family without anyone getting hurt, especially my sweet Itay, who I loved more than my own life. So why, I wondered, was Danny the one who suddenly felt frustrated and embittered? Logically, he couldn't have dreamed of better conditions than those I was now offering him; in effect, the opportunity to realize his own career goals and aspirations without having to worry about money.

The fact that Danny had been seething with such difficult emotions below the surface, emotions I had been completely unaware of, rattled me to the bone. It was obvious to me that the angry, almost volcanic, eruption that had taken place when I was trying to give him what I saw as happy news, could not have come from nowhere. And since I saw nothing rational in his behavior, I had no choice but to assume that his motives, and his actions, were completely irrational.

If I had been him, the only thing I might have been upset about was the fact that I hadn't shared the negotiation process with him. Maybe that was what had hurt him so badly, I thought regretfully. Danny had never liked surprises. He had even warned me once never to throw a surprise birthday party for him. Even his marriage proposal wasn't exactly a surprising, grandiose event, and only came after a long series of mutual discussions about the subject.

And so, the following morning, as soon as I entered Doron's office, I said firmly, "I'm sorry." I sat in the chair facing his. "I should have told Danny about our negotiations from day one. It's just that I wanted to make sure this is really happening. I know how sensitive he is about my professional career, but I thought he and I would be able to discuss this like adults. Then, yesterday, when I told him about this new job, he didn't react as I expected him to."

"Nicole," Doron intoned, "you don't need to explain anything to me. I think you're definitely up to this job; if I didn't, we wouldn't have offered it to you in the first place. But we are talking about a highly sensitive and demanding position and I need to know if you still think you can do it, in spite of your husband's reservations."

"Doron, in the same way you don't look into a man's family life when you're considering him for a senior position, I don't think you should be looking into mine as a woman. You can rest assured I'll fill this position and do the job required in the best possible way, and with the utmost loyalty and dedication."

When I got home, I wanted to make up with Danny, but I knew he had to first agree to come to terms with my new job at the commercial television channel. Over the ensuing weeks he did make efforts, and I respected him for that, but unfortunately, it just didn't work. Our

relationship continued to falter for long months, caus-
ing us both grief and stress, until it finally died out
completely.

*

"Good night, cutie," I sighed as I tucked Itay up in his bed.

"Why are you sad?" he asked, his lovely brown eyes
wrinkling in concern.

"I'm not sad, I'm just thinking about how much I love
you." I gave him my usual reply at such moments.

"I love you, too." He hugged me in his slender, delicate
arms. "More than anything in the world."

"And I love you more." I smiled sadly, wondering how
much time would pass before a man would hold me in his
arms again. Not that I thought I would ever stop being
thrilled by my sweet son's embraces, but all the reminisc-
ing I had done suddenly made me yearn for a different
kind of thrill, butterflies dancing in my stomach, and that
delicious feeling only a new man could breathe into life.

Once Itay was asleep, I rose and tiptoed out of his
room. I went into my bedroom and called Anna. Anna
was my closest friend. As well as being intelligent and
having a heart of gold, she was also a great dentist. I
had first gone to her for treatment after a friend recom-
mended her to me. I knew she'd be the only one who
would be able to understand me, perhaps the only one
who would listen. And I also knew she understood more
than I meant her to. Immediately after I told her how I

missed the feeling of a man's touch, she had said intui-
tively, "So, there's someone new? Tell me all about him
right now!"

"Well, it isn't exactly someone new," I muttered hesitantly. I was finding it hard to admit, even to myself, that
I actually missed Razi. "And there's nothing much to tell,"
I went on, realizing that I actually wanted to talk about
my date — the fiasco — with him. Perhaps I was hoping
that Anna might be able to understand what I didn't. I
took a deep breath and then blurted it all out. "Look, I
met someone who wouldn't stop chasing me for three
days; then, after our first movie and dinner date, which I
thought was fun, he disappeared into the night without
asking for a second date."

"So, just call and ask him out," she said, her voice
clearly filled with surprise. "What are you, some kind of
insecure high school girl sitting at home, all depressed
and waiting for a phone call?"

"I guess you're right, but I don't have his number," I
said. At that moment I thought I heard a light tap at the
door.

"Anna, let me call you right back," I said and finished
the call. I thought it might be that irritating neighbor
from the homeowner's association coming to collect the
check for my dues. Then, I remembered that he always
rang the doorbell, despite my repeated entreaties for him
not to wake my son. The light tapping made me think
that, perhaps, he had finally gotten the message and was
being a little more sensitive.

Nothing prepared me for what was waiting behind the closed door when I finally opened it wide.

It was Razi and his ravishing smile.

Chapter 4

"What are you doing here?" I whispered in amazement.

"I missed you."

He embraced me and moved me backwards into my apartment, still holding me in his strong arms.

"But why..." I stammered. I always seem to stammer when things take an unexpected turn.

"Leave the questions for later, just be spontaneous for now," he whispered in my ear. His whisper sent a tremor of anticipation rippling through my body.

It was at that moment that I decided to let go. *Que sera, sera.* If the worst came to the worst, I'd earn myself a passion-filled, electrifying night with a man who looked like a movie star. What could possibly be wrong with that?

I had barely reached that conclusion when Razi started pushing me into the bedroom, turning off the light on the way. He pressed me against the wall, opened the light nightgown I was wearing, and gave me a long, spine-tingling kiss.

"You are simply breathtaking," he whispered, his mouth wandering up and down the contours of my neck. "I've never been so attracted to a woman. From the first day I saw you in the pool, I haven't been able to stop dreaming about your eyes...your lips...so much beauty...." Razi stripped the nightgown off my body with one hand, then he took me back into his arms and carried me to the bed. He quickly undressed and leaned over me, never once taking his lips off my skin.

I was all too aware that Itay was sleeping in the next room, despite the blazing passion that quickly spread through my limbs, as Razi's manly touch lit the fires of ecstasy. It soon became obvious that he belonged to that special breed of men who think not only of themselves in bed, but of their partner's pleasure as well. He completely immersed himself in the sexual act, his extreme excitement spurring me on as well. Just looking at him was enough to make me forget everything and be swept away, in a kind of pure, sensual pleasure which I had never experienced before that night.

Despite the passion, though, I was also confused by this sudden, unexpected development, and I tried to understand Razi's true intentions as he declared he had found the love of his life. As we lay in the aftermath of our love-making, I heard him say softly, "That was the most intense sex I've had in my entire life!" Then he moved his mouth next to my ear and whispered, as we lay comfortably in each other's arms, "You're simply an extraordinary woman. I sensed it the moment I first saw you. That combination of beauty and intelligence, but still overflowing with sexuality. You have no idea how rare that is. And it was the reason I invested so much energy trying to find you."

For a moment, the thought flashed through my mind that Razi simply knew how to use the words a woman wants to hear to get her into bed, but I quickly pushed that thought to the bottom of my mind and let it sink.

"Don't exaggerate," I said and leaned my head against his chest. "How hard can it be to find a woman named Nicole who works as a CFO for a television channel in Israel?"

I was thinking about his hyperbolic show of emotions, and I couldn't help wondering what his true intentions were, but Razi simply pushed all my doubts back into a dark corner. He showered me with compliments, and told me of the efforts he'd made in his attempts to locate me. "You think that's all I've done?" he stroked my hair gently. "That evening, after we met at the pool, I searched every building in the street, looking for your name on a mailbox. It was only after I'd been up and down the whole street twice that I realized most mailboxes only have the resident's' last names on them. So, I tried something else. I decided to look for you by calling every television station in the city."

"Are you serious? You actually went looking for my name on every mailbox in the neighborhood?"

I thought any woman would be flattered by such a romantic act, but, at the same time, I was a little bothered by the obsessive nature of everything he'd done. Such obsessiveness, I thought, wasn't really compatible with my own personality. I considered myself to be a rational, steady person. So, what was going on? How had he managed to sweep me off my feet with his charm and charisma? And then I thought that I might have answered my own question. Was it possible, I wondered, that I needed more love and warmth than I consciously cared to admit to myself? And was it possible that Razi was meeting that need?

"Dead serious." He kissed my neck again. "And I have to tell you, that night I hardly slept. I was too stressed thinking I might not be able to find you again."

"Don't you have some kind of artificial intelligence in your high-tech company that's capable of locating a girl in your neighborhood?" I laughed. "You know, you could just have waited until you saw me again at the pool, then asked me for my address and telephone number."

"Yes, but how could I be sure no one else would have snapped you up by then? I don't need to be an Einstein to realize just how special you are."

His tone was utterly serious and I turned to look up at him. I could see his white teeth glinting through his smile in the half-light.

"Are you kidding me?" I cupped his chin in my hand. "If you were really so stressed about someone else 'snapping me up', why did you disappear on me for a whole day? And without asking me for another date?"

I regretted the questions as soon as they had left my mouth. I knew that in the game of not showing too much enthusiasm during the early stages of courtship, I had just lost a few valuable points.

Razi surprised me again. The smile vanished from his face and he said, sounding as if he was speaking from the bottom of his heart, "Nicole, I think you don't understand how smitten I am with you. I felt so stressed, lost, when I realized I had finally met a woman I would do anything, and I do mean anything, to be with. You've torn down all my defenses. When I'm with you, I feel helpless and lose every ounce of my common sense. I'm not used to feeling like that, so I felt I simply had to take some time out, to ask myself whether I was really willing to let something like this happen."

I said nothing for a moment, shocked by the intensity of his declarations. I was convinced that Razi, with his impressive appearance, overflowing charisma and social status, would appear desirable in the eyes of just about any woman on the globe. And maybe that was the reason I suddenly felt my heart melt and open up to him, this charming man. A man who had lowered all his defenses for me, who had put aside his ego and admitted he felt helpless when he was with me.

I hugged him tightly and said, trying to keep a rein on the excitement I was feeling, "You have no idea how much I appreciate what you've said, Razi. I don't think I've ever met a man so brave and honest."

From that night on, Razi and I were a couple. We met two nights a week, and on the weekends when Itay slept at his father's. We managed to do so much together during that period. We went to the movies or the theatre, ate in all kinds of restaurants, and, of course, we spent a lot of time in bed. On the weekends, we went to luxury hotels and romantic cabins all over the country, and even, sometimes, abroad.

Razi was the perfect partner and companion. He seemed to love all the things I did, from visiting museums to taking nature hikes, to sprawling lazily on a beach sunbathing, interrupted by frequent games of friendly paddleball. Shopping was the only thing that bored him a little, but he still came along whenever I felt the need to do some store-hopping, and he never pulled any 'what am I even doing here' faces on me.

I was floating on air in those early days of our relationship. I could feel myself glowing with happiness, beaming at everyone and feeling as though I was walking on pink clouds of sheer joy. It must have showed, judging by the clever remarks I got at work, even though I did my best to maintain a professional, matter-of-fact appearance. Actually, I couldn't have cared less about my work colleagues so blatantly trying to pry into my personal life.

In fact, in those first six magical months, I didn't care about almost anything else in the world, other than my son. I was head over heels, immersed in the happiness that seemed to be flowing like an endless stream through my life. And I ignored everything and anyone who might try to ruin it for me.

Then, one morning, I woke up to find a mysterious text message on my cell phone.

Chapter 5

I could hardly breathe. I felt as if a giant fist had smashed into my stomach and all the blood had drained from my body. My head was spinning and I dropped dizzily into a chair, trying to regain my breath even as I kept on staring at the telephone screen.

'Razi is married.'

Who could have sent me a message like that?

My mind whirled. It had to be a mistake. Who even knew about our relationship, and why would anyone send me such a message?

My first impulse was to call Razi, but I remembered he had told me he was taking his children, Oren and Gaya, on a trip up north. My mind whirled with thoughts about the message. There was no room to misconstrue what it said, written, as it was, in no uncertain way. Messages like that didn't just pop out of nowhere, it would be easy enough to check if it was genuine, and the sender would have known that. Inevitably, I started thinking back over our conversations, and the more I did, the more I realized Razi had never actually said he was divorced. He had always diverted the conversation when the question of his marital status came up. And me, being so gullible, had believed him when he said he was, "…free as a bird and owing no one anything."

I was filled with turbulent, conflicting emotions. Primarily, I was furious with Razi for having deceived me in such a low, even sneaky, way, and yet, I felt my insides shriveling in fear because I realized I would have no choice but to end my relationship with him. I also realized doing so would break my heart.

I wondered who had been so cruel as to send the message. I thought it must be someone who wanted to damage our relationship, or, perhaps, wanted to put an end to the lie I had, all unknowing, been living?

All through that day, I lay curled up in the fetal position on the living room sofa, my knees pressed up against my head, my eyes shut tight, as if trying block out the horror. I tried to think of what I should do. And, all at once, as I lay there consumed by fear, doubt, sorrow and anger, the dam broke and the tears began to flow. Floods of them. I had invested all my feelings, all my love, in Razi. I cried with rage and humiliation and pain. And I didn't, I couldn't, hold back. I cried because, now, I had no choice but to kick out of my life the man who had brought so much passion and warmth into it.

At about seven-thirty in the evening, the telephone suddenly rang, startling me. I lunged at it, thinking it was Razi calling and I could vent my anger and humiliation by hurling harsh words at him, words that would leave him, and me, no hope for the future. But it wasn't Razi, it was my friend, Anna, on the line, and she was startled by my tear-choked voice.

"Nicole? What's happened to you? Are you sick?" she asked, her voice anxious.

"No," I sniffled, and I told her about the message I had received. Anna was silent for a long moment, then, when she realized I was done, asked in a stunned voice, "And you actually believe a text message sent from an unknown number?"

"Who would bother to send me a false message?" I said. I could hear the desperation in my own voice. "Where there's smoke, there's fire. It must have been his wife."

"How do you know it was his *wife* and not his deranged *ex*-wife, pretending to be his wife? Some women refuse to accept reality."

I was surprised. Anna has always had a decidedly negative opinion about all men, in general, and here she was defending Razi. She had met him a couple of times, and I knew she had been taken by his charm and charisma. She had even let me know that, thanks to Razi, she was almost considering giving the male of the species a second chance.

So now I, of course, expected this new development to make her step back from her optimistic intentions, which was why I was even more surprised when she added, "I think you need to talk to him and give him a chance to explain what's going on."

"Are you serious?" I was amazed. "It's completely obvious! The bastard is living with his wife and children and has been playing me for a sucker for six months — that's what's going on!"

"Exactly, Nicole." Anna was calm, unruffled, and when she spoke it was with the voice of sweet reason. "You've been together for six months and he hasn't given you any reason at all to think he's a liar. Not even once. So why don't you try asking Razi himself what's going on in his house, instead of just accepting that some mysterious text message is true? There's a serious chance whoever sent it is just jealous and wants to ruin things for you."

"You think?"

"Of course. Razi is a once in a lifetime kind of man, and I wouldn't be surprised if someone out there is trying to mess it up for you two."

I began to calm down a little, but a tiny worm of unease remained. Anna was my closest friend at the time. She was intelligent and had a heart of gold. Still, I suspected she was lacking in the intuition department, which was why she tended to be attracted to the wrong type of man, usually backward, macho types, or men so inclined to jealousy that they made her life a living hell. It was why she divided men into two categories: the kind who are jealous and possessive and ruin your life, and the kind that aren't jealous and possessive simply because they don't care enough.

When Danny had started pestering me about quitting my job, Anna vehemently claimed that his behavior derived not only from jealousy of my successes, but also jealousy of me.

In other words, he was afraid my success in the

business world would eventually cause some of my amo-
rous colleagues to woo me until I started believing what
they said and came to the conclusion that I deserved a
more successful and accomplished husband. That was
one of the main reasons Anna liked and appreciated Razi
so much, because he wasn't the jealous type. On the contrary, now and then, he would even tell me how flattered
he felt when other men looked at me with admiration in
their eyes.

"So, what do you think I should do now?" I asked
tearfully.

Anna quickly replied with a question of her own.
"When is he supposed to be calling you?"

"Razi decided to use the holiday vacation to take Gaya
and Oren for a trip up north, but he still calls me every
evening at around eight."

"All right, so in half an hour you'll know for a fact
whether he's just a chickenshit bastard who's addicted to
thrills and has been caught red-handed, or if he has some
logical explanation for this whole thing and his intentions are genuine. Personally, I think the second option
is what's coming."

"And what am I supposed to tell him when he calls?"
I asked desperately.

"Just tell him exactly what's happened and give him a
chance to explain, that's it," Anna replied calmly. "Then
call me and tell me what he says."

"I don't understand what you think he's going to say,"
I said hesitantly.

I was thinking hard. The fact that Razi called every evening made me feel that he cared for me, loved me and was worried about me. Maybe if I confronted him, he would just invent some false excuse so he could go on seeing me. I was afraid that feeling so passionately about wanting to stay with him would interfere with my critical faculties so much that I would 'buy' his story — until, that is, reality ended up blowing the cold wind of truth straight into my face.

"I don't think anything, and you shouldn't be making any assumptions either," Anna said firmly. "Give him a chance to explain and then we'll think about what to do next. My own opinion is that Razi is the sort of man who's worth falling in love with, and it would be a shame for you to give him up too easily, Nicole. You don't meet men like him every day. Yes, you can always break up with him, but it would be better for you to keep that option for the next stage, after you hear what he has to say in his own defense. All right?"

"All right ... I think," I answered skeptically.

"Nickie, I understand you want to use the justified anger you must be feeling right now to kick him the hell out of your life." Anna hadn't finished. "Because if you don't do it now, while your emotions are high and making you strong, you're afraid that in your head-over-heels in love condition, you'll let him dazzle you with excuses until he gets fed up. But I still think you don't just dump a man like Razi because of a single, dubious, suspicious message."

"I suppose," I said, after giving it some serious thought. "All right, Annuch'ka, I'll give him a chance to explain."

"Attagirl." She sounded content.

The ten minutes I had to wait for Razi's phone call seemed like an eternity. He called right on time, as he had done every evening since he'd left to go on his trip with Oren and Gaya.

"Hi, Nicole, how are you?" he asked, his tone warm, interested.

"Fine," I answered in a tense voice. "Other than the fact a little bird told me you're happily married and that you're living with your wife and children."

"What?" he sounded stunned. "Who told you something like that?"

"What does it matter?" I asked angrily. "Is it, or is it not, true?"

The long silence from the other end of the line turned my heart to ice. It testified in a thousand silent voices that there was some truth to the mysterious message.

"Listen, Nicole," Razi finally spoke. His voice was calm, and it seemed as though he had been able to regain his composure, "I just didn't want to get you involved in the mess I've been living in, which is why I haven't told you everything. The truth is ... the truth is ... I do live in the same house with my wife, but not happily."

"Will you get to the point?" I could feel rage taking over. "Are you married or not?"

"I'm separated," he answered quickly. "We live in the same house, but we have an agreement we had drawn up by a lawyer. She is committed to divorce me as soon as my company attains a high enough value."

"Is there anything else you haven't told me? I mean, other than the small fact that you're married?"

"Hold on, Nicole. You have to understand, my company has vast, huge potential, but it relies on a technological development that has yet to be completed. That artificial intelligence I told you about. My wife, soon to be my ex-wife, is a greedy woman. She doesn't care that I don't love her anymore, that I actively dislike her. All she cares about is getting her hands on the money. She's the patient sort, so she's not in any hurry to give me a divorce before my company completes developing the artificial intelligence, and she gets to earn from it. I need you by my side, Nicole. I know her, she'll never divorce me if I put too much pressure on her. She'd refuse just to spite me. And that's why I've agreed to her terms. She enjoys our financial and social status, so she turns a blind eye to the way I live my life. We haven't been sharing the same bed for years, and ... well ... she's not entirely stupid. She knows I've had extramarital affairs, excuse me, I mean an affair, and she doesn't care. How else do you think I could spend so much time with you, and go on all those vacations and weekends with you?"

"I ... suppose," I replied. I was trying hard to stay calm. I couldn't help but wonder if this was the ultimate excuse, one that would allow him to drag me along by my gullible nose for years until he finally got a divorce — or dumped me. "How long do you think it will be before your company starts making money off this new ... whatever it is?"

"You know as well as I do it's impossible to accurately estimate that sort of thing." His voice was still measured, still calm, still patient. "I told you once that this development will change the world. I've been meeting Russian oligarchs, who aren't exactly my cup of tea, to try and raise more money to speed up the process. I can assure you, it's what I dream about every night, when I'm not busy dreaming about you, that is. As far as I'm concerned, this could happen even as soon as tomorrow."

"And what is your company's financial situation?" I wanted to know because deep inside, I realized that Razi was a rare man. In the divorced singles jungle, it was hard to find a man who looked like a movie star, yet didn't act like a showoff, was highly intelligent, a man of the world who liked museums and fine restaurants, and was also a kind and sensitive lover. And yet, despite all these qualities, Razi had persistently wooed me for six long months. He made me feel as though I was the center of his world and he couldn't live without me.

The fact that he was still married and bound by an agreement that linked his divorce with a technological development was the only drawback I had been able to find in him to date.

"Nicole, I didn't want to bore you with stories from work. You haven't told me too much about your job either. I just assumed you preferred that we dealt with more… interesting things when we spent time together."

"That's right, but if there are work-related issues that directly impact on the future of our relationship, then they should definitely have been shared."

"You're right, and I'm sorry." Now he was speaking in a soft, indulgent tone. "When there's anything new about the development, I'll be sure to tell you, all right?"

"Fine," I answered in a formal voice. I still felt a little angry with him. Also, I didn't want him to think I was just going to forget the fact he'd been hiding the truth from me for the past six months.

"So … goodbye for now," he whispered. "And don't forget, I love you more than anything and miss you no end. I dream about you every night, my beauty."

I wanted to call Anna after we had hung up, but I felt I had to listen to myself first, understand my own reactions to the conversation I'd just had. I decided to take a shower before I phoned her. Under the stream of cascading hot water, I went through what Razi had said. The way he told it, it made sense. I knew of more than a few women who stayed in shitty, emotionless marriages just for the money. And if that was truly the situation Razi and his wife were in, why shouldn't his wife only agree to divorce him after she got the best deal she could? True, it wasn't exactly an ideal situation, but after six intensive, love-filled months, I was sure I knew Razi, and I was convinced that he loved me. It was nothing like the relationship

I had had with Danny. I knew I was much more in control.

I knew I could handle a relationship with Razi — even if it was a little complicated.

As the water ran down my body, I decided.

I chose love.

Chapter 6

Week by week, my relationship with Razi settled into a somewhat strange routine. We went on meeting and going out whenever Itay stayed with his father, but we were both aware, in some unstated way, of the cloud of uncertainty about our future that was hanging over our heads. And that cloud, at least for me, dampened the pure joy I had felt before I found out that Razi was married.

I tried to convince myself that the fact we weren't free to establish our relationship any time we wanted to, did not pose a real problem. I was young, with a promising career and had a son of my own so, on the surface, I shouldn't have been in any rush. But to be honest, I knew this was all true only in theory. Actually, I felt constricted and owned by the relationship, as if I was caught in a tangle of alien systems and considerations, none of which depended on me, and all of which had been forced upon me. The fact that I had to hide Razi's existence from my family, and that he hid me from his, did not help to improve my feelings. I came from a warm, tight-knit family and had been brought up never to hide anything — or to lie. My parents' concerned looks, especially on Friday evenings and holidays, pained me on the inside. I knew they ached for the fact that I was all alone. And not being able to tell them the truth made me feel physically ill.

I was unable to hide my emotions from Razi, who tried to cheer me up without much success. He promised me that our relationship was steady, rock-solid, and that it would soon be made public and official. Then, one evening, he called me, sounding particularly excited.

"Sweetheart, I have some wonderful news," he said over the phone.

"I love wonderful news," I said, not hiding my excitement. "All right, what is it?"

"Pack a bag, we're going to the Hilton Dahab."

"Hmm…" I said, a little reserved. "We just got back from a weekend at a hotel, I'd much rather spend this one at home. Why don't we cook something together?" I suggested.

"You're right, my beauty, but the sort of news I have should be told against the background of a turquoise-blue sea. We have the rest of our lives to cook together!"

*

The Hilton Dahab was a real desert pearl, its numerous, low-rise buildings sprawling around the shores of a magical lagoon. Between the whitewashed buildings were beautiful gardens in which grew flowers of every conceivable shape and color, and a swimming pool that blended in with the view. The lagoon itself, less than three feet from the hotel, boasted a spectacular coral reef which was home to the shoals of colorful fish that thronged in and around it.

Razi decided to take a diving course. He suggested that I join him, but I preferred to simply dive along the reef with a snorkel. My plans for that vacation, other than listening to Razi's exciting news, involved resting and sunbathing, preferably both.

I began the following morning with a half-hour swim in the pool. Then I spoiled myself by having breakfast at the hotel buffet. After that, I sprawled on a tanning bed on the beach with Garcia Marquez's, 'Love in the Time of Cholera'.

I took an occasional dip in the sea, sometimes with, sometimes without, the snorkel, to cool myself off a little. I love Sinai and its laidback atmosphere. When I'm there, I always feel that time slows down, especially when set against the dazzling pace of the modern world. And, of course, I enjoyed the primordial and magnificent views the area has to offer. Tall cliffs painted with a palette of sandy colors, and beautiful, endless blue sea on the other side of the road.

Razi finished the first day of his diving course at noon, and I saw him waving to me from a distance. I waved back and motioned for him to come over as I wanted to sit with him at the bar by the beach. He marched towards me, smiling, the clear white of his teeth contrasting brilliantly with his deep tan. I had to admit he was the handsomest man in the place.

"How's the book?" he asked, after kissing me and dropping into the bar chair beside mine.

"It's a classic; a love story that began in secret and lasted a lifetime." I smiled at him.

"Just like ours," he muttered cynically.

"Don't count on it." I smiled again. "I don't have the patience the girl in the book has."

"Neither do I." His turn to smile. "Tonight, you'll find out what we're here to celebrate, but in the meantime, let's order some calamari, I'm famished. Don't forget I've hardly eaten anything since this morning."

"I'll settle for some *labneh* cheese and a salad, I don't feel like eating too heavily in the middle of the day. And maybe I'll have one of his cocktails." I pointed at the barman who was pouring the contents of a blender into a large glass.

Razi ordered everything I had asked for, and a large bowl of fried calamari and a similar cocktail for himself.

I looked at him as he hungrily tackled his calamari, and thought about how he addressed everything in life in a similar energetic way.

In my heart I was wondering why he had bothered to arrange an entire vacation around this mysterious good news. After all, he could have told me over the telephone, or even in a fine neighborhood restaurant. I assumed the news had special significance, and must be meaning-ful and important to him. I appreciated the fact that he wanted to share it with me so badly.

"I'm really happy you insisted we come here," I said. "I

have a feeling this vacation is going to be different — and special."

"Me too." Razi smiled and sipped his cocktail.

I couldn't help but think I had made the right decision in staying with him after I had found out he was married. I had always believed in positive communication, especially in challenging times, which was why Danny and I had managed to maintain a good relationship after our divorce, and also the reason why Razi and I were allowing ourselves to sit together as if we were in heaven, happy and carefree.

Razi finished devouring his pile of calamari, gulped the rest of his cocktail, and asked, "Are you finished eating? Shall we go to the room for a quick nap?"

I finished my cocktail, slid off my barstool, and we went to our room. On the way, we passed some vacationers sunbathing on the beach. As we walked by, my eyes fell on a young, blonde woman with an especially shapely body. She was lying on her back in a red, and less than minimal, swimsuit, I noticed Razi scrutinizing her, his eyes raking her from head to toe. The look must have lasted only a second or two, but it seemed a lot longer to me. I wanted to protest, but I said nothing. As we entered our room, Razi turned and pressed me against the wall. He literally tore off the swimsuit and the shawl I was wearing. "You're stunning, Nicole. More than any other girl on this beach," he whispered, his lips touching my ear. It was as if he was reading my thoughts, that he had somehow divined my discomfort at his looking at another woman. His words, and the soft touch of his lips, sent a tremor of desire coursing through my whole body.

*

Later that evening, we walked arm in arm to the poolside restaurant. We began drinking more of the cocktails we'd had earlier in the bar, wanting to maintain that nice fuzzy feeling we had felt surrounded by after some intense activity in our room.

"What would you like to eat?" asked the swarthy waiter who served us our drinks.

"I'd like Caesar salad and calamari and shrimps in butter and garlic," I said.

"I'll take a Caesar salad as well," Razi said. "And a fillet mignon, medium-rare, and fries. Oh, and a bottle of wine."

When the waiter moved away, Razi took my hand in his and said, "I swear I could spend my whole life here with you." His eyes enveloped me in the warmth of his feelings. "In a perfect world, this is exactly how I would have wanted to live, with the woman I love more than anyone, in the place I love more than anywhere."

I squeezed his hand, excitement melting my heart. "Go on, then, turn your world into perfection." I smiled teasingly. "It's up to you."

"I wish it was only up to me," he sighed. "Unfortunately, it depends on a number of other elements."

"I see," I answered. Disappointment and impatience

surged in me. I realized the conversation wasn't taking the 'wonderful news' direction I had hoped and had, to be honest, expected it to take. I went on, hearing the disapproval in my own voice. "It depends on your wife and the technological development in your company. But what if it takes another ten years before its ready, and you can't sell the company till then? Do you really think 'the woman you love more than anything' will wait that long?"

"Nicole, why are you being so pessimistic?" Razi asked pleadingly. "Isn't it better to be an optimist and believe it's just a matter of a few months before we finish developing the software?"

"You told me your father had invested in the company."

"That's right, and he did that because we have an extremely attractive product. Artificial intelligence is the future, Nicole."

"But what if you aren't successful? I read somewhere there are four-thousand start-up companies in Israel, of which only five percent will survive, and an even smaller percentage will actually make a successful exit."

"Nicole, I'm not some computer geek teenager sitting at home and dreaming of making millions."

"Of course not, or at least, I hope not."

"I'm going to change the world," Razi interrupted. Then he said in a more assured tone, "You need to trust me and believe that I know what I'm doing."

"Of course," I replied.

"The others only want money," he said, meaning his

wife and investors, but I'm dreaming about turning the world into a better place and leaving my mark on it."

"And what if you don't? What if … I don't know … something happens? This is our future we're talking about, Razi," I said. I didn't bother to hide my agitation.

"It won't make any difference as far our relationship is concerned."

"Why won't it make a difference?" I inadvertently raised my voice and noticed the couple sitting at the next table were staring at us and exchanging whispers in French.

But I did not relent and Razi, trying to calm me down, exclaimed, "Because Dorit and I are getting divorced." He flashed a triumphant smile at me.

"What?"

"Yes, Nicole, darling. Dorit and I are signing the divorce agreement this very week."

"What?" I said again, my voice rising. Now I cared even less about the French couple and their reproachful looks. "But what about the value of the company and the new software?"

"My father is prepared to sign a written guarantee that she will get her money, adjusted to the real value of the company, right after the development is completed, or in five years at the latest."

"What?" I realized I was in danger of sounding like an echo, but I couldn't help myself.

"My lawyer spoke with her and showed her the astronomical figures she can expect, assuming she agreed to divorce me immediately. Do you see, Nicole? It means Dorit will get her share, and, more importantly, I will have the freedom to be with you. It's all signed and sealed — or at least it will be by the end of the week."

"Razi," I said, relief and joy flooding through me, "this is wonderful news."

It was only after Razi had said the things that I had so desperately been yearning to hear that I realized how badly the uncertain nature of our relationship had been affecting me.

Razi poured wine into our glasses and said, "Let's raise a toast to us, and to the freedom of being together."

"Oh, yes," I breathed. I clinked my glass with his, wanting to treasure this magical moment.

"Hold on, why did it take you so long to tell me?" I smiled to take the edge off my words.

"I want things to always be interesting when you're with me." He laughed. "That way, you won't ever be bored and want to leave me."

When we finished the meal, we went to the hotel's Bedouin tent where we lounged on the large pillows, drank *sahlab*, and watched a belly dancer performing. When Razi took me in his arms, I felt, no I *knew*, I was the luckiest woman on Earth.

*

The following days drifted lazily by. Our schedule, such as it was, remained pretty much as it had been on the first day. Razi woke very early and went diving, while I would rise somewhat later and swim in the pool for half an hour. After a pampering breakfast, I would lie on the magical beach and read. Now and then, I would take a quick swim, or snorkel along the beautiful reef.

At noon, when Razi came back, we would sit together at the beach bar. We would eat and drink heavenly-tasting cocktails. Then, for dessert, we would retreat to our room and wallow in afternoon sex.

In the evenings, we would go out to dine, and watch the belly dancers in the Bedouin tent, or take a walk along the moonlit beach. On one of our evenings, we talked about a brother or sister for Itay, something I wanted so much to give my son. Talking about Itay suddenly made me remember I hadn't called him at all that day. I left Razi to watch the belly dancing and hurried back to our room to call my son before his bedtime.

As I walked quickly back to the room, I pondered on how amazing it was that Razi always managed to detach me from reality, and he did it every single time. However, as much as I was wrapped up in Razi and our love, I also knew I had a son who needed my attention, and I wasn't about to neglect him in any way. I quickly went into our room, opened the safe and took out my cellphone. When I switched it on, I saw another message had arrived from an anonymous number.

Chapter 7

'*Nicole, Razi is the complete opposite of the man you think he is. And he's dangerous.*'

I read and re-read the message. This was the second one I had received from an anonymous number. But this time, it was more personal, the sender using my name and bluntly warning me off Razi. I wondered who it could be, and why whoever it was considered Razi to be dangerous, and what it was really all about.

I tried to reply to the message, to discover the sender's telephone number and identity, but I wasn't able to. Whoever had sent it knew how to block any response. For a moment, I forgot all about my original intention of calling Itay before he went to bed. But only for a moment.

I quickly called Danny's number. Itay answered. "Mommy!" He sounded excited, "I was waiting for you to call."

"And I was waiting to talk to you, sweetie. Are you having fun with Daddy?"

"Yes, when are you coming back?" he asked eagerly, with the bluntness of youthful innocence.

"Soon, very soon." I felt emotion swell and it took all my mental strength to go on speaking in a normal, steady voice. "I called to say I love you."

"I love you too, Mommy."

Later, after the call, I sat on the bed holding my head in my hands. Thoughts swirled and pounded in my mind. Who could have sent me such a message? I thought it had to be Razi's wife. I tried to convince myself she was trying to ruin things for us, trying to prevent her divorce from Razi from going ahead, despite the new agreement he had told me about. For a moment, I thought I should tell Razi about this new message, then I thought better of it and decided it would be better not to tell him anything. Then I wondered if maybe someone was trying to protect me from something Razi had been hiding all through our relationship.

I came to a decision. The first thing I had to do was sort this out with Razi's wife. I would call her as soon as Razi and I got back from our vacation. And if she didn't explain what the messages were all about and give me a convincing story, then, and only then, would I confront Razi.

When I got back to the tent, Razi was lying on the cushions, a glass of wine beside him. "That was a long telephone conversation. I was starting to miss you," he smiled.

I don't know what made me lie to him, but I said instinctively, "Itay's not feeling well."

"What?' he looked at me, surprise in his eyes. "You're not thinking about going home, are you?" he asked. "We're here now, and we still have two more days to enjoy this paradise."

"I'm sorry," I said. "I talked to him and promised I'd

go back to take care of him. You can stay here if you want, I'm fine with that."

"Hold on." Razi straightened. "Can't Danny take care of him? I'm sure he can take him to the doctor, can't he?"

"Razi, I've also had a ton of urgent messages from work. I love you, but everything that's happening back home is getting to me, making me feel ... unsettled. I'm really sorry."

He sighed. "Okay, so we'll go back day after tomorrow, right after I finish the diving course. All right?"

"Fine."

*

I decided not to tell Danny and Itay straightaway that I was home. I needed a day to myself to try and make sense of that latest mysterious message. I took a long shower, then I called Anna and invited her over. I had to tell her about all of the exciting news and, more importantly, get her opinion.

My loyal friend arrived in no time, bearing a bag with two bottles of wine and appetizers, which she quickly arranged on the living room table.

"All right," I said, as I opened one of the bottles and poured wine for us both. "Ready to hear my Sinai Desert adventures?"

"I've never been readier." She sat beside me and clinked her glass against mine. "Start talking."

I told her everything from the beginning, about the

technology Razi's company was attempting to develop, his divorce, and the strange new message I had received.

"Unbelievable, I don't have that many adventures in ten years!" Anna exclaimed.

"Well, I'm happy you're having fun listening to my stories," I grumbled, "but the intention wasn't for you to be entertained. I was hoping you'd be able to help me understand what's going on."

"What do you mean?" she said almost disbelievingly. "The only thing that's going on is that your hunky, gorgeous Prince Charming is going to make it big time in the not-so-distant future, and people are trying to damage him in some way. Face it, Nicole, you've won the jackpot. What more do you want?"

"What I want is to know who exactly sent me that message, and why."

"Don't be naive, Nicole."

"What do you mean?"

"You're a big girl. You know how to handle yourself. Why don't you talk to Razi's wife and tell her to stop sending them?" Anna suggested.

"That's what I had originally decided to do. But now, I just don't know… it feels like a betrayal." I sighed. "I even had to lie to Razi when I told him I had to come home because Itay was sick. It makes me feel uncomfortable."

"Why? Didn't he keep his marital status a secret from you? Yes, he did! Well, now you're even," she said.

"And what if the first message was actually true?" I finally got to the question that had been bothering me the most. "How do I know the message was a lie? Anna, do you understand what that would mean?"

"All right, settle down," Anna said soothingly. "This isn't a horror movie. If you really want to know the truth, just call his wife and ask her. I'm sure she'll be happy to tell you how the prince turned into a monster." She laughed and emptied the bottle of wine into our glasses.

"That's exactly what I'll do," I said. I suddenly felt determined, purposeful. I guess the wine must have put me in a courageous mood. "In fact, I'll call her right now. When Razi dropped me off, he said he was going to his parent's house, so he won't be there."

"All right, hold on a second." Anna fiddled with her cellphone and several minutes later said, "Here, write her number down. Even Google's working with you on this."

Before I could hesitate, I dialed the number, swallowed what remained of my wine, and pressed the call button.

"Hello?" a drowsy feminine voice responded.

"Hi, is this Razi Zonenberg's wife?" I asked quickly, subduing the sudden urge to hang up the phone.

"Yes, why? Has anything happened to him?" the voice was awake now, and sounding a little panicky.

"No, he's fine," I answered in the most soothing tone I could muster. "I wanted to ask you something about him."

"Who are you?" her voice was suddenly suspicious and alert.

"My name is Nicole, and I know you're the one who's

been sending me those anonymous text messages. I just wanted to tell you that it's not going to work on me."

"Don't you have any sense of shame?" Mrs. Zonenberg lashed out without waiting for me to finish speaking. "You filthy slut, who do you think you are to call me and ask questions about my husband? It's beneath me to talk to a woman like you!"

"Wait a minute, aren't you two getting div..."

I heard a loud click. Razi's wife had hung up. I just sat there holding the phone in my hand, stunned, humiliated, and now extremely nervous.

"I can't believe she hung up on you like that," Anna said. "No wonder Razi wants to divorce her."

"Well, it makes sense. I'd react the same way if someone tried to pry into my private life."

Anna nodded in agreement, and it seemed to me she didn't want to put into words the obvious conclusion.

"If it wasn't her," I wondered aloud, "then who sent me those messages? And why?"

"Based on the way things are going, I have a feeling you're going to find out very soon."

I didn't have to wait long. Only the following morning, I realized just how perceptive Anna had been.

Chapter 8

That morning I woke with a massive headache. I swallowed two aspirins and as I was already up, decided to go in to the office early. I walked into the building parking lot, my head teeming with a list of tasks I knew I had to tackle as soon as possible. Remorse for having left so many matters untended threatened to overwhelm me. I had received countless emails over the past two days, which was typical of the intensive nature of my day-to-day work, certainly after several days' absence. New, unexpected problems arose every day, and we had to solve most of them on the fly.

The parking lot was fairly empty for a weekday, which was why, as I approached my car, I couldn't miss the young, athletic-looking man who was leaning over the driver's door. From where I was, it looked as though he was tampering with it.

I tensed and looked around to check if there were other people in the parking lot. When I saw there were, I hurried over to him and said loudly, "I don't think you should break into this car, sir, there's nothing valuable in it."

The man was obviously startled and turned so quickly his sunglasses were thrown from his face and fell to the concrete floor. The scared look in his eyes almost immediately morphed into bewilderment. It was a good recovery, but I knew I had not mistaken the alarm I had seen.

"Excuse me," he said quickly, "but I can't imagine how you got that impression. I have no intention of breaking into your car."

I looked at his hands and saw they were empty, and he wasn't carrying a bag in which to hide any tools. It occurred to me I might have been mistaken — but when I lifted my eyes again to his face, I realized he looked familiar. He had a handsome, Slavic face and large blue eyes. When he bent down to pick up his glasses, I remembered I had seen those same eyes at the country club swimming pool, in line at the supermarket, and in the café I had been to several times with Razi. I remembered vaguely thinking he must live in the neighborhood and hung around the same places everyone else did. But now, having seen him so many times, it seemed a little strange for him to be taking an interest in my car.

"What is it you mean to do, then?" I asked loudly. From the corner of my eye I saw I had managed to get the attention of a few of the neighbors who were on their way to their parked vehicles. Others glanced curiously at us from the open windows of their cars.

I stared at him. "It looks to me like you've been following me, and I want to know why," I said, still speaking loudly. "And if you don't tell me right now, I'm going to call the police."

The drivers around us went on watching with interest,

but refrained from interfering. On the other hand, the man standing by my car did appear to be concerned. He said, "What's wrong with you? Are you paranoid, or what?" He turned and started to walk away, but I wasn't about to let him go. I marched after him, emboldened by the fact that we were surrounded by a group of onlookers.

"Listen," I called after him as he stopped at a vehicle and took car keys out of his pocket. "I'm not going to just let you go without an explanation. If you drive away, I'll write down your license plate number and file a complaint with the police. I don't think you want to get into trouble."

"Need a pen?" shouted one of the drivers still watching from a distance. The others burst out laughing, and none of them seemed in a hurry to leave.

I walked closer to the blue-eyed man who had opened the door to his Subaru and climbed in.

"You were the one that sent me the message, weren't you?" I hissed, lowering my voice this time. "I suggest it's in your interest to cooperate with me. I know your intentions aren't bad; otherwise, you wouldn't have sent me the message. I just want to know why, that's all."

The young man looked at me angrily for a few seconds. Then the tension seemed to leak out of his face. He sighed and said, "All right, so long as you get these people..." he indicated the spectators watching us "... to go on their way."

"I'm not sending anyone anywhere until you explain

what's going on here." I wasn't backing down. "Why are you following me and who sent you?"

"I'm a private investigator," he grudgingly answered in a low voice.

"No way!" I was surprised, and not a little stressed. What possible, logical reason would anyone have to pay a private investigator to follow me? "Do you have a business card?"

"I do." He took a business card from the glove compartment and handed it to me. I examined it closely. The card read, *'Ron Bondi — Detective Agency'*. A shiver rippled up and down my body. I understood none of this. Why would anyone have me followed? And who?

"Who hired you? It isn't Mrs. Zonenberg; I know that because I spoke with her..."

"No..."

"Then who the hell is it?" I demanded.

"It isn't her — Mrs. Zonenberg." He eyed me pensively and was silent for a long moment. Then he spoke again. "Look, I could get in a lot of trouble for telling you this, but I don't want Mrs. Zonenberg to get the blame. It's the widow of the scientist who was a partner at SEG."

"Razi's company? I didn't know he had a partner ..."

"Maybe you should get to know your boyfriend a little better."

"I know him very well."

"I'm sure I could surprise you. Got time for a cup of coffee?"

I was curious, very curious. Even so, I still deliberated

about whether or not I should find out what lay behind this young man's surveillance of me. I was a cautious and suspicious person by nature.

Finally, I decided to trust my instincts, which were telling me Bondi had no intention of harming me. Additionally, the nearby neighborhood café was always busy at that time of morning.

"All right," I said. "We'll go to the café across the street," I pointed, "but it'll have to be brief, I don't have much time."

"Fine," he said. He got out of his car and locked it.

The drivers watching us looked everything from surprised to disappointed when we started walking together towards the café. The man who had offered me a pen honked and shouted, "Lady, is everything all right?"

"Everything's fine," I said, so they all could hear. "Thank you, you're all dismissed!"

"Everyone's bored in this country," Bondi hissed under his breath as the cars moved off to the parking lot exit. "Sticking their noses where they don't belong."

"I think it's nice," I smiled. "At least a woman can feel safe when she's being followed."

"Whatever." He shrugged.

We sat at the only available table in the café, possibly vacant because it was situated in the sun rather than the shade. The waitress bustled over and we ordered two lattes. When she had gone, Bondi lit a cigarette and gave me a hostile look. "Well, what do you want to know?"

"Everything," I said defiantly. "Who sent you to follow me and why, God damn it?"

"I'll tell you everything, but first, I need you to promise me you won't say a word to anyone else about this... this meeting, and anything you might hear in it."

"I can't promise you anything before I hear what this is all about," I snapped impatiently.

"All right," he replied, his tone now sarcastic, "I guess it won't surprise you to hear you have a lover called Razi Zonenberg, right?"

"Funny!" I said making it clear I thought it was anything but. "Let me remind you, I can call the police at any moment."

"All right, I get it." He suddenly smiled, just as the waitress came back with our lattes. She put them down on the table.

"So, it goes like this." He took a sip of coffee and began. "I'm sure you know that Zonenberg is the CEO of a high-tech company called SEG, a company that deals with technological developments in the mapping and storage of data derived from photographic images. It's all based on artificial intelligence."

"Yes, so what?" I kept my expression blank.

"And I assume you've also heard their new creation is based on an idea originally conceived by a doctor of optical physics called Giora Golan — who killed himself a year ago."

The utter amazement that washed through me wiped

the blankness from my poker face for a moment. I'd known nothing of this … this … insane story.

Bondi was watching me carefully. "I see you haven't heard about it," he said with obvious satisfaction. "And if that's the case, I bet you also don't know that Shraga Zonenberg, your Razi's father, went to see the scientist's widow while she was still in mourning, still traumatized over the recent death of her husband, and bought all her husband's company stock from her for a pittance."

"That can't be true," I said. I couldn't believe him. It all sounded surreal. As if it was a story from a third-rate telenovela rather than real life — certainly not my life.

"Oh, it's real all right," he answered quietly. "Mrs. Olga Golan realized what Shraga Zonenberg had done only six months later, when she happened to read a newspaper article about a group of Russians who were offering to purchase the Zonenberg's company for twenty million dollars. The Zonenbergs paid her only a hundred thousand dollars for her stock!"

"Maybe, when the scientist passed away, they hadn't realized they would be able to sell the company for such big money?" I found myself trying to defend Razi and his family.

"You think?" Bondi smiled apologetically, the way someone would smile at an innocent little girl. "First off, he did not just 'pass away'; he committed suicide, and even that isn't a certainty. Secondly, it's a type of fraud, isn't it? You, as a financial expert, should know that better that me."

I flinched inwardly as he corrected my knowledge of how the poor doctor had died, as if he were trying to hint at something I could not entirely understand. I also had nothing to say to contradict his second argument, because I knew very well what he meant. No one invests in digital developments before they conduct feasibility studies, which would include an estimate of the final product's worth.

"Furthermore," he verbally pounded on me, "the deceased left three children behind. The psychological treatment they need by itself costs a fortune. And when the widow went to Shraga Zonenberg asking him to at least pay her a few hundred thousand dollars more after the sale, so she could care for her children and see to their future, he set his lawyers on her. They threatened to sue her for trying to breach a signed contract."

The disgust I felt upon hearing the story was more than I could bear, but I did not forget, even for a moment, that I still had to get to the office. If I just went on sitting there, listening to something that sounded like it was straight off a television screen, the authenticity of which I couldn't be sure, I would not get there, even by tomorrow.

"Listen, Bondi," I said impatiently, "this whole story sounds terrible and really doesn't sound like the man I'm going out with. I don't understand what you want from me. Why are you following me, of all people? And why did you send that message?"

"To be honest, I thought you knew much more," he

explained. "I've been dealing with this case for several months now, trying to find out what exactly happened to Dr. Golan. Shraga Zonenberg is a suspicious man. In fact, he is so discreet that he and his wife hardly leave their house. Razi, on the other hand, is very active, dynamic even. It was only after I'd been following him for three months that I realized what was going on in his love life — the romantic triangle with you and his wife. That was when I decided to concentrate my efforts on you. You seem to have a much more intimate and communicative relationship with Razi than his wife does."

"Really?" I gave him a piercing look. I wanted to know if he truly meant what he'd said, or whether he was trying to soften me up with compliments so I'd promise not to say anything to Razi. "And how would you know that? Have you bugged his house, planted cameras and microphones?"

"Let's just say I have my sources." Bondi stifled a smile.

"All right," I said and decided to use Bondi's knowledge to my own ends. "So maybe these 'sources' have also told you Razi and his wife have a separation agreement, and they are about to divorce soon?"

The investigator said nothing and seemed lost in thought for a long moment. "My sources have said nothing about an agreement, but from what they have said, I know he and his wife live in a sort of cold peace. Very cold. When he stays in the house, he mostly sleeps in their living room, and they hardly ever talk."

"I understand," I said keeping my expression blank,

trying to conceal just how pleased and content this information made me feel.

"But if you like, I can ask my sources to find out if they're really about to sign a divorce agreement," Bondi offered.

"But only if I don't tell Razi about you and that you've been following him?"

"You're catching on fast," the detective smiled.

I glanced at my watch. Time had flown, it was already ten."

Before we left the café I said, "Tell me, Bondi, what do you think really happened to Dr. Golan?"

He looked around shiftily and spoke cautiously. "Look, the police enquiry determined he killed himself by jumping from the twelfth floor of the Europa Hotel in Tel Aviv. But I have to say, it's my impression the police have been negligent in their work."

"Why?"

"There are all sorts of strange details that don't mesh well with a suicide. A day after the suicide, Razi invited engineers from Lock-space, who had come to Israel solely for that purpose, to a presentation at the Raja Hotel, which is only about three hundred feet from the Europa Hotel. On the day of the suicide, around noontime, Giora called Razi and they had a thirty-four-minute telephone conversation. A few hours later, Giora 'jumped' from the hotel roof without leaving a note or any other indication of his intent to commit suicide."

"So, Razi is involved?" I whispered hesitantly, and felt chills run down my spine.

"I'm certain of it."

"And what did Razi say to the police?" I suddenly felt ludicrously like a detective in a crime series on television.

"Your boyfriend claimed that Golan had a strained relationship with his wife, that the scientist was often nervous and on edge when he came in to the office, and that he, Razi, thought the suicide had something to do with that."

"This is the same wife who is now your client?" I asked.

He nodded. "She categorically denies this claim. She admits their relationship wasn't exactly rosy, but that was hardly a reason for him to kill himself."

"So, what does she think actually happened?"

"Olga told me that the tension between Golan and Razi started when Razi allowed his father to invest in the company instead of trying to raise money from an outside investor. By doing that, they held on to the majority of the company's shares."

"So, what you're saying," I said slowly, "is that Razi and his father intentionally reduced Golan's percentage of the company shares, and increased their own so they could control all of the decision making."

"You need to understand, Nicole," Bondi said earnestly, "this science of artificial intelligence is still taking its first baby steps. But those who know a little something about it have already realized it's capable of changing the world order, and is worth a lot of money."

"So actually… she suspects they are… responsible for Golan's death?" I asked hesitantly.

"More or less." Bondi put his sunglasses on and looked directly at me. "She didn't speak about it right after his death, but then she told me that artificial intelligence had been the topic of Golan's PhD thesis, and that when they had established the company, Razi promised him they would go hand in hand all the way. It was only after Razi's father's behavior during the mourning period for her husband that she began suspecting something was very off about the Zonenberg family."

"And the police have never suspected them?" I asked in a defensive tone.

"Apparently not. Look, Shraga and Razi are both very persuasive and well-connected," he said. "Although I have to admit this whole suicide story sounds illogical."

"So why didn't the widow say anything to the police about her suspicion that her husband's death wasn't suicide?"

"Because she was shocked and devastated. And the Zonenberg family had gone out of its way to support her during the first few months after Dr. Golan's death. At least, they had until she asked them for financial aid. Then they showed their true faces and set their lawyers on her."

"Don't say 'they'!" I shuddered. "You have no proof

that Razi knows anything about his father instructing lawyers to act against the widow."

"You really believe Razi doesn't know anything?"

"I believe a person is innocent until proven guilty, and so far, it seems to me all you know for sure is that Razi's dad acted like a crook and a bully, not Razi himself!" I said defiantly. "Besides, if Mrs. Golan suspected her husband had been murdered from the first moment, why did she agree to sell the company shares to Shraga for a pittance?"

"Maybe because she was still in mourning and was shocked by the whole affair and under the influence of psychiatric medication?" Bondi replied in a decisive tone. "People in that sort of state tend to make bad decisions."

"All right." I took another glance at my watch. It was eleven thirty. "I have to get going…"

Bondi flagged the waitress who came across to our table. He paid the check and stood up. I rose heavily after him, deeply troubled by what he had told me. We walked in silence to my car, and only when we reached it did Bondi come to the main point. He said, "The morning after Golan's suicide, Razi and his father's telephone numbers and devices changed. Razi keeps both SIM cards from the old devices in his wallet."

"What are you trying to say?"

"That if there was a way for us to locate those SIM cards, we might know for sure whether or not Razi and his father were involved."

"And if we don't?" I asked.

"Nicole, do you want to live with a dubious man? One you suspect of doing evil things?"

I stopped in my tracks and Bondi stopped with me. I looked into his blue eyes and said, "Razi is my companion. Everything you've told me is based on a theory devised by a woman who takes pills to control a psychiatric disorder. Bondi, I had to lie to Razi because of your message, and I have no intention of spying on him or snooping in his wallet, so please, leave me alone."

"You have my phone number," he said as I got into my car. "I know the truth is important to you. I'll be waiting for your call, Nicole."

"Forget it," I snapped. "It isn't going to happen." I started the car and quickly drove to work.

Chapter 9

When I got to the office, I felt an inexplicable motivation to quickly and efficiently deal with the list of tasks piled up on my desk. So, I immediately summoned the staff to a quick meeting, the sort that would make me forget about Bondi's stories. But even as I listened to other people talking, my mind was still seething, still troubled by unsolved questions that made everything a confused mess.

I had enough questions to confront Razi with, but I couldn't help also wondering about the questions that now concerned the Zonenberg family. What kind of person was Razi's father to rob a widow with three children as Bondi had described?

When the meeting was over and the staff had left my office, I took the card Bondi had given me out of my purse. I had to hold something tangible, something that would confirm the meeting had actually taken place, that I hadn't dreamed or imagined it.

I looked at the card in my hand. The words were clearly printed in bold black ink, 'Ron Bondi — Detective Agency.' Beneath, in smaller print, were two telephone numbers beginning with a '03' area code, which meant his office was somewhere in or around Tel Aviv. I still couldn't understand why Bondi had assumed I would cooperate with him. What did he actually know about me?

Suddenly, I saw Shay Barkay, the company's content vice president walking down the corridor. I remembered how he had sought out my company soon after my divorce. Shay was about my age and came from Kibbutz Beit Hashita. Like me, he had also enjoyed a career that included rapid promotion. At the same time, he had studied film at Tel Aviv University, and had started working as a screenwriter and television director for the Israeli Educational channel. He soon became its chief director. When the commercial channel was established, he had been offered the role of content vice president, which carried a generous salary package, so he would agree to leave his position with the Educational Television channel. Our resumes had a lot more in common than Razi and I had.

'My girlfriend from the valley,' was how he referred to me when he was in a light-hearted mood, because he had grown up in a small town not far from Beit Shean, the city in which I had been raised.

"I wish I'd known you back then," he once said, smiling at me, exposing two sweet dimples that creased his cheeks. "What a missed opportunity! I would have gladly given up Tel Aviv to go back to the peace and serenity they have up north, and live there with you."

We occasionally discussed this subject during the rare breaks I allowed myself throughout my intense working days. He didn't bother to hide the fact that he liked me. He told me he had grown tired of meaningless dates, and that he felt he was ready to settle down and start a family. He also never bothered to hide his desire to become a father. Despite his open attitude, I had never succumbed to his attempts to woo me, even though, on paper, he had all the positive qualities I was looking for in a man.

Razi, on the other hand, was a man who had the innate ability to thrill a woman. That he had lived his life pulling out all the stops, challenged me. I wasn't innocent or naive, and I was still convinced that everyone had a couple of skeletons hidden somewhere in their closets, and that included Shay. One of the things I had learned in my relationship with Danny was that everyone has secrets, and no one ever tells everything — even to those who are closest to them. It isn't that a man plans to hide things, he simply chooses not to talk about them. Now, I suddenly had secrets from the man I loved, secrets I wouldn't have had if Bondi hadn't decided I should be the one to help him. I told myself that what was important was that my lies had no evil or harmful intentions; they were simply white lies. And I almost believed it.

Did Bondi really think I would spy on my own boyfriend? That I would rummage through his wallet, steal the SIM cards and hand them over to him? Soon, Razi would divorce his wife and we would be living together, so why would Bondi think he could recruit me to help him with his mission? The more I thought about the messages, and about the attempt to break into my car, and the way he had tried to manipulate me in the café, the angrier I became.

Whatever happened, I was sure I wasn't prepared to live a life of constant uncertainty and uncomfortable feelings caused by spying on Razi. In the end, I was sure I would find there was no problem with him and everything would be fine. I've heard many stories about good relationships falling apart because of unfounded suspicions. By the time one party or the other discovered the suspicions had no basis in reality, the damage had already been done, the rift too deep to mend. A good relationship, like the one I had with Razi, wasn't easy to come by.

I was damned if I was going to be a pawn in whatever game Bondi and Mrs. Golan were playing. They were wrong to think they could influence me enough to hide what they were doing from Razi. I had to tell Razi about the mysterious messages, about my call to Dorit and about my meeting with Bondi. I was sure Razi would have a logical explanation for the scientist's suicide.

*

It was already four in the afternoon by the time Razi entered the apartment. I had called him earlier and told him there was something important I wanted to discuss with him before I picked Itay up from Danny.

When he came in, I was sitting in the kitchen with two wine glasses waiting on the table. There was a plate of bruschetta beside the glasses, some of them spread with sliced cherry tomatoes, mozzarella cubes and basil, others with pesto and goat cheese.

I got up to greet him and we hugged and kissed. I realized he had seen the open suitcase on the floor when he drew back from me. He said, "I see you haven't unpacked, yet."

"I'll take care of it later on."

I was hoping he wouldn't sense the tension in my mood, so I tried to be as calm as possible.

Razi looked at the set dining table. "The bruschetta certainly look appetizing," he said. But instead of sitting at the table, he went to the refrigerator. "Would you like a glass of water?" he asked.

"Yes, please." I smiled at him.

"It's been hot today," he said.

"Yes," I said pensively.

We both sat at the table. He took a sip of water and asked, "So what is it you wanted to tell me?"

"That Itay's not really sick."

"I see," he said. "Then why did we have to come back early?"

"Because when I went back to the room to call Itay, I saw this message." I switched my phone on and showed him the message.

"What is this?" he said. "It says here that you shouldn't believe a word I say and that I'm dangerous. Who would have sent you a message like this? You think it was Dorit? She's insane, that woman." He paused, and when he spoke again, I heard a trace of nervousness in his voice. "Why on earth would she send you a poisonous message like this?"

"It wasn't her," I said quietly.

"How do you know? She's capable of anything."

"Because I asked her," I replied. "I called her. That's the real reason I wanted to come back early. I wanted to check it out with her before I told you."

"And you believe her?"

"Yes. It wasn't her."

"Who else could it be then?"

"A detective."

"What?"

"Before I go any further, I want you to swear you won't do anything with the information I'm about to give you. And that you won't reveal any of it to your father. I promised to keep this a secret."

"My dad? What's he got to do with this?"

"Razi!"

"All right, all right," he grumbled. "I swear."

"The widow of the scientist who was a partner in your company, Dr. Golan, has hired a private investigator to find out more about the death of her husband."

"Okay." Razi reacted to the news cautiously. "It wasn't an ordinary death anyway. The man committed suicide."

"They're trying to find out why," I replied.

"What?" His eyes narrowed as he watched me. "And just how do you know all this?"

"I met him this morning."

"Met him? The detective? When did that happen?" His voice rose. "And you didn't tell me about that either! What else have you been hiding from me, Nicole?"

"Hold on, Razi, that's not why I asked you to come here."

"I don't believe you."

"Razi, I understand you're under pressure because of your company and the divorce, but I can't go on just accepting all the secrets and plots I seem to be uncovering every day."

"What secrets and plots?"

"Well, for a start, that you're married, and that you had a partner who killed himself. I don't know what else is waiting around the corner to jump out at me. I need you to tell me everything, because I'm just not built for this."

"I've told you about my relationship with Dorit, and you know we're signing the divorce agreement on Thursday."

"That's right, I know that. But what… what about…?"

"What else do you want to know, Nicole?"

"Did you have anything to do with the scientist who killed himself?"

Razi was silent for a moment. I could almost see the cogs of his agile mind meshing, and when he answered my question, it was obliquely. "When I graduated from university with an MBA, I preferred to go straight into the business world and establish a company in a developing field that had a lot of potential. I had become familiar with the world of artificial intelligence during my army service days. Back then, it was still in its infancy, and Dr. Giora Golan, who was considered an expert in the field, offered us guidance. At a certain point, I decided I should simply take the plunge and establish a startup company. I invited Dr. Golan to join me as a partner and he agreed."

"And what about your father?"

"I needed money and connections. I used the fact that my dad had built top-secret facilities in the country and had him join us as an investor in return for shares in the company. His financial input was exactly what I needed."

"So, you were the one who actually set up the company?"

"Yes," he replied laconically. It was evident he wasn't too thrilled to be talking about the subject.

"And Dr. Golan already had a family?"

"Yes."

"What about your brother, the one who lives abroad? Does he have anything to do with the company?"

"My brother, Ronen, is a professor of statistics and research methods at Stanford University in Stanford, California," Razi said. "He doesn't hold any official position in the company, but he helped us find investors in Palo Alto, which is very close to Stanford."

"Was he also the one who found Lock-space for you?"

"Wait a minute, who told you all this?"

"The detective I met with."

"I see he's been thorough in his investigation," Razi said. And there it was again, that tiny hint of nervousness.

I went on pushing as I picked up a bruschetta and bit into it. "And your brother simply volunteered to work for you?"

"My dad asked him to help." Now Razi sounded impatient. "Why are you suddenly so interested in my family history?"

"No particular reason, it's just that it sounds like an interesting story to me," I said. "And I'm sure it involved a lot of serious emotion. After all, your brother, despite being a professor and helping you look for investors, still didn't become part of the company. Didn't he feel frustrated because of that?"

"Why would he feel frustrated?" Razi said. "He's the one who insisted he stay on at Stanford. He has a weakness for academic degrees and he loves studying, so we let him do whatever he wants. If you ask me, he'd rather spend time with his adoring female students than be stuck in an office all day looking at algorithms."

"He's not married?"

"Married with three children." Razi was sounding more and more frustrated. "And you've nothing to worry about him or his children. I suppose he's the first of my siblings mentioned in my parents' will, so financial difficulties should be the least of his, or even his grandchildren's, concerns."

"Why the first? Is he the oldest?"

"Yes, and he's the favored one." He sighed heavily. "I've been the black sheep of the family all these years. In my family, an MBA is the equivalent of what a high school diploma is for a normal family."

"Why didn't you study for a PhD, then?"

"Because the academic world didn't interest me," he

said. He changed tack suddenly. "I don't get it, why all these questions all of a sudden?"

"Like I told you, it just sounds like an interesting story," I replied quickly. "Despite the fact that I'm in accounting, or maybe because of it, I plan to one day write a book, or a screenplay, about a particularly interesting human story."

Razi burst into laughter and sat down. "Are you serious?" he asked as his laughter faded. "Do you really harbor that fantasy?"

"Why not?" I pretended to be insulted by his words. "Don't you think I might be good at it?"

"You would be good at anything you decided to do." He leaned over to stroke my hair. "It's just that I had no idea you were so romantic. Where do you picture yourself writing this book, some remote little garret in Paris?"

"Actually, since I met you, I've been thinking about writing a script." I stroked the muscles on his tanned chest. "You remind me of George Clooney, and I'm considering giving him the lead part in my movie."

"You don't say…?" My compliments were melting Razi like butter — which was exactly what I had planned. "And who would I be playing? Myself?"

"I haven't decided, yet," I went on caressing him. "I'm just gathering material for now, which is why I asked you to tell me about the poor doctor. Maybe, together, we'll figure out why he killed himself."

"What else do you want to ask?" Razi didn't sound hostile anymore.

"How old was he when you started the company?"

"He was forty. Married with three children. He met Olga, his wife, when he was working at LSB Defense Technologies. She immigrated to Israel while her family stayed in the Ukraine."

"Really?" I was beginning to understand why the widow needed financial support. "And they stayed on friendly terms with you?"

"Oh yes. Golan was my partner and we had a good relationship," he replied. "And despite what you think about my parents, we adopted Golan and his wife and children into our family. Giora Golan came from some far-flung kibbutz, and had a very tenuous relationship with his parents and brothers, so he and his family celebrated holidays with us."

"And now that he's dead, you still have a warm relationship with Dr. Golan's widow and her children, yes?"

Razi shook his head. "No, not really. Actually, she drifted away from us after some sort of financial argument."

"The widow? For real? Do you mean to tell me she didn't appreciate everything you'd done for her?"

"Apparently not," he replied. He seemed pleased by the tone of my last few questions. "That's just the way the world goes, there's no lack of ungrateful people."

"What happened? Did she ask for millions in return for her dead husband's shares?"

"Sort of," Razi mumbled. Now he seemed a little embarrassed. "Not millions, but a million dollars. However, because Giora committed suicide before the company was fully developed, it wasn't worth much at the time. My dad felt sorry for her and gave her a lot more than she actually deserved for the shares. But that wasn't enough for her. In fact, only recently, she's started asking for more and has even threatened to sue us. So, I'm sure you can understand, it's difficult to maintain a friendly relationship under those circumstances, no matter how sorry we all feel for her."

"How much did she get?"

"A hundred thousand dollars."

"And she's not suing you? Where does the matter stand now?" I feigned a shocked expression. "You know, Razi," I said, "a woman in such a difficult position, a widow with three children… with no one in the world to care for her… Your dad could have helped her with a little more money as a gesture of good faith, especially seeing as today the company is worth a lot more than what he paid her."

"But…" Razi suddenly looked surprised and a little helpless. He stopped and started again. "This thing isn't going to end with just some money changing hands," he said, "and the truth is, I haven't really been dealing with this. I've been uneasy about her whole situation, especially because of the friendly relationship I had with Giora. In any event, my dad was the one who conducted the negotiations with Mrs. Golan, and I have no idea what his considerations were. I think he was hurt by the fact that she decided to fight us, after everything we'd done for her."

"I don't understand how you, as the company CEO, weren't involved with your father's considerations."

"First of all, because he's the company's principal investor and is, therefore, its board manager. Secondly, because he thinks I'm too soft and don't have enough of a killer instinct to become an excellent businessman like him." Razi's voice rang with bitterness.

I said nothing. I could feel tension slowly spreading through my limbs. The use of the expression 'killer instinct' made me shudder. I wondered if what Razi's father had really meant was that his son was too soft to order the murder, in cold blood, of a partner who was resisting diluting the company shares.

I stood up. "Would you like an espresso?"

"A tall macchiato, please," he said.

"Tell me, does it bother you that your father thinks you're not tough enough?" I asked as I turned the espresso machine on. "Why did you allow him into your company in the first place?"

"No, you tell me, Nicole, does anyone remember who the shareholders in Apple were? Does anyone know who the investors were? It doesn't matter, does it? What matters is who gets to make the crucial decisions. Like I've told you, I want to make a difference in the world, and if that means I have to deal with my dad, or with Giora — and believe me when I say I don't have a clue why he chose to end his life at such a critical moment for the company — then I'll just have to live with it, no matter how hard it gets."

"All right." I smiled at him.

"See?" he said. "I haven't been hiding anything from you."

"Okay."

"But you're hiding things from me!" He suddenly erupted. "And that's wrong."

"What am I hiding?" I felt my face paling.

"The detective's name."

"I can't tell you that, Razi." I told him firmly. "He asked me not to share any of the details of our meeting with you."

"Nicole, we're a couple, for God's sake. You have to tell me!"

"What you're asking me to do is really unfair," I said quietly. I had my back to him as I spoke.

Razi got up and took a step towards me. "Nicole, I'm about to divorce my wife for you. Do you understand what that means?"

"You're not divorcing for my sake, Razi. You're divorcing to regain your freedom and for your own personal reasons." I turned to face him, holding two cups of coffee, one in each hand. Razi was less than a foot away from me, his face was flushed.

"You lied to me," he accused. "And now you're hiding things from me. I'm not leaving until you tell me the name of the idiot who's been following me."

"You? He's been following me, Razi! And the way you're trying to portray me as being unfaithful is very irritating. Don't forget, if you hadn't been such a coward, you wouldn't have hidden the fact that you're married from me for six whole months!"

"Don't you dare call me a coward!" His face darkened and he took another step towards me, his eyes now blazing with sudden anger. "Do you hear? Don't you ever dare call me a coward!"

I was so scared by Razi's sudden and utter transformation that I started to retreat from the kitchen. I took one step backwards; my foot caught on the edge of the open suitcase and I fell backwards into it. Pain surged through me as the iron edges of the case smacked into my back. Fortunately, the two cups of coffee didn't hit me as they fell and shattered on the floor. Scalding coffee splashed in every direction but, luckily, none of it went on me. The pain in my back was so sudden, so severe, that I groaned aloud.

Razi was suddenly terrified, mortified. "Forgive me, Nicole, I'm so sorry." He leaned down to offer me his hand. I grabbed at it and tried to get up, but my back hurt so badly I couldn't move. A great, paralyzing fear flooded through me, and all I could do was hope the awful pain was emanating from pulled muscles, and not from any deeper, and more abiding, damage to my spine.

Chapter 10

Razi bent down and tried to steady me in his arms. "Are you in a lot of pain?" he asked softly when I groaned again.

"Yes," I muttered, "but... I... can't... spend the rest of my life in a suitcase, can I?"

"I guess not." He smiled compassionately and gently picked me up. I almost screamed with the sharpness of the pain, but I bit my lip and used the deep breathing technique I had studied in my *Lamaze* class. Despite everything, I was able to take encouragement from the fact that I could still move my limbs, a sure sign that no irreparable damage had been done.

Razi gently carried me through to the lounge and lowered me onto the sofa. He quickly cleaned up the remains of the coffee, picked up the broken glass, carefully helped me drink some water, and then picked up the telephone and called the number for Emergency Services.

"I have an emergency here," he said. "My girlfriend's fallen on her back and is in excruciating pain. You need to help me find a doctor or an orthopedist, or at least a first-class chiropractor who can get her up on her feet again."

"There's no need," I shouted at him, and tried to get up off the sofa, but I simply couldn't, the pain was paralyzing.

Nevertheless, I called out to Razi again. "Razi, just give me a few minutes and I'll be fine." But he ignored me and pressed on, holding the phone away from his ear and explaining,

"We'll use your private medical insurance; I'll get you the best orthopedist."

Razi looked at me, his eyes soft, enveloping. "Don't worry, Nicole, you'll be fine. Your muscles are strong."

"There's no need, really," I whispered and tried to force myself to slowly rise. It was no good, the pain was too great. "Ouch, I can't sit up," I moaned and leaned my head back against the cushions.

Razi looked at me in silence. He put the phone down and I could see he was thinking about what to do next.

"The pain must be coming from my muscles cramping after the sudden fall backwards," I said, trying to calm him. "I don't think it's serious. For now, could you please bring me a painkiller? They're in the bathroom cabinet."

"But what if the situation gets worse instead of better?" Razi asked, still sounding stressed as he walked to the bathroom.

"Then I'll let you get me that expert orthopedist," I replied, and carefully tried to straighten my back.

Razi came back from the bathroom with a painkiller. He put it on my tongue and gave me some water. "Now what?" he asked. "Where's the ice?" He went to the refrigerator, wrapped some ice cubes in two dishtowels and came back to the sofa. Slowly, gently, he helped me turn around and carefully put the dishtowels under my shirt.

"The ice cubes will help prevent inflammation," he said in an authoritative, doctor-like tone.

The pill I swallowed took effect relatively fast, so it wasn't long before I was able to lever myself into a sitting position on the sofa on my own.

"I want you back up on your feet as soon as possible," he said, his tone concerned.

"Of course you do," I feigned a sigh.

"Stop it, Nicole, why are you being so cynical?" he said. He sat beside me and gently stroked my head. "I'm sorry about that stupid argument. Really. Do you forgive me?"

"I don't know yet," I answered. I realized I was still angry.

"I'm sorry, my lovely," he leaned over and kissed my clenched lips. "Are you hungry? Do you want me to order us something to eat?"

"You could do that." Actually, now that the pain was receding, I was starting to feel a little hungry again.

Razi picked up the telephone and ordered several dishes from the neighborhood Thai restaurant. Then he came back to sit beside me and went on stroking my head and apologizing.

"Nicole, you're right," he suddenly admitted. "I really am a coward. I'm afraid that I won't be able to fulfil my destiny, in spite of the heavy price I'm paying."

"What price?"

"In a few days, I'll have to face my children and tell them I'm leaving the house. I'm afraid to face the tears and the accusing faces of my children when they realize I'm about to ruin their world. After all, none of this is their fault, right?"

"Right," I answered, although his question sounded rhetorical. "But this is just the way things are in this imperfect world of ours. People get divorced. It happens all the time, and not just to entrepreneurs with big dreams."

"This isn't right, everything you said before. It would be much nicer if you actually respected what I'm trying to do in this world instead of interrogating me as if I'm in some police investigation. It would be nice if you cooperated with me and helped me face the people who are trying to hurt me. Trying to hurt both of us, really."

"Of course, but why do you think I'm not being cooperative? I've told you everything."

"Except for the name of the person who's been following me, sending my girlfriend messages from an unlisted number, inviting her to have coffee so he can falsely accuse me of God knows what, and manipulating us into having an unnecessary argument…"

Much to my relief, the sound of the doorbell interrupted his diatribe. Razi went to take the food from the delivery guy, then sat beside me and started feeding me like he was a devoted nurse, occasionally tasting the food and making happy sounds. When he finished eating, he turned the television on and started channel-surfing, while I sat there asking myself how I'd gotten into a situation where I was sitting beside Razi and fishing the last rice noodles out of a box, instead of having my arms around my son.

"Razi, I'm going to pick Itay up from Danny's," I said.

He turned the television off and stood up.

"Can you help me get to the car?" I asked.

"Sure," he said. He helped me up, took my bag, and went down in the elevator with me, all the way down to the parking lot.

"I'll manage from here," I told him as I climbed carefully, and not a little painfully, into my car. "Thanks, Razi."

"What for?" He smiled. "Seriously though, call me when you get back," he said. Then he added, "Nicole, I don't think I've ever loved anyone as much as I love you."

"I love you, too. But now let me go get my son before he forgets he has a mother."

"Sure." It looked like it was hard for Razi to let go, but, finally, he closed the door and turned to his own car.

When I got to Danny's, I called him from the car and asked him to come down with Itay. My son was napping in his father's arms, so Danny placed him in the back seat and buckled his seatbelt.

"Hi, sweetie, I've missed you," I whispered to the sleepy Itay, but when I tried to get up from the driver's seat, a sharp pain seared through me. "Ouch," I groaned. "Danny, give me a hand."

Danny gave me a surprised look and helped me out of the car. I went to the back seat and looked at Itay. It seemed to me he had grown over the past few days while I had been away on vacation. I kissed his drowsy face.

Danny, who was standing behind me, helped me straighten up. He had a worried expression on his face.

"What happened to you?" he demanded.

"I fell," I replied. "Razi was at my place. We had an argument. I didn't pay attention and tripped on a suitcase."

"How do you trip on a suitcase?" he persisted.

"I was too lazy to unpack it and left it open in the living room. I took a step back, tripped, and fell on top of it."

"I don't believe you," Danny's voice was raised. "Did Razi push you? Because if that asshole touched you…".

"Shh…" I whispered. "You'll wake Itay — and *no*, Razi didn't push me." I denied Danny's unrealistic accusation. "I took a step back without looking, tripped on the suitcase and fell. I should have paid better attention."

"He tripped you," Danny insisted angrily, his old jealousy getting the better of him. "God, Nicole, if you hadn't tripped, he might have ended up hitting you.

I swear I would kill him if that had happened! I don't understand why you're having a relationship with such a lunatic."

"Razi is not a violent man," I replied firmly. "You're exaggerating. He was just angry at me for calling him a coward. But he never raised a hand to me or anything like that. I was just a little scared by his reaction. It was out of proportion. As you know, personally, I don't stay in relationships that aren't good for me."

"What can I tell you?" Danny looked defeated, but the worried expression did not leave his face. "For your sake,

I hope I'm wrong. Need any help with anything before I go back up?"

"No," I said. "Just help me get back into the car."

When I was seated in the car — with Danny's help — I heard my cellphone bleeping. Looking at the screen, I saw it was a new message from an unlisted number. I tapped the link attached to the message and was directed to an online article featuring an interview with Razi. The title read, *'Artificial Intelligence in the Service of Satellite Technology. Razi Zonenberg talks about his million-dollar deal with Lock-space.'*

My eyes darted over the headlines, but I simply couldn't take it all in. My eyes felt leaden with tiredness. I put a sliver of mint chewing gum in my mouth to help me focus and drove home.

Chapter 11

Razi decided to take a few days off to spend my sick leave with me. His desire to support and help me warmed my heart and brought me closer to him, although, deep inside, I still felt confused over his angry outburst that had so thoroughly surprised me. I felt I had been exposed for the first time to some hitherto hidden, damaged aspect of him, possibly rooted in his childhood. I hadn't suspected such anger existed in him, but, in his defense, he had apologized, his contrition apparently genuine. And his caring attitude towards me caused my love for him to blossom to the degree that I found it easy to repress the memories of the events that had led up to that painful fall. I had more or less forgiven him, and somehow managed to stop thinking about those awful events, as they seemed to contradict so strongly with Razi's normal bearing and behavior, his family and general background. I realize now that social stigmas also helped me convince myself that what had happened had been a one-time outburst and not a reflection of Razi's normal behavior. The many hours we had spent together in the apartment proved to me that our relationship was constantly growing stronger — at least it was, as long as the outside world did not interrupt us. Razi arrived every morning at around eight and made breakfast for both of us while I read the newspaper. Then, we would take out our laptops, place them on the table and work like a couple of carefree students.

I was happy when he asked me to help him prepare a presentation for the roadshow[1], to help him raise funds for the company. It was one of the aspects of my work I liked best. In light of the data sent by the company's CFO, it appeared we would need to raise about twelve million dollars for us to develop the artificial intelligence.

The company had achieved two significant milestones that were crucial to highlight in the presentation. The first was related to the company's intellectual property, based on the patent Dr. Golan had sold to it in return for shares. The first time I came across a document approving the patent, and bearing Dr. Golan's name, I couldn't help but feel a certain uneasiness. But after Anna convinced me it wasn't my job to set myself up as the law, I tried to repress the story of his suicide, although it did still continue to bother me. The second milestone was the million-dollar deal signed between SEG and Lock-space for artificial intelligence-based cameras.

"Lock-space paid you a million dollars?"

"Yes." Razi smiled. "It's a huge deal, and it proves the market is willing to invest money in the technology."

"But the technology doesn't exist. Is this why you're doing the financial road show?"

---

1. A marketing process in which companies present their capital-raising intentions to investors.

"You're right, it doesn't. But we don't have to deliver the technology for five years. And that gives us enough time to take a trip around the moon!" Razi smiled, and smoothed his hair back with one hand.

"I'm fine right here on Earth," I said.

When we finished preparing the presentation, I was convinced that would be the last of the volunteer work I had to perform for my future husband's company.

*

One evening, about two weeks later, Razi and I drove to ancient Caesarea. We ate at a fish restaurant built on the cliff above the sea. We strolled among the summer festival stalls showcasing local handicrafts, and we watched the movie, 'Gone with the Wind, shown on a giant outdoor screen.

And all the time, Razi somehow created a bubble of romance around the two of us that left me in no doubt about the genuineness of his love for me.

On the drive back to Tel Aviv, a long silence settled in the car, and I sensed Razi was troubled by something.

"Nicole," he suddenly blurted, breaking the silence. "We need your help."

"Oh, is there something wrong with the presentation?" I asked.

"No, it isn't that. Open the glove compartment, please." I did as he asked and took out a folded newspaper.

"Have you seen the article in it?" he asked. I unfolded

the newspaper and looked at the article it featured. I glanced at the headline and my heart froze. It read. *'Court orders SEG's financial roadshow delayed until lawsuit brought by the company's senior partner's widow is examined.'*

The headline was enough to make my breath catch in my throat, but I went on reading the article itself. It stated that a month or so earlier, underwriters representing SEG had started talking to potential investors as part of the planned financial roadshow that was supposed to take place on the twenty-second of the following month. But after it had been disclosed that Olga Golan — widow of the scientist who had been the brain behind the invention — had filed a lawsuit against SEG. Mrs. Golan claimed the company had misled her by giving her a false assessment of the company's stock value, and demanded to be compensated for the difference. The court had accepted her request to block all company activity, specifically the fundraising that was aimed at recruiting new investors in return for shares.

Countering the widow's allegations, the Zonenberg family claimed that as the share transfer agreement had already been signed, Mrs. Golan's lawsuit was frivolous and had been lodged with the intention of harming the company.

"I can't believe it," I said. "She just won't give up."

"I told you, she's crazy. No wonder Giora..."

"All right," I said, stopping him from mentioning the scientist's suicide. "So, what do you need from me?"

"As I'm sure you know, a company that announces a financial roadshow and then cancels it is likely to be perceived as 'problematic', and its value and credibility are equally likely to be hindered. If we can't somehow make Olga withdraw the lawsuit, we'll lose everything. It would be years before we'd find another opportunity like this, if ever." Now Razi sounded very upset.

"And how much do you have in available cash?"

"The money is running out fast. Engineers, artificial intelligence experts, are the most expensive employees in the market. We're talking about salaries starting at twenty-five thousand dollars a month."

"Yes," I mused. "I remember that particular figure from when I was working on the presentation."

Razi didn't reply.

"Wow, I just can't believe it," I continued. "And you can't reach a compromise with her?"

"She won't talk to us; she's motivated by revenge. She knows she'll eventually lose, but by then, the damage will be done — and it will be irreversible."

"And the development of the artificial intelligence will be delayed as well," I said.

"I'm afraid we won't be able to get out of this," Razi said gloomily.

"But what do expect me to do?" I paused. "Hold on, when you said 'we', who did you mean?"

"Me and my father."

"So, he also knows about the business with Olga and the detective?"

"You didn't really expect me to hide that sort of information from him, Nicole, did you?"

"You promised it would stay between the two of us."

"This is my father we're talking about. He's invested a million dollars in the company. I can't hide crucial information like that from him."

I was silent for a moment.

"You do understand, don't you?"

"I guess," I replied hesitantly.

"We need you to meet with that mysterious detective again, and get Mrs. Golan to back away from the lawsuit."

"Razi, are you sure you want me to get involved in all this? Last time it happened, you'll remember, we had a big fight. I don't want anything to hurt our relationship, certainly not money or work."

"Nicole, there's no other way. I have no choice. Without you, the company will fall apart, and I..." he paused and let my imagination complete what would probably happen if I didn't cooperate.

Chapter 12

"I was expecting your call," Bondi said to me when we met two days later at the same café. His habitually tense expression had momentarily become one of amusement.

"Why?"

"Don't act naive, Nicole, you know that but for our legal move, I would never have heard from you again."

"That's right, because you tried to force me to become part of your mess," I replied, anger welling sharply.

"You broke our agreement not to tell anyone about our meeting. You told Razi!"

"And you, Bondi, have been following me. Like I told you, Razi is my boyfriend. I'm not the issue here."

"No," Bondi agreed, "justice is the issue here. A man doesn't take his own life for no good reason, Nicole. I'm sure you understand that as well as I do."

"But what does any of this have to do with me? With my relationship with Razi? If you want to check on someone, you should check his father," I said.

"Good, which is why I need you."

"You need me?" I snorted in disbelief. "Don't get me involved in this, Bondi, please."

"Nicole, if you marry Razi you're going to be living on, enjoying, blood money. So, you're already involved."

I said nothing, and Bondi went on, sounding

impatient. "All right. I can see where you stand. I don't have much time, so if you don't want to move forward with this…" He stood up and half turned to leave.

"Sit down, Bondi," I said firmly.

He hesitated, looked hard at me, and sat down again. I couldn't read his expression.

"What is it you want from me?" I asked.

"I want the SIM cards."

"Razi's father's?"

"His and Razi's," he replied in an uncompromising tone.

I had no choice but to cooperate with him, or at least to try and improve the terms.

"And what do I get in return?" I asked.

"The postponement of all legal proceedings."

"I want them terminated in no uncertain way, no matter what happens," I insisted.

"That's not up to me, Nicole…"

"You do realize the company will hire the finest lawyers, the sharpest legal minds available, and they will crucify Olga on the stand. She signed an agreement. I think she would be unwise to use the power the court has given her."

Bondi got up again and this time left the café. I sat and sipped my coffee for a few minutes, bothered by the fact that it looked like I was being forced to spy on Razi.

Bondi walked back into the café. He was smiling. He sat in front of me and said, "She's approved it."

"Good, and she understands that you can use whatever

you find on the SIM cards, but if there's nothing there, the lawsuit will immediately be terminated, and she will stop harassing the Zonenberg family." For a moment, I felt as if I was speaking like a lawyer representing the Zonenberg family, but at the same time I felt it was a decent offer that did not overly favor either side.

"Here's the device." Bondi opened a cardboard box and took out a black, oblong device the size of a matchbox. He said, "This will copy the SIM cards in a matter of seconds, as soon as you connect them to this input point here." He pointed.

"I feel like I'm in a movie," I said quietly. "This is mission impossible."

"It's definitely possible." Bondi handed me the device and said earnestly, "I trust you."

"All right," I replied. I stood up.

"Nicole, if I find information you ought to know about Razi on the SIM cards, do you want me to share it with you?" he asked looking up at me.

"Keep it to yourself," I said defiantly, and quickly left.

*

"How did it go?" Razi asked tensely.

"It went well," I replied.

"Have they agreed to cancel the lawsuit? Can I tell the underwriters they don't need to cancel the financial road show?"

"Not yet."

"What do you mean 'not yet'? You said it went well." Razi's voice rose.

"Razi, I don't work for you, so please lower your voice."

"Forgive me, Nicole, you're right. It's just that my dad's driving me crazy. I can't take it anymore…."

"I understand."

"What are we waiting for, then?"

"Olga," I answered.

"She wasn't at the meeting?"

"No, just the detective and me."

"What did you tell him? Did you explain why they should stop the lawsuit?" he asked.

"Of course. I did what you asked me to," I replied, my voice steady.

"So, when will we know?"

"In a few days, I suppose."

"That's not good," Razi said in a pensive tone.

"Why?"

"Our underwriters have sent us a notice stating we have to tell them whether or not the widow is cancelling the lawsuit within forty-eight hours. After that, they'll cancel the road show themselves. And that would be the end of the road for us."

"Forty-eight hours?"

"Yes."

"All right, so let's meet and plan what to do next," I suggested.

"I can't. You haven't forgotten it's my son's birthday tomorrow, have you? We're taking him out to a restaurant this evening, and tomorrow Dorit has invited the family to our house."

"We can't meet then?"

"No, we can't. But Itay is at home with you now, anyway. You don't like it when we meet on the days he's not with Danny."

"Right, but..."

"Nicole, the children are here. I have to hang up," Razi said, and terminated the call.

*

Razi had hung up and left me without answers and without a solution. How could I copy his SIM card within forty-eight hours without meeting him? I had no other choice. I called Bondi and begged him to trust me to get the cards for him. I also asked, again, if they would terminate the lawsuit, but he refused to relay my request to the widow. He claimed she was in a fragile mental state and might not believe him if he told her he trusted me; basically, because everyone who had promised to help her over the years, had ended up turning their backs on her.

I woke up at two in the morning feeling uneasy and upset. *'I'm hiding things from Razi again,'* I thought. *'And it's because of Bondi this time as well. What can I do? If I tell Razi about the offer, he'll simply deny he has the SIM cards and will make them disappear.'* Not only that, I knew we would have another terrible fight.

At six in the morning I wrote him a message. *'I'm retiring, Razi. I can't take this anymore.'*

Razi called me immediately. "What's happened?" I could hear the stress in his voice.

"I haven't slept all night. What happens if Olga doesn't agree to withdraw the lawsuit? All the responsibility for the fundraising and the development, as well as for our relationship, comes down on my shoulders."

There was a long silence. I said into it, "This is all too much for me, Razi."

"I'll be at your place at eight. Wait for me."

"What for?"

"I'm coming over," he said, and hung up before I could respond.

*

At eight o'clock on the dot the doorbell rang. I opened the door to Razi and kissed him hello. In that brief instant, I could feel the tension in his body. We went into the kitchen and he sat down.

"What are you drinking?" I asked.

"Espresso. I waited to have my first of the day with you," he said. He smiled but I could tell he was forcing it.

"I've had three already," I said. "I'm exhausted. I didn't sleep all night."

"Why? What's happened?" he asked calmly.

"Razi," I replied, my tone betraying the nervousness

I was feeling. "I'm under a lot of stress because of this whole situation. It's all too much for me."

"There's no need for you to be feeling any stress, darling." I smiled at him and he went on, "Whatever you decide to do is what will happen. Period."

"I'm glad to hear you say that."

"But of course!" he said, sounding surprised. "You're my woman, aren't you? Who would I care for, if not for you?"

I smiled at him again. "And what about the fundraising?"

"I really don't know," he said and looked thoughtful. When he saw my expression he added quickly, "My dad's been giving me a hard time. He's blaming me for this entire mess."

"Don't let him bother you, then. Doesn't he see the stress this is putting you under? You're his son!"

"I've tried to tell him, but he's a difficult man."

I felt my mood changing. Frustration was building. "Then what about me?" I asked angrily. "Why did you get me involved in this thing in the first place?"

The long silence that followed chilled my heart.

"Listen." Razi spoke in a calm, assured voice. "I didn't want to get you involved in this, which is why I have to admit, now, that I haven't yet told you everything."

The hairs on the back of my neck tingled, as I waited to hear 'everything'.

"Look," Razi continued, "we both know that Bondi

is the one at fault here, he's the one who's insisting on communicating only with you."

"What does it matter whose fault it is?" I raged. "Both of you are endangering the only thing I want."

"Which is?" asked Razi, as if he didn't understand what I was looking for from our relationship.

"A normal relationship with the man I love!" I felt tears pricking behind my eyes and turned away from him to face the coffee machine. I pressed the button and watched as dark coffee started to trickle into the glass jug.

Razi stood up and crossed the room to me. "Oh, darling! You know I want the same thing," he said in patient, measured tones. "The divorce agreement with Dorit is ready to be signed, and I've been doing everything in my power for months to try and overcome the loss of Giora. You won't believe how much the company will be worth once we finish developing the software. We'll be rich and, more importantly, finally free to love each other."

He put a hand on my hip and gently pulled my body towards his. As I yielded to him, he slid his other hand under my thin shirt and caressed my back. Sensations flooded every fiber of my being and I stood immobile, reveling in the sensuous touch of his warm hands gliding over my responsive skin. Then I allowed him to lead me to the bedroom.

"Tell me, Razi," I was curled up in the security of his strong arms, "could it be that you've lured me into bed just to soften me up? I almost feel like you're trying to bribe me sexually." I wasn't serious, I was just teasing, even as I gave in to him.

I felt his hard body tense for a moment, then he relaxed and burst out laughing wildly.

"Are you nuts?" he asked when he finished laughing. "I never mix business with pleasure, and certainly not when I'm in bed with the world's sexiest, most amazing woman."

The passion with which his lips caressed my neck, and the magical touch of his hands fluttering on my body both gently and demandingly, sent a thrilling wave of warmth through my naked body. I cuddled in against him, with a satisfied sigh of release, feeling my body melting. But Razi wasn't finished. He went on moving beneath me, filling the quiet air with brief groans; moving and groaning, until he pressed my body hard against his for a long moment, and then he relaxed, breathing heavily.

"Nicole, you're a sorceress..." he whispered in my ear. "I want to spend my whole life with you. We won't let anyone ruin it for us."

I kissed his tanned face, then remembered the crucial question that had been bothering me, *'How far would I be willing to go for the man I love?'*

*

When he got up to shower, I got out of bed, too. I took his wallet from his jeans pocket and opened the zip to the inner compartment. But before I could do anything,

I heard Razi coming back into the room. The wallet was in my hand. I wanted to put it back into his jeans pocket, but I knew I didn't have enough time.

"Sweetheart," he said as he walked into the bedroom. I quickly slid his wallet under the blanket and sat on it. "Where do you keep your towels?"

"Oh, right here." I retrieved a green towel from the closet and handed it to him.

"Thanks." He blew me a kiss in the air and headed back to the shower.

Thirty seconds later the black device Bondi had given me contained all the information copied from Razi and his dad's SIM cards.

Razi emerged from the shower a few minutes later. He dressed and said casually, "Please do this for me, Nicole. You're the only person who can get Olga to back off and cancel the lawsuit."

I didn't reply. For a moment, I had an overwhelming urge to confess what I had just done. When I accompanied him to the door, he looked down at me and said, "Don't give up, this is about our future."

"All right," I replied submissively.

"Promise? I trust you."

"Yes," I answered. I kissed him and closed the door.

An hour later I called Bondi "I've done my part," I said.

"All right. As soon as I see the information, I'll tell Olga."

I had decided, just to be on the safe side, to transfer

the information from Razi's SIM, now held on Bondi's device, to a USB flashcard. It gave me just one small chance to take some control.

"Bondi," I said. "For now, I'm transferring *only* the information contained on Shraga's SIM. Once the lawsuit is withdrawn, I'll transfer the information from Razi's SIM too."

"Nicole, she'll never agree to that."

"Bondi!" I snapped angrily, "Promise me."

"All right, all right! I give you my word. Just send me all of the information and I'll see to it that the lawsuit is withdrawn."

*

"Didn't I tell you that you are a sorceress?" Razi said enthusiastically. "I just got a fax informing me that the lawsuit has been withdrawn. We're contacting all the underwriters to tell them the news right now. And it's all thanks to you, Nicole. Thanks to you, developing the software can go ahead as planned."

Three weeks later, while at work, I was leafing through the Glo-bus financial newspaper and came across an article reporting that SEG had successfully raised the sum of twenty million dollars.

It excited me to read a quote from Razi, *'We're proud of the trust we have been given. These investments will allow us to take the development of artificial intelligence to the next level and into the future.'*

Chapter 13

While Razi was away on the financial road show, I was busy dreaming. I imagined our house as a happy place, a haven of peace and contentment for his children, as well as for Itay and the three other children we would have together. I wanted a large, happy family, and I was utterly convinced Razi would eagerly go along with my dream.

'I wonder what Razi will be like when we get old together?' I thought to myself. I'd heard it said that people either become like their parents, or turn into their complete opposites.

"My father is a cold man," he had once told me, when I asked why his father had never called to thank me for my part in getting Olga to terminate the lawsuit. It always seemed to me that Razi strictly censored his proclamations about what he thought about his father. I couldn't help feeling he only told me what he wanted me to hear, holding back all the real stories.

When Bondi told me they had found correspondence between Shraga and Razi, which raised suspicions that Shraga might have been somehow involved in Golan's suicide, on the SIM cards, I was afraid the fundraising might be at risk again. But as no concrete evidence had been found, Bondi and Olga were unable to try, for a second time, to thwart the fundraising.

Two weeks had passed since I had last seen Razi, which was a little off. Since we had first been together, Razi had always made sure we met at least every two or three days. And if he did not have the time, he would meet me for a brief lunch between his various meetings. But the fundraising period was intense, even for a gifted man like Razi.

"I hardly have time to go to the bathroom," he bitterly complained during the few telephone conversations we had. "We're out there travelling all day so we can fit in four or five presentations. Remind me never to do this again," he said jokingly.

"I'm sure this will all pass, and you guys are going to make it, big time," I told him.

I never doubted any of his stories because I was convinced that he loved me with all his heart and truly couldn't live without me. Still, I found it hard to understand why, after the road show had ended successfully, he vanished for three whole days and didn't answer any of my calls.

Every time I called, he sent a text message saying he was busy and would get back to me. He never bothered to update me in real time about the successful outcome of the fundraising, which, according to the newspaper article, had finished two days before. On top of that, he hadn't even bothered to tell me he had, at last, left the marital home and rented a new apartment.

My hands trembling with an anger that made my

body tingle, I dialed his cell phone number again. This time Razi answered after two rings.

"Nicole, darling," he sounded excited. "What do you have to say about the road show?"

"Actually, I don't have too much to say," I spat the words at him. "In light of the fact that you've not bothered to tell me anything about it, or that you've left your house and rented an apartment."

"Why are you angry?" he asked, sounding mystified. "I wanted to surprise you and invite you over when the apartment was furnished. I'm in the middle of getting everything ready right now. I took two days off just to do that. Why don't you drop by tomorrow after work?"

"All right," I answered. I was still seething, but the fact that he had wanted to surprise me suddenly seemed very logical. Razi was like that, a man of dramatic gestures. Still, I couldn't help but think he always managed to somehow manipulate me into thinking I was being unreasonable, while he escaped unscathed from situations that could, theoretically, get him into trouble.

I found it hard to focus on my work for the rest of that day. I was confused. I felt there was a lot of grace in Razi's childish desire to surprise me with the new apartment, but I still thought he should have done it differently. Leaving me hanging, with no word for three days, couldn't be right. Could it?

I would have been surprised and happy enough if he'd come to me carrying suitcases and asked me to look for a new house with him.

I prayed the new apartment Razi had rented would be to my liking. If it was, I thought, I would be able to rent my house out as quickly as possible and move in with him.

Razi's new home was located in a northern Tel Aviv neighborhood, just one block away from his ex-wife's house. Worse, still, was the fact that, although pleasant and picturesque, it was tiny, scheduled for demolition, and utterly unsuitable for a family.

Razi was waiting for me in the yard, sprawled on an outdoor chair, a broad smile lifting the corners of his mouth. "Nicole," he cried, and motioned for me to come closer. "Look what a nice porch this place has, just like they used to build in the good old days."

I couldn't help smiling at his enthusiasm, but I still insisted he open the door properly for me. Climbing over a porch fence wasn't part of my immediate plans, especially as I was wearing high heels.

"Welcome!" Razi hugged me long and hard as soon as he opened the door. "What do you think of the love nest I've arranged for us here?"

I was curious to see the house, so I freed myself from his embrace and walked in. I could hardly believe what I saw. Though Razi had obviously invested a lot of effort in arranging the house, nothing could hide the fact that it was a classic bachelor apartment. It had one bedroom, which could only be reached by crossing the spacious living room, which also opened onto a kitchen that looked like it had been renovated at least a decade ago.

Shocked, I went into the bedroom, hoping to discover another room beyond it, but in that, I was disappointed — there was none.

"Well, what do you think? A fantastic house, isn't it?" Razi asked. He hugged me from behind. "Shall we try out the bed?"

"Are you serious?" I turned around quickly and pushed him away from me. "Is this the house you want us to live in? And only a block away from your ex-wife?"

"Why not?" he asked, his surprise obvious. "This is a beautifully renovated apartment, and there's even a great porch. Besides, I need to be close to my children for the foreseeable future, so what's the problem?"

"How about the fact that there's no room for Itay here?" I said bitterly.

"Itay?" He looked genuinely stunned. "Why should there be a room for him here? Even my own children don't have a room here. You must have noticed that. I planned for this to be our love nest, a place where no one else would be able to bother us."

"Razi, a love nest is good for a young couple living together, not for the family we're planning to start," I said. I felt like a headmistress talking to an errant pupil.

"Right, but we're not in any hurry, are we? What's so bad about spoiling ourselves here for a year or two, and then starting a family?"

"Are you serious?" I was amazed. How could he be so blindly stupid? "Just to remind you, the whole idea of us living together is about expanding our family. Razi, look at me! I'm not some twenty-year-old bachelorette!"

"Judging by the way you look, no one would believe that!" He moved in again and tried to hug me and calm me down. I fought free of his arms. "You'll stay young forever, my Nicole," he said.

"Don't try to dazzle me with compliments!" I was even angrier now. "Razi, Itay will be studying in first grade next year, I want him to grow up having a little brother or sister."

"It isn't that much fun growing up with a brother or a sister…" Razi started to say.

But I pushed him hard and spoke over him. "Not having a brother or a sister is one of his biggest frustrations. Why are you arguing with me about things you obviously don't know the first thing about?" I suddenly felt helpless. I realized he was serious. As far as he was concerned, he intended to go on leading me by the nose for another year or two without making any commitment. I said, "I've never hidden from you that I've been waiting for the moment you'd finally be available because I want to marry you and start a family."

"I want to marry you, too," he said, his voice pure velvet, "but don't forget I've just escaped from a long and depressing marriage. You need to give me time to rest, calm down, and to understand what's going on with me before getting into another relationship."

"Wait a minute! Now you're not even talking about a year or two?" I was boiling again, and I refused to calm down. "What are you actually trying to tell me? That you're not even sure you want a steady relationship with me? I thought you wanted to leave Dorit to live with me because I'm a hundred-and-eighty degrees different from her."

"You really are a hundred-and-eighty degrees different from her," Razi said quickly. I could hear an apologetic note in his voice now. "Which is why I want to marry you. But why does it have to be now? Why can't we enjoy a fun and carefree relationship for a while? Liberated from any formal ties. What does it matter how long it will take, as long as we're enjoying it together?"

I was almost too angry to speak. Everything he was saying was the complete opposite of all he had declared and promised me before that moment.

"Because I don't want it," I said defiantly. "It's been two years since I divorced Danny, and that's quite enough for me." I paused, took a deep breath and went on. "I've waited for you, Razi, because I believed you were a family man who simply chose the wrong woman. But if that's all you have to offer, 'a fun and carefree relationship' that would finish any time either of us got fed up, then I'm out! Get it? I really don't feel like playing the part of the nagging woman who's running after you, tongue lolling, asking you morning, noon and night, when you'll finally be willing to marry me. I don't deserve this, Razi. Certainly not after everything I've done for you in recent months."

Insistent tears made it hard for me to breathe as I

neared the end of my surprising, and dramatic, speech. I turned to leave, to get out of the romantic love nest my boyfriend had prepared for us as quickly as possible. As I ran from the house, I didn't even hear him screaming my name. I only realized he had been yelling after me when I saw a few neighbors peeking from between their window shutters.

By the time I reached my car the tears were running freely down my cheeks. I started the engine quickly and drove out into the road, tires screeching. Suddenly I saw Razi standing in the middle of the road waving his arms, trying to make me stop. I was too angry, too disappointed, too damn hurt, and I had no intention of stopping. I put my foot down and drove full speed ahead. I pressed down on the horn and screamed aloud, "Just leave me alone. Let me have a normal relationship with someone else!"

I could see the fear mounting in Razi's face as the car sped towards him. Then, luckily for him and at the last moment, he leapt onto the sidewalk. I saw him tumbling as the car rushed past him. I was in turmoil, so full of anger and frustration that I could have run him over.

Gladly.

Chapter 14

I called Anna as soon as I got home. I must have sounded devastated because she was at my house inside fifteen minutes. I had managed to take shower. As the water cascaded over me, I had a chance to relax a little from my anger-fueled crying fit, but I was still trembling wildly.

Anna listened to my story in silence. She looked at me with compassion in her eyes, showing neither surprise nor shock. She had strangely always given Razi the benefit of the doubt, which was completely out of character for her. But somehow, he had gotten through her defenses. *What would she say now*? I wondered.

"Poor thing." She wrapped her arms around me once I was all talked out. "You've had quite a day, haven't you?"

"An insane day. Did I tell you I almost ran him over as I left?" I tried to smile. "Never in my life have I been so filled with fury."

"Too bad it was only 'almost,'" she muttered, then added in a matter-of-fact tone, "but as running him over isn't really an option, I'd like to know what you intend to do now."

"What do you mean, 'what I intend to do now'?" I couldn't understand what she meant. "I'm going to do what I've been thinking of doing all along, kick that son of a bitch out of my life once and for all."

"Are you sure it's going to be once and for all?"

"Sure I'm sure," I answered confidently. Fury and frustration were fading into cold determination. "You think I'm going to waste even one more minute on him? I just can't believe I let him pull me along by the nose all this time. He deluded me! The way he was able to play with my very soul scares me."

I tried to calm down, but the sentences kept flowing on their own, "I should have known that after his divorce he'd be thinking only about himself and the fun he could have with me! 'Why don't we experience a fun and free relationship for a while?'" I imitated Razi's voice, even as I swore to myself that I would be strong and never go back to him. "He," I vehemently declared, "has lost me."

Anna just listened as I ranted on, and then, as I wound down, she said in a very quiet voice, "I'll tell you why you didn't realize this was going to happen. It was because, deep inside, you felt he really loved you."

I could see her, swallowing hard. She was very shaken up. In her eyes, I saw how deeply disappointed she was in Razi, and perhaps in herself, for not seeing any of this coming.

"That was what made you believe he'd marry you as soon as he divorced his wife. And to be honest, that's what he kept telling you all the time."

"I have a keen sense of intuition. I knew it was trying to tell me something. Why did I insist on not listening to it?" I said. "The ability he has to act like the ultimate lover is insane!"

Anna was still trying to calm me. "Why don't you talk to him?" she suggested to my surprise. "Hit him with an ultimatum. Commitment to you, permanently, or nothing. No more you. And if that doesn't work, break up with him. Send him on his way. If you do that, whatever the result, you'll feel more at peace about the whole thing."

"I can't believe you, of all people, are telling me to do something like that!" I was appalled. "Give that maniac another chance? Why? So, he can break my heart into little pieces again? So, he can mop the floor with me and my emotions in that sordid 'love nest' of his?"

"No." Anna was still talking quietly, sensibly. "If you show him you're determined any relationship you have will be on terms that suit you both, then he'll yield. It will be a test for him" She smiled a devilish smile, giving me and Razi — and her ideas about love — one more chance.

*

Razi was on my doorstep at eight in the evening, sharp, carrying a bouquet of flowers in one hand and a bottle of wine in the other. He looked incredibly excited and enthusiastic. I realized he was too excited to sense my own nervousness.

"You're the absolute best," he whispered in my ear as he pressed me to his heart. "You've really gone all out, haven't you?"

I had. Mainly with the setting and arranging of the dining table. I had spread a white tablecloth with golden tassels. On it I had placed a dinner service in matching colors, and two elegant wine glasses. I scattered gold-painted acorns Itay had made in kindergarten, and put two crystal candlesticks, with tall candles, in the middle of the table. I lit them the moment I heard Razi knocking on the door. The food, on the other hand, was mainly comprised of warmed-up dishes my mother had sent me, the exception being a lettuce and cherry tomato salad I had sprinkled with glazed pecans and grated blue cheese. That I had made myself.

"Here's to a happy life together," Razi cheerfully declared as he poured the wine he had brought with him.

"To a happy life," I echoed and clinked my glass with his, reminding myself that from now on, I firmly intended to make my life, and Itay's, happy — with or without Razi.

"So, what's on the menu?" he asked, lifting the lid from one of the serving dishes.

"We'll start with some *harira* soup," I declared, and poured the reddish liquid with the turmeric aroma into two matching bowls.

Razi carefully took a taste of the soup and immediately expressed his delight. "This is amazing! How did you concoct this? It's magical!"

"It's a secret." I smiled mysteriously. "A recipe passed down from generation to generation in my family."

"And a delicious secret at that," he muttered, and ostentatiously slurped the remaining soup from his bowl. "Can I have some more?"

"Not before you eat your first course," I said. I placed

a portion of *chraime* — fish in spicy tomato sauce — on a clean plate and put it in front of him.

"The sauce is a bit spicy, so dip a little *challah* bread in it first to check if you can take it."

"Take it? Are you joking?!" Razi exclaimed. He dipped a piece of *challah* bread in the sauce and bit into it, lifting his head and savoring the taste.

"Drink?" I poured him some water, but he insisted on more wine.

"Help! I can't take it anymore! Where has all this amazing food come from? What have I done to deserve all this goodness?" he asked when we moved on to my mother's famous couscous and a meat-stuffed potato dish called *mafroum*, both well-known and loved in my large family.

"That's exactly the point," I said seriously. "You've won a once in a lifetime opportunity to have all this goodness every Saturday for the rest of your life." I spoke quietly, in measured tones. "I'm saying it's a once in a lifetime opportunity, because if, by the end of tonight, you don't make the right choice, there won't be any more opportunities."

"What?" Razi stared at me, his eyes astonished and slightly glazed. "What do you mean there won't be any more opportunities? You're not going to cook dinners like this for me anymore?"

"Not only will I not cook any more dinners for you, I won't see you at all." Again, I spoke quietly, looking straight into his eyes.

"I don't understand." He looked confused, even stressed. "You're... you're breaking up with me?"

"No, my dear, you're the one that's breaking up with me," I said firmly. "Unless you accept my generous offer of finding an apartment large enough to expand our family."

"You're so intent on getting married, you're prepared to put pressure on me like this?"

"Razi, I don't understand why we're even having this conversation. How come this isn't coming from you?" My head was in turmoil, but I still tried to maintain a poker face. "I thought you meant all those pretty words you used to shower me with, about wanting to marry me and spend the rest of your life with me."

"But who told you that…" he started to say in a defensive, whiny voice.

"No 'buts,'" I flatly interrupted him. "This is about my son and our love — if it's genuine. You tell me where exactly the problem is here?"

"The problem?" he muttered bitterly. "There's more than one problem. For a start there are two children who've just been traumatized because their father's left the family home.'

"You didn't think about that before you declared your love for me and your desire to settle down with me in an enduring relationship?"

"What are you talking about? That's not the point," he said darkly, his eyes looking anywhere but at mine. He was clearly nervous. "Don't you feel any pity for my poor children who haven't done anything wrong? When you and I were enjoying ourselves on our hotel vacations, they were peacefully sleeping in their beds, believing their parents would keep them from harm. Nicole, they had no idea their father was about to turn their lives upside down."

"Oh, I definitely have pity for them," I could not avoid slipping a hint of cynicism into my voice, "but am I not supposed to have pity for myself, too? I haven't done anything wrong to anyone either, and I certainly don't deserve to live with a married man who didn't bother to tell me he was married until I was already in love with him, and that…"

"If you're in love with me," he interrupted, "why is it so difficult for you to have a little patience? A year, a year and a half from now, once they're used to the fact their father won't be coming back, we'll find an apartment that will be suitable for all of us. Nicole, you need to understand this! You have to, even if it's just because I'm so much in love with you and I can't think of living my life without you."

"Razi, you asked me to wait until you got a divorce, and I waited. You asked me to help you with the fundraising for your startup because you were under so much pressure, and I helped…"

"Nicole," Razi sighed. He got up from the table, took a few purposeful steps, and threw himself into an armchair in living room. "Why are you doing this to me?"

"I can't believe you have the gall to accuse me." I, too, got up from the table. I realized that dinner was over and confronted him. "I've had it, Razi. I'm sick and tired of having an intimate relationship with someone, but feeling that I'm alone. Do you understand what I'm saying? I'm tired of hiding. I'm tired of being alone at social and family gatherings, I'm tired of hiding you from everyone, most importantly, from Itay. Itay is five now, and he's so lonely. When am I going to give him a little brother or sister? When he has his Bar Mitzvah?"

I choked on my tears as I stumbled over the final few sentences. I turned and fled from the room, escaping to the bathroom where I washed my face. But that didn't stop the errant tears. Razi followed me into the bathroom as fresh tears flowed down my cheeks.

"Nicole, dear," he said, hugging me from behind. "I'm really sorry. The last thing I want is to make you miserable. Trust me, I think of these things all the time too, but there's nothing I can do…"

Anger flared again, stemming my sobs temporarily. "Oh, there's a lot you can do," I turned to face him, no longer caring if he saw my tears. "Our future depends on you. On you, Razi. And I won't have you playing games with me anymore."

"I don't know what to do."

"Do what your heart tells you to," I lashed the words back at him, fighting the urge to throw myself into his arms. "Because you've run out of time for playing games, Razi. With me, in any case!"

"Stop threatening me!" He pulled my body hard up against his and held me there with the power of his arms. "It doesn't become you."

Maybe Razi considered this to be a compliment, but

I simply felt he was bragging. I gathered all my strength and pushed him away — before I could lose control and find myself in a dangerous situation. Despite the confusion in my mind, I remember thinking the whole scene was like something from a movie — when the two tortured lovers are unable to fulfil their love, and act out of desperation. Assertively, I turned away from him to the dining table, picked up my glass of wine, and drank deeply to regain my resolve.

By the time Razi came back into the room I was ready to face him. I stood with my hands on my hips and hissed at him angrily. "As much as it doesn't become me, this is my ultimatum to you, Razi. Unless you start taking real, practical steps towards building a shared life with me right now, I'm leaving you."

"Right now?" Flustered, thrown off balance because his natural charm had failed to work its usual magic on me, he glanced at his watch and said, "It's nighttime, Nicole. What do you expect me to do 'right now'?"

The anger I was feeling mounted until a red mist seemed to form in front of my eyes. The guy was stupid enough to try to be funny when I was, literally, fighting for my life. Either that or he was demonstrating a cynicism that was mixed with sheer evil. Either way, he was making a fool out of me. I was on a merry-go-round that he was controlling, and I knew I had to stop it. Coldly, calmly, with contempt underlining every word I spoke, I said, "Our relationship is dead, finished. And I'm warning you right now to stop bothering me. I want nothing more to do with your obsessive ways. And I'm also telling you not to try to interfere or hinder me from having a healthy relationship with another man, a normal man. Now get out of my house. Go look for another victim!" I pointed to the door.

"But…" Razi looked as if his whole world had just fallen apart. "No good will come of this, Nicole. It will only make everything worse…" He was pleading, trying to convince me.

"If marrying me means 'making everything worse', then you're right!" I lashed back at him.

"My Nicole," he suddenly softened his voice. "Of course I want to marry you; I dream about it all the time, but I also need to think about what it would do to other, innocent people, mainly to my children. Moving too quickly could ruin them."

"That's fine," I said, my heart aching from the entire situation. "And you must do what's right for you. But I've been considerate towards you, your wife, your children, and your parents for too long. Now I have to do what's right for me — put myself and my own child first and foremost."

"Are you serious?" He moved towards me with his arms outstretched. "I can't believe you're leaving me. Nicole, I love you as I've never loved anyone else in my life. Is this how easily you're willing to throw our love to the dogs?"

"I'm not the one throwing it all away, Razi, you are," I spat at him. I quickly moved away from him, closer to the door. "Now go, Razi. And tell Olga Golan to stop sending me messages because I'm no longer part of her investigation team."

"What? What investigation? What's your connection to Olga Golan?"

Too late, I realized I might have said too much. "Razi, that's not the issue here, just leave me alone, all of you."

"Nicole, what are you talking about?"

"I don't know, she sent me a recording of one of the employees from Giora Golan's team, but I haven't paid any attention to it," I replied.

He stood there, in my kitchen, as still as a statue. Amazement and disbelief flitted across his handsome face. Then, for a millisecond, I saw in his eyes the same insane madness I had seen when we had had our previous fight. I quickly opened the door and shouted at him "Leave!"

He didn't.

"I can't believe this," he said. "I can't believe you're actually cooperating with that woman!" He started moving purposefully towards me.

I put my hands out, as if ready to push him away. "I'm not cooperating with her, Razi," I said. "She sent me the recording. I haven't even listened to it — because I couldn't care less."

"Was that why you invited me over for dinner? I see it now, you've been plotting this for quite some time, haven't you?"

"Plotting what?"

"Plotting to blackmail me into marrying you."

"You're out of your mind," I told him levelly, although I was furious.

"You'll be sorry for this," he hissed and stalked past me. "You'll never find another love like ours. Never."

"Maybe, but perhaps it's better this way," I said, speaking to myself more than to him.

"What's better?" He turned and blocked the door. He was standing too close to me.

"Anything would be better than madly loving a narcissistic man who loves when it suits him and lives a delusional life. A paranoid who is constantly convinced he's being chased and followed." I lifted my chin and stared directly at him so he would realize I meant every word.

"You admitted that it's…"

"Just go, Razi. What I need is a steady, balanced love with a normal man," I interrupted, "and you can't give me that." I motioned again to the door, urging him to leave the house.

"You won't have that," he hissed meanly. "I will personally see to it!" Then he was gone.

I stood in my kitchen trembling. It took several minutes before I felt my body returning to normal. And then I felt a pressing need to send a message to Olga Golan. It was brief and to the point: *'Razi and I have separated. Please stop sending me messages. If you don't, I will involve the police.'*

Chapter 15

The first few weeks after I broke up with Razi were hard. I admitted to myself that I still loved him, even though he had hurt me so badly. I found it hard to forget the smile that had lit up my nights, his arms which had always made me feel safe, and, of course, his soft demanding touch that excited my body and ignited the flames of my desire.

If I was honest with myself, I also realized that some of the distress I was feeling came from the fact that Razi had not tried to contact me since that awful evening. While it proved to me that he had finally gotten the message, and that he wasn't trying to toy with me anymore, it also seemed that our breakup wasn't bothering him. Despite the bombastic declarations of love that he had made at our last meeting, and his resolute statements that he couldn't live without me, the echoing silence on his part proved the opposite.

I tried to lose myself in work, because in the moments when I did not have to deal with day-to-day problems, he was there, in my mind. At the same time, I allowed myself to flirt more openly with Shay, until he mustered up the courage to ask me out on a Friday night date.

I invited Anna over for coffee and cake and deliberated with her about whether I should ask Danny to switch weekends, or if I should go out with Shay the next weekend.

"I think you should go out with him sooner rather than later," my friend solemnly declared. "Mainly so you can forget about that Razi person as quickly as possible."

"Oh, yeah?" I smiled sadly. "So now you no longer think he's a 'rare man, and there aren't many like him to be found?'"

"When I said that, I had no idea how childish, indecisive and narcissistic he was." She shrugged. "Forget him, Nickie. That man will always live his own delusional life. You don't need a partner who'll always love himself more than he loves you."

"True." I nodded gloomily and cut into my slice of home-made apple pie with my fork.

"And that is why — because of *that*, and because he makes you miserable," she pointed at me — "you need to go out with Shay this Friday, if you can."

"So, I ask Danny to switch?" I put my hand out toward the telephone.

"No," she said decisively, stopping me. "Danny could spoil this relationship for you with that horrible jealousy of his. It's better he doesn't know about the thing you have with Shay, at least until it gets a bit more serious."

"What should I do, then? Postpone the date until next Friday?"

"No," Anna stretched herself in the armchair. "Talk to Eilam, your brother, and Ravit, your sister-in-law. Itay likes being at their place more than anywhere else. Tell them we're both going to some cabin up north and ask them to have Itay over for the weekend. That would be ideal, right?"

"Actually, it would. That would make everyone happy." I tried to feel excited over the prospect of going out with Shay. "Itay will be in seventh heaven. He's normally only allowed to sleep there on vacations."

"Great." She pointed at the telephone. "Call them right now."

Eilam and Ravit said they would love to have Itay over for the weekend. When I told Itay, he couldn't get to sleep because he was too excited. I was the only one who seemed to be experiencing confusion, and that was because I was finding it difficult to muster the same enthusiasm that seemed to have gripped everyone around me.

Luckily, Shay was out of the office for the two days before our date, so I was spared having to pretend I was excited by his presence and the prospect of going out with him.

Friday finally arrived. I was so restless that I was unable to properly focus on my work. Then Shay walked into my office, looking a little exhausted, but his eyes twinkled with enthusiasm.

"Hi," I said in surprise. "Where did you disappear to the past two days?"

"What, didn't I tell you? I took two days off to work on my new television series. It's being screened today in a special premiere at the Cinematheque. I came to ask if you'd like to come with me."

"What do you mean?" I was confused, and even a little hurt. "We have a date tonight, don't we?"

"Yes, but the screening is from six to eight," he explained, "and it's not really a dating style screening, because there will be too much commotion. If you want, you could just join me there, and then we could go on to the restaurant I've reserved for us at nine. Or I can just pick you up from your place at eight-thirty."

I understood, and his considerate attitude made it easier for me to decide. "Do you want me to come to the screening?" I asked.

"Of course I do!" His embarrassed smile and the dimples in his cheeks won my heart all over again. "It's just that I wasn't sure you'd feel comfortable with all the silly personality cult thing that revolves around the makers of the film, you know. There'll be lots of speeches, and everyone will say how brilliant and talented I am, but you should know it's all an act. They say that to everyone."

"I'd love to come with you, Shay." I smiled at him, liking him more and more. "And I don't need any speeches to tell me you're brilliant and talented."

At four that afternoon, I drove Itay to my brother's house. The child couldn't stop talking eagerly about all the things he'd be doing with his cousins over the weekend. Then, suddenly, he stopped chattering and asked hesitantly, "Mom, where are you going with Anna?"

"I told you, to a cabin up north," I answered quickly. I hated lying to him.

"Where exactly up north?"

"… Achziv," I stuttered, compounding the lie with an achingly guilty heart.

"And what will you do there?"

"Hmm… there's a beautiful beach there, and an ancient castle that's nice to visit."

"Why aren't you taking me with you, then?"

"Sweetheart, I thought you'd rather play with your cousins instead of spending time with two boring old ladies like Anna and me." I tried make light of the situation.

"You're not old, you're the most beautiful Mommy in the whole world," he said decisively.

"Thank you, sweetie," I said gloomily. I promised myself that if and when my relationship with Shay became serious, I would immediately introduce him to Itay and never lie to my son again.

"Mommy, do you know, we have a girl in my kindergarten who has two mommies?"

"Of course I know, Itay, honey. It's Noam," I said, demonstrating my knowledge of the latest kindergarten gossip. The fact was that I already knew about the two mothers because they were Danny's neighbors, and were very good friends of his.

"Right," Itay said, "and now they had a baby sister for Noam. Her name is Yael."

"Really?"

"Yes!" he was suddenly brimming with enthusiasm. "So, I thought maybe you and Anna could get married too, and give me a little brother?"

My surprise was so sudden, and so complete, that I burst into laughter despite the instant pang of sadness that pierced my heart. My innocent, sweet son had just expressed what I had long sensed. For some time now, I had been thinking he needed a new little soulmate in the house, and I suspected he had been longing to have a little brother or sister. And all this time, his mother — me — had been busy playing make-believe games with a man who had no serious intentions.

"Why are you laughing, Mommy?" Itay sounded hurt. "I really would like to have a little brother. I promise, I'll take care of him when you and Anna are out at work."

'Don't worry, sweetie, you'll have a little brother much sooner than you think,' I promised him silently, in the secrecy of my heart. And I swore to myself I would have a healthy, loving relationship with a man who would give Itay the little brother he so longed for.

Chapter 16

I got home earlier than usual and went straight into the shower, pulling off my clothes as I went. I carefully washed my hair and then scrubbed hard at my skin until it almost glowed red, as I tried to eradicate any lingering traces of Razi from my body. Then I sat for a long time in the bathtub, thinking about how my life had been since I met him.

I found it hard to understand how I, a rational, clear-thinking person, had allowed myself to fall in love with a married man, one I had allowed to delude and dazzle me for so long.

When I could find no one else to blame, I finally had to admit to myself that I was responsible for everything that had happened to me. I was the one who had stubbornly refused to acknowledge all the bleeping, red warning lights I had encountered along the way. I promised myself I would get out of this madness, and comforted myself with the fact that I was starting a new relationship with a serious and normal man. While I didn't know where this would lead me, I was convinced my life would be much more relaxed with Shay.

I reminded myself of my mother with the submissive behavior I had been displaying, although she, at least, had nurtured a warm, wonderful family. It was this latter point, I thought, that justified her. But I also knew she had had to pay a heavy price. The fact that she had never developed a successful career with all her unusual talents saddened me. I took comfort from the fact that I had started my career at a relatively early age, but then my heart immediately soured when I thought what a shame it would be if I failed to have a successful, meaningful relationship.

By five in the afternoon, I had begun to consider the heavy question of what I should wear to the premiere. I had visited the Cinematheque quite a few times, but never before had I accompanied the creator of a television series to its premiere screening.

To be on the safe side, I searched Google for media mentions of the event. In an online article I found, I read about Shay and his series.

'The fact that Shay Barkay is a creative genius,' the article stated, *'has been well-known for half a generation, but this time he has outdone himself with this magnificent drama series written and directed by him. 'The Dream Factory' is not merely a funny and emotional series about growing up, it is also an important document about the choices we make in life, and about destiny. With incredible sensitivity, Barkay has drawn, with a masterful hand, the imaginary fate of an entire generation that has grown up determined to fulfill itself.'*

It certainly felt good to read all the superlatives written about my date. I even felt a little excited for him, although he had warned me in advance not to get too excited because he said, "That's just the way they talk about any creator whose work is screened at the Cinematheque." All these thoughts and deliberations did not help me decide what to wear. Most of the clothes I had were either too elegant or too laid back for the event. Finally, I found a floral Laura Ashley dress in the closet. It was elegant, but not too much so, and despite the fact that I didn't wear it often, it emphasized all my natural advantages, including my tan. I confess its bright and somewhat colorful nature did not sit well with my normally under-stated taste but, this time, for the premiere screening of a television series at the Cinematheque, it fit like a glove.

*

When Shay arrived to pick me up, his green eyes examined me admiringly. I felt happy at having chosen to wear that dress.

"You look stunning!" He gently kissed my cheek as I sat in his car. "I wish you would dress like that when you come to work."

"Yeah, right..." I smiled. "As CFO I have to maintain an elegant dress code, or wear pencil skirts suitable for a staid businesswoman," I answered in an amused tone. I changed the subject. "Are you excited?" I asked. He started the car and we moved off as I examined his attire. Shay was wearing a pair of jeans and a white, buttoned shirt. The shirt emphasized his tanned, muscular body and gave him a festive appearance that was atypical for him on a day-to-day basis.

"Excited by our first date? Very." I noticed the dimples deepening in his cheeks as he spoke. They complimented his face.

"And by the premiere?"

"By that too, but not as much," he said smiling, and the dimples deepened. "I'm used to premiers. I've directed more than enough movies in my life."

"Still, I read every conceivable superlative about your new series online."

"I've already told you, you shouldn't believe what people say," he sounded amused, "or what they write, either. Anyway, let's hurry up before they decide to screen a more interesting movie."

It was clear to me that, unlike Razi, Shay did not make too much of himself, and was more modest.

"If everyone thinks it's perfect, why should you think differently?" I wondered aloud as we reached the Cinematheque.

"I know." He sighed as he parked the car. "Maybe I'm too much of a perfectionist."

"I'm sure the series is perfect." I smiled and held his hand in mine.

A large crowd filled the Cinematheque plaza, much larger than I was used to seeing at premiere screenings.

I wanted to ask Shay why he was being so honored with a red carpet event, unlike the premiers of other movies I had seen, but before I could say anything, a multitude of people rushed at him, shaking his hand and speaking excitedly. And, of course, the massed photographers began clicking their cameras.

I was embarrassed. I wanted to slip away from the carpet, but Shay drew me to him, holding my hand tightly and whispering in my ear, "You're not going anywhere."

So, I stayed. Actually, it was a unique experience, being exposed and looked at by everyone under the spotlights, side by side with the star of the evening. But this was Tel Aviv and not Hollywood, and all the people massing around us looked like my neighbors. Most of the men were dressed in an ostentatiously casual and bohemian way, and only some of the women were well-groomed and elegantly dressed.

Against that human background, I unexpectedly saw him. He stood out with his elegant appearance, erect as a peacock, staring at me with those piercing eyes. I was shocked, dumbfounded. I found it hard to believe I was seeing him only thirty feet from where I was standing with Shay.

Shock quickly became anger. *'What the hell is he doing here?'* I thought. *'Is he following me?'*

*

"Nicole, I'd like to introduce you to Noa Moyal, my producer." Shay's voice seemed to be coming from somewhere far away.

I metaphorically shook myself and forced my attention

back to Shay. "Yes, yes," I extended my hand to a young, smiling woman with an exotic appearance. She squeezed my hand firmly and said, in a hearty voice, "Pleased to meet you."

"The pleasure is all mine," I answered, my mind still seething with the shock Razi's presence had caused me.

"Where has Shay been hiding you?" She was smiling at me. "If I had known he had such a charming girlfriend, I wouldn't have gone on trying to hit on him all this time," she said in an easygoing, humorous way, as if she had known me for years.

"What?" I responded in confusion. "Are you being serious?"

Noa and Shay burst out laughing, and that further confused me, especially because I could feel Razi's eyes watching me from afar.

"Actually, she is." I was surprised by Shay's apparent confession. "But I kept telling her we're not suited. Do you know how many times she arrived at work in the mornings with a hangover? If she wasn't the best producer in town, I'd have fired her ages ago."

"He just doesn't know how to live, this guy." Noa clapped his shoulder fondly. "I hope you'll be able to teach him that life's not just about working."

Far from receding, the sense of shock I was feeling gradually intensified. Up to that moment, I had had no idea that Shay had a fun and 'devilish' aspect to his personality. To me, he seemed like a solid guy who was looking for a serious relationship, flirting only with women he thought suitable for his plans. And if all this wasn't enough to completely put me off balance, I suddenly saw that Razi wasn't alone. A blonde woman, about his age, stood beside him holding tightly onto his arm. It must have been his wife, because she looked like the woman in the family photograph he kept in his wallet. I looked at her. She was relatively well-groomed, but not exceptionally beautiful or sexy. She turned her gaze to me and our eyes met. There was venom there, but before it could become too intense, I moved closer to Shay and joined in the conversation he was having with one of the actors.

A man in an evening suit appeared and asked the audience to move inside the theater. Like a small tide, everyone started flowing inside. Still, I could feel Razi's eyes burning on my back as Shay led me to the bar.

I sighed in relief. Until that moment, I had not been fully aware of the tension Razi's presence had caused. I was even happier when Shay told me we would be the last to go in, which gave me more time to settle my ravaged senses.

"Shall we have some champagne?" Shay suggested, and immediately put a glass in my hand. He raised his own glass in a toast. "Cheers," he said.

"Good luck," I responded, and I meant it. I tried to forget Razi and focus on Shay as I clinked my glass with his. "The series is going to be a hit, I can feel it in my bones, and you should know that my intuition is never wrong."

"Thanks." He smiled happily and sipped some

champagne. "It's a good thing you agreed to come. I don't know how I'd have survived this evening on my own."

"You're not on your own. Look how many people have come here just for you."

A bearded man approached and said, "Barkay, they're about to call your name. Go in, go in!"

Shay took my hand and pulled me along after him. The lights dimmed as we entered the movie theater. A single spotlight found us as we made our way to the front row.

"Ladies and gentlemen," the announcer declared. "Will you please welcome the series creator, Shay Barkay!"

The whole audience was on their feet, clapping furiously. My stomach churned as I walked beside the star of the evening, who charmingly flashed embarrassed smiles in every direction. Inside, I was furious with myself. Instead of celebrating with Shay, I couldn't stop wondering how Razi had known I would be attending the premiere. And why he had gone to the trouble of coming to the premier with his ex-wife. And, perhaps more worryingly, what was he planning? After all, I had learned that with Razi, nothing happened without a reason, and it didn't happen at all unless it was in his interest.

"We're here," Shay finally whispered with a sigh of relief, and he sat in one of the reserved seats in the front row. I dropped as elegantly as I could into the seat beside Shay's, happy to discover that the spotlight that had been trained on us had been turned off. Silence settled in the theater as the credits appeared on the screen and the first episode of the series began. I quietly took a deep breath, just as Ruthie, the yoga instructor, had taught me. I focused on trying to slip into an alternative and drama-free world.

On the screen, the main protagonist in the series, a theater director who dreamed of establishing his own theater, is told by his mother that the factory his father had established and run is in deep financial difficulty, and now faces bankruptcy. He is forced by these circumstances to return home and offer to manage the factory himself in a last-ditch attempt to save it from financial ruin. He does this on condition that he can use the factory compound at night as a location for the acting classes he teaches.

In between these dramas, Shay has gently woven the emotional relationships between the protagonist and his parents, his students, his teaching, and between him and a young woman who is two years his senior, with whom he had been in love as a child. Now, over ten years later, he has decided to reveal his true feelings towards her.

The intermission caught me by surprise and left me eager to see more episodes. I immediately began to question Shay. I wanted to know which of the stories we had seen were based on his real life, and which he had completely invented. I was especially curious to learn whether he too had a mythological lover like the hero of the series. But before Shay could answer, he was surrounded by what seemed to be a million people, all congratulating and showering him with praise.

I used the opportunity to go to the ladies' room. There, as usual, I found a long line, as if someone was handing out gold inside. I stood at the end of the line, lost in my thoughts about the character on the screen who had had to give up on his dream to save his family.

"So, my body's not yet cold and already you're with another man?" Razi's voice, quiet, unmistakable, spoke from behind me.

I turned with a start, and found myself staring nervously at his cynical smile. "Hello to you, too," I said defiantly. "And there's no need to be so dramatic, you know. We've all moved on."

"What do I know?" he bitterly interrupted. "I never would have guessed you'd be so cold, so calculating. Jumping straight into the arms of the next man you'd meet."

I felt my face reddening. "First of all, he's a work colleague and I've known him since before I met you, if you don't mind." I replied sharply. And immediately I was annoyed with myself for the note of apology I heard in my voice. "Besides, what right do you have to reproach me?"

"The right of a man whose heart is broken," he lashed back at me. "Since that night, I've hardly been able to sleep. I barely think of anything else, and I'm almost unable to function — while you've just moved on without a problem..."

"Looks to me like you're functioning just fine," I answered sarcastically. "I wouldn't call going out with your ex-wife for a cultural Fun Night at the Cinematheque dysfunctional."

"Fun Night?" Razi looked confused. "What are you talking about? I'm here with Dorit because she practically begged me to come with her. This is how I punish myself for not being able to do what I had to, so I could be with you. Do you understand, Nicole? I'm being punished here, tortured every moment, while you're celebrating with a new man." He almost screamed the last few sentences, and, from the corners of my eyes I was aware that people around us were beginning to stare.

"People are staring at us," I hissed. "Lower your voice, please."

"How can I lower my voice when my heart is bleeding?" he exclaimed, his eyes misting. "I guess you're not the woman I thought you were. A woman with a heart and soul would never have treated me like this."

"Great!" I tried hard to lace my voice with contempt. "So now you know who I really am, you can forget all about me." I shrugged in an attempt to demonstrate indifference, even though my heart was breaking at the sight of the tears in his eyes. "Take care, Razi, have a good life."

I raised my chin, turned, and marched to the end of the line to the ladies' room, which had drawn further away from me. I was hoping Razi would understand this was the end of the discussion as far as I was concerned, but my hope faded as I heard him speaking close behind me again.

"A good life? Is that what you're wishing me? Is there no end to your cynicism? You are an evil woman, Nicole, and if there is a God in heaven, he will repay you for what you've done to me. He will make your life a living hell. Mark my words…"

I escaped into the ladies' room, assuming he wouldn't follow me in. The whole situation, pathetic as it was, had unnerved me.

Panting, I leaned on the marble counter and looked at myself in the mirror. I was convinced I'd see white strands appearing in my hair after the emotionally-charged encounter with Razi, but, to my surprise, I looked the same. My eyes glinted with a suspicious sparkle. Suddenly, I felt that familiar choking feeling in my throat telling me tears were on the way.

Despite all the cynicism I had mustered up to help me as I spoke to Razi, I could not help feeling sorry for him. I believed with all my heart that he had spoken from the bottom of his. He still loved me, a deep, great love, but I knew he did not have the courage to do what it would take to fulfil it.

"Who was that gorgeous hunk I saw you talking with by the restrooms, and what have you done to make him so angry at you?" Noa Moyal was standing behind me. "He looks kind of familiar. Is he an actor or something?"

I used every ounce of my mental strength to gather myself. Shay's flirty producer was the last woman on Earth I would want knowing anything about Razi and me. I was convinced Shay would be the next person to hear about it when she tried to hit on him. I knew she would use the opportunity to blacken my name.

"He's not an actor in the sense that you mean." I turned to her and spoke sweetly. "He's just a guy I used to know."

Noa smiled. She was about to say something when I saw a restroom stall had been vacated. I quickly moved in and closed the door firmly. Luckily, she had gone by the time I came out, allowing me to quietly powder my face in front of the mirror and, mainly, to calm down. It was obvious to me that unless I regained my composure as quickly as possible, the entire pleasant evening I had planned to spend with Shay would be utterly ruined.

Chapter 17

By the time I got back to the auditorium, the lights had already dimmed. I quickly took my seat beside Shay, determined to forget the emotionally charged encounter with Razi. But I found I wasn't quite able to, and it was hard to focus on the next two episodes. The suffering on the hero's handsome face, up on the screen, as he discovered his mythological love preferred someone else to him, reminded me of the pain in Razi's eyes. I drifted off into doubts and contemplations regarding his love for me.

In the battle that raged in my mind between the logical and the emotional, the rational finally gained the upper hand. Logic dictated that if I was really that important to him, as he had declared morning, noon and night, he would have done whatever it took to live with me. The fact that he had chosen not to, seemed to me to be proof that his declarations were one thing, his real intentions something else altogether.

It took all my mental strength to force these indulgent deliberations from my mind and focus on the drama unfolding on the screen. The fact that the crowd around me was totally immersed in Shay's television series, occasionally bursting into fits of surprised laughter, demonstrated to me I was missing out. But how could I focus on other people's dramas when the lead actor in the drama of my life was sitting just a few rows behind me?

When the screening was over, the long and tiresome part of evening — the 'thank you' speeches — began. I found it difficult to focus on the relatively brief speech made by the star of the evening, but still applauded enthusiastically as I tried to smile. I really didn't want Shay to know my mind was elsewhere, floating in other worlds.

Finally, we went out into the cold night air, and I, at last, felt relief. Razi was nowhere to be seen. I believed he had gone home to spend another dreary evening in his illustrious bachelor apartment.

"Did you enjoy it?" Shay asked me as we sat in the car.

"Very much," I answered. "The first episode was really powerful, and the other two as well. Is it going to be broadcast on television?"

"Yes," he nodded. "And the French Cannes-Plus channel just purchased it as well, as you heard yourself."

"Of course," I lied through my teeth. "I meant to ask where it's going to be broadcast here in Israel."

"The commercial channel is currently interested in it." He turned to me and flashed me a forgiving smile. "We spoke about it in the speeches…where were you?"

"Actually, I admit that I was drifting off a little," I said in embarrassment, "but not because it wasn't interesting, it was just because…I ran into my ex-boyfriend during the intermission, and he made an unpleasant scene."

"Was that why you disappeared for so long?" He was interested, but showed not a hint of hostility.

"Yes," I sighed, "but let's change the subject, he doesn't deserve to be discussed. What restaurant are we going to?" I asked curiously.

"Bella Italia, it's a great Italian restaurant in the Florentine neighborhood. It has a fine antipasti bar and some delicious main courses for anyone still hungry after the premiere."

"Great, I'm really hungry." I tried to speak with enthusiasm. "And I'm crazy about Italian food."

*

Bella Italia did look interesting and was spectacularly colorful. The buffet-style antipasti bar also included cheeses and delicious, special cold cuts.

Shay ordered us a bottle of Chianti in a basket and would not stop praising the food. I couldn't help remembering the nonchalance with which Razi had dined with me in the finest restaurants, almost as if he had been born in one. I found it difficult to decide which impressed me more. Shay's open, almost naive, enthusiasm did have something childish about it, but it was also very genuine, especially when considered against the background of one of the scenes from his series. The scene showed the hero arriving at the house of an army friend and lustily devouring the homemade food that his friend's mother had cooked. It was easy, watching the scene, to understand the guy's enthusiasm for delicious, well-cooked food, as he had spent his childhood eating a kibbutz kitchen's tasteless, boring food.

Suddenly, Shay stretched and said, "It seems to me that you're still thinking about that meeting with your ex. Want to talk about it?"

"No!" I replied, too quickly, my voice unintentionally rising.

"Listen, Nicole." He smiled sadly. "I invited you to come with me to the premiere for a reason, and it's certainly not because I wanted you to hear how successful and gifted I am. I don't know how much of the series you were actually able to see, but the hero's story is a lot like my own."

"I imagined as much," I said.

"All right, but the love story part is also very similar," he went on, as if wishing to expose a story he had kept to himself for too long. "I really was in love with a girl who was two years older than me. She didn't know I was alive. There were many girls my age, or younger, who liked me, mainly because I was a bit of a wild child, an endearing rebel, but I, like an idiot, instead of forgetting about her, kept right on dreaming about her — even when I joined the army, served with the Navy Seals, and became a much sought-after bachelor."

"Then, one day, the woman I'd been in love with for so long started flirting with me. Then she finished her army service, went off to South America and left me hanging. In short, my dreams about her had gone on for so many years, they damaged any prospect I might have had of forming a normal relationship. It wasn't the only factor, of course. There were lots of girls, just as hazy as she was about what they wanted to do with their lives. Eventually, she came back to Israel and moved to Tel Aviv. I met her by accident one night in some bar. It was pretty obvious she still had a thing for me, and we quickly moved in together. What can I tell you? We spent two insane years living together, two years full of love and passion, but there were also endless dramas and arguments. And then, at some point, I realized she wasn't the woman I wanted to live my life and start a family with."

"I'm so sorry" I said sympathetically, looking into his eyes, lightly touching his hand.

"Breaking up was hard," he went on, "and we got back together more than once, but in the end, I realized I was wasting my time with her and that all I wanted was a good woman who could see something other than herself and who shared similar dreams about children and family. In short, someone I could have fun with, but also someone I could enjoy being bored with. I didn't want a woman who would always be obsessively seeking thrills. We broke up for good two years ago, and I've been looking for that special woman ever since…"

Shay was silent for a moment. He looked at me, then went on softly, "And for a while now, I've had a very strong feeling that woman is you, but I need to know you're walking into my story with a clear head, and not with some mythological ex, like that girl was for me. I don't want a woman with an ex-boyfriend who would climb back into the frame any time he felt like it and ruin things for us."

I stared at him in amazement. I found it hard to believe he was exposing himself to me like this.

"All right," I said finally, "that was a little heavy for a first date confession." I thought that maybe Shay was moving forward too quickly. I was still struggling to get over my breakup with Razi, but how was I supposed to say that to Shay without hurting his feelings? He was my work colleague, and I really didn't want us to start getting hostile with each other, not at all. I told myself that I just had to find the right timing to share what I felt with him. I was sure he'd understand, because he himself had gone through a fairly similar experience.

"Right," the dimples in his cheeks deepened apologetically. "I hadn't planned this, but as the evening passed, when I realized you were drifting in other places, I had to unburden my heart."

"I understand." I held his pleasantly warm hand, "But... you have to take into consideration that I'm not necessarily as open as you are..."

"Yes, I've seen that you're a little withdrawn, even suspicious." His smile widened to light up his green eyes.

No wonder so many women are wooing him, I thought. Not only does he look good, he also has this captivating sincerity, a pleasant way that was lacking in Razi, who constantly played games and suffered mood swings.

"But I can understand it," Shay was speaking again. "Especially because you have a small child for whose sake you need to constantly be on your guard, to be sure you aren't bringing unsuitable people into his, and your, lives."

I suddenly felt tears stinging my eyes as he spoke to me about Itay. This kind man had so much empathy, consideration and understanding, that I could not avoid comparing him one more time to Razi, who, unlike Shay, thought of no one but himself. In that single moment, I decided I was crossing out, with a thick black line, the insane relationship I had had with Razi. Deleting it. If Shay had managed to forget that legendary ex he'd lived with for two years, then I could leave behind the man who had agreed to do nothing in order to live with me. And the sooner, the better.

Yes, in that instant, I made a decision, but I failed to consider the fact that it had taken Shay years to be free of his ex, while I decided to mechanically, sharply, instantly forget the man with whom I had been head over heels in love with up to less than a month ago.

Chapter 18

And so, I found myself easing into a relationship with Shay Barkay, a relationship that was fun in the best sense of the word, predictable and straightforward.

In those first few weeks, we were unable to keep our hands off each other, but then the sex became less passionate and less frequent. I almost suspected that Shay loved intimate conversations more than he liked sex, because he would often prefer the two of us to simply lie in each other's arms and talk.

Shay did not hide his feelings towards me, but Razi did not relent either. Since the evening at the Cinematheque, he made a point of sending me emotional, passion-filled emails.

'Nicole, my love,' thus started one of his emails. *'I'm not sure you will understand me, but I must still try to explain what is tearing me apart on the inside right now. I feel as if two different entities reside within my soul; they keep taking turns, switching places. One of them yearns for you, the other stops it, and when the second one is grim and depressed, the first one toys with it, extending a hand towards the locked gate.'*

I felt as if I was reading a romantic love poem from the Middle Ages with a knight expressing his yearning for an unattainable maiden. I did my best to ignore the emails, persisting in keeping my promise to give my relationship with Shay a chance, even if it was devoid of fireworks.

I did not reply to any of Razi's emails. Some I deleted, others I marked as 'unread' as soon as I had finished reading them, reminding myself that Razi had failed in the past to deliver on his promises.

Razi did not give up. He continued sending me mail after mail after mail. *'My dear Nicole, I am in China now and can't stop thinking about you,'* he wrote in another email. *'I know I do not have the right to do that, because you are with someone else now, but no matter how hard I try to stop thinking about you, I simply can't. I breathe you in with every breath. I have never loved anyone as much as I love you, and it is important to me that you know that. I no longer care what you do with this knowledge, especially here, at the far end of the world. I am detached from all pressures and removed from my conflicted emotions about the children. I feel the purity of the love I bear for you. I love every part of you, and the graceful wildness you have that ends up becoming feminine sweetness. This love I have can never end, yet I do not know how to fulfil it.'*

I did not feel guilty reading Razi's emails. I told myself that reading them was a kind of a test — to see if I could withstand Razi's attempts to win me back. But as they began to pile up, I began to fear that they could, somehow, without me noticing, sabotage my relationship with Shay.

*

It happened one Saturday evening, when my mother asked me why I never brought my boyfriend over to have dinner at my parents' house. My parents and brothers already knew about Shay, I had told them a little about him, but I still kept him a secret from Itay, God only knew why. We had been in a relationship for three months, and I really had no excuse, or reason, for keeping Shay a secret from my son.

"Itay still doesn't know about him," I answered hesitantly.

"And what are you waiting for?" my mother asked cynically, "the Messiah?"

"Of course not," I replied hurriedly. I decided it would happen soon. Itay had not stopped asking when I was going to bring him a little brother. I was convinced he would be happy to meet the man who would be the father of that brother. After all, Shay, my boyfriend, was sweet and charming, and my son was sure to like him.

After that weekend, Shay was supposed to go to Paris for a week to sign an agreement with the Cannes-Plus channel regarding the sale of his television series. I wanted to join him, but as fate would have it, Danny was supposed to travel to the US that same week. So, I decided that during the week I would spend alone with Itay, I'd start preparing him for the fact that I now had a boyfriend. Later, when Shay was back from Paris, I'd get them together during the weekend at one of the fun activities Itay liked best.

By the time I had to leave work to take Itay out of

kindergarten, I had already decided how I would introduce to him to Shay. But then, as if my life was governed
by some madcap Murphy's law, my office telephone began
to ring.

"Hello?" I answered impatiently, praying silently it
wasn't one of the senior managers, deciding to detail me
with some nagging task.

"Hi, Nicole." I heard Shay's warm voice. "How are
you? Judging by your tone, I'd guess you're already out
the door."

"Actually, I am. I'm in a hurry to pick up Itay from
kindergarten," I explained. "Can I get back to you a little
later once I get home?"

"Of course." He sounded pleased with himself.
"Call me at home. I'm coming back to Israel early —
tonight."

"What? Why?" I wondered. "You said you were
coming back on Thursday. What's the matter, Paris isn't
romantic enough without me?"

"Actually, it isn't." To my surprise, he sounded serious.
But you need to go now, so we'll talk when I'm back in
Israel, all right?"

"All right," I replied, still feeling confused.

*

By the time I was able to call Shay, I was pacing the house
like a nervous tigress trapped in a cage. My thoughts had
been running around in a giant maze of possibilities.

My biggest fear was that he had somehow discovered, the devil only knew how, that Razi had been sending me emails. I was also worried that his negotiations with the French television network had gone awry.

Luckily, Itay was tired that evening and seemed happy to just sit and watch the Children's Channel. I felt so absentminded and devoid of energy that I let him eat his dinner in front of the television.

Finally, when Itay was asleep, I called Shay.

"Hi, Nicole." The warmth of his pleasant voice enveloped me. "I'm sorry for being so mysterious, it's just that something ... well ... defining has happened, and I felt I had to tell you about it face-to-face."

"What happened? Is it good or bad?" I asked, my heart pounding.

"Good," he said firmly. He sounded amused and happy. "I understand that you're with Itay now. Is there any chance you can get someone to babysit for him?"

"Of course," I answered, desperately trying to think who I could call on at such short notice. "But you could come over here. He's a sound sleeper."

"All right. I'll be over in half an hour," he said and disconnected.

Tense, I immediately went into my bedroom and changed the sheets. Then I put the dirty ones in the washing machine with the house dress I had worn the day before.

I was planning to delete all the emails Razi had sent me, but I was so nervous that I was afraid to open the computer. I was afraid I'd find more emails from him and be tempted to read them.

Shay arrived half an hour later. He looked a little tired, but very excited. When he hugged me, I caught a whiff of his manly aftershave and pressed myself against him. "I've missed you," I whispered.

"Me too," he kissed me on the lips.

"Come in, come in." I took a step back and cleared the way for him. "Are you hungry, should I warm something up for you?"

"No, I'm just dead-tired, so if I could have a double espresso, that would be great."

"Coffee's on the way." I hurried into the kitchen and returned with a tray bearing an espresso for him, instant coffee for me, and two slices of my mom's cheesecake. We sat on the living room sofa. Shay took a sip of his coffee and started talking hesitantly. "Look, Nicole, I've never kept the serious intentions I have for us as a couple a secret from you, right?"

"Right," I answered, holding my breath, trying to ready myself for any possibility.

"Fine, and it's why I've decided I have to share this offer I've received from Cannes-Plus with you as quickly as possible."

"What offer" I asked, confused. "You went there to negotiate with them about the possible purchase of your television series, didn't you?"

"Yes. The negotiations are going along fine, but while we were negotiating, they made me an offer to relocate to Paris and become their content manager. And they emphasized to my French agent that they'll still pay what's due to me as the series creator, whether or not I agree to accept their job offer. The salary they're offering ... well ... I could only dream of such figures in Israel!"

"Shay, this is incredible." I was thrilled for him. "Cannes-Plus is the largest television network in Europe. This is an offer you can't refuse," I said enthusiastically.

"I've always dreamed of spending a few years in Paris. That's why I've been studying French for several years now." He took my hand in his. "Nicole, you do realize I'm not going to make this move without you?"

"What?" I stared at him, confused and amazed. "What are you actually trying to tell me, Shay? That you want me to move to Paris with you?"

"Look." His grip tightened on my hand. "I understand this is complicated for you, especially because of Itay, but I thought we could do this gradually. He can get to know me first, as I'm going back and forth from Israel to Paris. Then you two could come and live with me before he goes to first grade. There's an excellent Jewish school in Paris. With the insane salary I'll be earning, we'll be able to afford for you to get pregnant and not work for a while. And Itay will be happy to finally have a brother or sister. And also, you know, living abroad would be a great adventure for a six-year-old, meeting new friends and learning a new language."

I stared at him in utter shock for a few moments. The

thoughts running through my mind were that he was moving way too fast with our relationship. Perhaps it was my fault for allowing him to feel that way? I felt like I had to, in all honesty, talk to him.

I was certainly flattered by the fact that Shay had already planned everything down to the minutest detail, but I was also stressed by the thought that I might be misleading him. And, in general, I found the idea that I should 'get pregnant and not work for a while' a little condescending and patronizing. Shay assumed I would be happy not to work for several years after having a child with him. I couldn't help feeling that sort of thinking was more in line with a Danny, than with an enlightened and creative person like Shay. I suddenly thought of a way to escape his entire offer without insulting him.

"Shay, you've forgotten about Danny, Itay's father," I gloomily said. "I'm not sure he'd let me take Itay out of the country for a few years."

Shay looked stunned, as if reality had fallen on his head like a ten-ton elevator.

"I understand," he finally said, "and I'm really sorry, Nicole. I'd forgotten all about Danny. Of course, it would be unfair for me to take Itay away from his father. But maybe you could still check with Danny. Living abroad for a while could be a great life experience for Itay."

Shay looked guilty and tortured, so I took him in my arms and hugged him. "Don't feel badly, Shay. I understand how you got so excited by that amazing offer from Cannes-Plus, you forgot all about Danny. If I'd received an offer like that, I'd have forgotten the whole world, at least for a few days."

"All right." He flashed a gloomy smile at me and stroked my hair. "I have no choice, then. I'll let them know I'm rejecting their offer."

"Are you crazy?" It was my turn to be stunned. "Who would reject such an offer? I just told you, I'd have snatched their hands off!"

"No." He put his arms around me. "You told me you'd have forgotten the whole world for a few days — but then I'm sure you'd have remembered you have a child who needs a good relationship with his father, and you would have rejected the offer."

"All right, but … Itay is my child, not yours."

"True, but I love you and want to tie my life together with yours." His arms tightened around me, pulling me hard against his heart. "And sometimes, you need to make a few concessions, compromise for the good of everyone. What can you do? It's much more important for me to spend my life with the woman I love than to be the new Cannes-Plus content manager. With all due respect to them."

"I love you, too," I answered, my heart aching, "but under no circumstances will I allow you to give up on an offer like this one for my sake. And you're taking things too fast — don't forget I only just recently broke up with Razi," I reminded him. "This is a crucial decision, and I don't want to take the risk that at some point in the future, should our relationship not go the way we want it to, you might suddenly feel frustrated and angry for having given up on that offer because of me."

"Nicole, I could never be angry at you," he said in a strained voice, "but I'd never be able to forgive myself if I let you go. Don't you get it?"

"Who said you have to let me go?" I tried to smile, although I, too, wanted to cry. I knew the scenario I was about to suggest had only a slim chance of really succeeding. "Take the job, Shay," I said. "You've earned it, fair and square. We'll see each other when we can, and we'll go on examining our relationship. After all, Paris is only four-and-a-half hours away by plane. This way, I'll feel more at peace with myself."

Shay had always said how level-headed and rational I was, which was why he came to consult with me whenever he was bothered by something. This time as well, despite his dismay, he agreed and thanked me for my honesty.

*

Two days later, Anna arrived at my house just after Itay had fallen asleep. As usual, she was carrying a basket filled with delicacies. As she placed the wine, cheeses and breads on the table, I felt I could no longer contain myself. I said, "Shay has suggested we move to Paris."

"What?" Anna looked up sharply.

"Yes, he's had an offer to serve as the Cannes-Plus content manager. It's a once in a lifetime opportunity."

"Wow! And what did you tell him?"

"That it would be complicated for Itay and Danny, and for my work here. But what do you think?"

"Me? Let me see … I would love to live in the City of Lights, surrounded by the scents of *boulangeries* when I wake up in the morning."

"Come on, be serious, this is really bothering me. How would we be able to have a long-distance relationship?"

"What's your alternative, getting back with … wait a minute, what's been going on with him since the premiere?"

"Nothing special," I answered.

"I know that sly smile." Anna was watching me. "You two are in touch?"

"Yes, I mean, no."

"Nicole!"

"He keeps sending me these delusional emails, and I don't reply," I explained.

"What emails? What are you hiding? Show me."

"It's nothing."

"Nicole!"

I brought the laptop into the living room and opened it in tense silence.

"I can't believe it," Anna hissed. She was standing behind me as I logged into my email account and we both saw a new incoming message.

'Nicole, my dear!' he wrote, *'I can hardly breathe with excitement to be writing you this news — I want to marry you! I can't stop thinking that maybe, maybe, if you haven't*

forgotten all about me … we can finally be together — just like we dreamed about for so long.'

"What's this?" Anna said. "You're with Shay now, remember? I thought you had severed all ties with Razi?"

"Shh … I can't focus on reading the email with you nattering on," I said. I couldn't help myself; I was smiling.

"You're cooperating with him," she went on, speaking over my head. "You should have told him to stop bothering you or you'd go to the police."

"Really?" I turned to look at her. "You think the police would arrest him for writing love letters?"

"No, but if you'd told them these emails were bothering you, they'd have warned him to stop writing them and that would have been enough," Anna insisted. "We both know he's guilty of following you."

"Stop talking about him like that." Sudden anger surged through me. To hide it, I turned back to my computer, staring at the email on the screen. "It isn't so terrible to want a moment of peace and quiet after your divorce. Besides, look how much he loves me. He hasn't given up on me, although he knows I've been with someone else for a while now. We both know that a man like him could easily have found a hundred younger and prettier girls than me."

"Shay could do that, too," Anna protested. "And he's not as messed up as your Prince Charming, who's in way over his head with a shitty marriage, plus two. I just don't understand why you insist on messing up your life when you have the opportunity to have a good relationship."

"Well, now," I turned to look at her again. "Suddenly you're the chief priestess of steady, long-term relationships?" I asked sarcastically. "May I remind you that you've been with your new boyfriend for a mere month?"

Anna smiled and said, "Well, the fact that we're still together is an accomplishment in itself, isn't it? All right, I guess I deserve to be laughed at. I admit that while you were having a monogamous relationship, and raising a model child, I was still fooling around with half the world. Even today, whenever I meet someone who looks like he might be serious about me, I can't help feeling apprehensive about making a commitment. But that doesn't mean I have to let you ruin your life."

"You're right. I learned my lesson when I let Razi influence me." I agreed with her and closed the computer. "Come on, let's go drink some wine and think together about how I can make Itay fall in love with Shay."

We were both drunk by the time the evening was over, but we also had a plan. I was supposed to suggest to Itay that we spend Saturday at the water park, with my sister, Bat-El, my brother-in-law, Moti, and their children, Ido and Shirel. I planned to invite Shay too, and pretend he was there by accident. Then I could introduce him to Itay as a coworker and let their relationship develop from there.

When Anna left my house, I could not subdue the urge. I opened my email account again and clicked on Razi's mail. All I felt was confusion. Did he really want to marry me, or was this just one more attempt to ruin things between me and Shay?

Finally, as I uprooted myself from the computer and dragged myself to bed, the phone rang. I answered immediately because I thought it would be Shay, who had not called that day. To my surprise, it was Razi. His voice was hoarse and excited.

"Nicole, darling, I'm so happy you answered the phone! Have you read the email I sent?"

"Yes, I have." It took all the mental strength I had left to speak with laconic restraint, despite the turbulence I felt in my heart.

"And how do you feel about it?"

"I ... this is really hard for me to answer, Razi..." I squirmed, torn — between my longing to be with him, to feel his spine-tingling touch and be burned with the fire of his love, and the remorse I felt over betraying the charming Shay, who had never wronged me in any way.

"Nicole, darling." His whisper sent another shudder down my spine. "It's real this time. I'm ready to accept your terms. Please, open your heart to me again ..."

"Razi ..." I hesitated despite myself. "I ... it's hard for me ..."

"Where are you? In bed?" he asked, breathing into the phone. "Because I'm downstairs in the parking lot. Would you like me to come up? Just for a minute? I just want to hug you. I've missed you so much ..."

"I ... I really can't see you right now ..." I was so torn. One part of me wanted to tell him to hurry up to me, to take me in his arms and ... Another, rational part, urged me to say goodbye and hang up the phone.

"I'm coming up," he said urgently. "If you want to, just open the door. If you don't, I'll understand and leave."

"Razi, no!" I tried to make my voice determined, but all I heard was the sound of the line being disconnected.

Five minutes later, we fell wildly into each other's arms.

Chapter 19

"Mom wake up! Mom, I'm going to be late for school," Itay's childish voice shouted in my ear.

I opened my eyes in panic and looked around to see if Razi was still there. The whimsical thought occurred to me that if he had still been in my bed, it might have made a highly amusing scene taken from some romantic comedy. The heroine spends an entire evening deliberating with her best friend about how she can introduce her new boyfriend to her little son, only for the boy to find her in the morning — in bed with her ex.

However, as this was reality, on reflection I found nothing very amusing about that scene. I was relieved when I recalled Razi had left at five that morning. I smiled at Itay.

"Sorry, sweetie." I hugged his slender body. "I was up till late chatting with Anna and forgot to set the alarm clock. You won't be late. We'll get organized lickety-split and get you to school on time." I jumped out of bed and quickly put on the same house dress I had worn the previous evening.

"You're going to work like that? In your pajamas?" Itay surveyed me with two round, wondering eyes.

"No. I'll take you to school and then come back here

and change." I pulled him along to his room. "Come on, let's get you dressed and go."

I quickly dressed him in his school shirt and he pulled on his jeans.

"That's it, you're ready. Just brush your teeth and we can go," I went into the bathroom to splash water onto my tired face.

"But when will you make me a sandwich?" he asked.

"You're right, my cute little thing." In something of a daze, I walked into the kitchen to make him a sandwich of cheese and vegetables, his favorite.

On the way to school, I chatted happily with Itay, so he would not notice how guilty I actually felt. Not only had I cheated on Shay, and in doing so had sunk back in the mud I had barely been able to rescue myself from before, I was also going to be late for work. If things continued like this, I would have to go on lying, not only to Itay, but to the whole world — and then some.

"So, are you and Anna going to end up getting married?" he asked.

"Of course not. Why are you asking?"

"Because you said you two chatted until late at night, and now you look happy, even though you're going to be late for work," he answered astutely, "so I thought you two must have been talking about something really happy."

Luckily, we were just arriving at Itay's school, so I was spared having to give him any more details. The bell calling the children to their classes was ringing in the background. So Itay hurried off with his question unanswered. He rushed out of the car and ran to class.

All that day, I walked about with a feeling that I was carrying a new burden, as if large chunks of stone had settled in my stomach. I couldn't entirely blame the bottle of wine Anna and I had demolished together the previous evening. There was something much deeper that told me, no matter how hard I had tried to expunge Razi from my life, I hadn't truly been able to do it. The truth was that I loved him, and craved the thrill of his touch. Still, I was with Shay now, a handsome, charming, talented man who wanted me in his life with no complications. Openly, so the whole world could see. I could not avoid thinking I might be harboring that destructive instinct Freud had called *Thanatos*, the one that causes people to be drawn to adventures and risks.

I wanted to call Anna and tell her everything that had happened since she'd left, but I was afraid she'd accuse me of the same things I was thinking myself — that I was ruining my life for no logical reason other than the fact that Razi thrilled me and Shay didn't. She would probably say it was all only in our heads, and that I should make a genuine, final decision to cut Razi out of my life.

And if that would not be enough to convince me, she'd add that my parents, my family and my friends would all prefer me to be with a single man my own age, rather than a man who was divorced, older, and who had two children of his own. She'd never understand that something inside me still craved Razi. And it was that 'something' which explained why I had remained relatively indifferent towards Shay. Despite the fact that the latter was a solid and successful man, I simply couldn't devote myself completely ... and introduce Itay ... to him.

Deep inside, I felt that Razi had needed to be rattled — really shaken up — to make him realize what he needed to do. The previous night, after having read his email, I had become convinced he had finally come to this realization, and that we were now nearer than ever to finally tying the knot that would bind us together forever.

Things had developed too rapidly, and quickly gotten beyond my control. I was confused and kept wondering how I could safely get out of the mess I had gotten myself into with Shay.

Two days later, when I had finally recovered from my confusing daze, I decided to confess everything to Shay and simply tell him the truth.

I told Razi what I was going to do and then met Shay for dinner. I held nothing back. I simply poured my heart out to him and apologized.

I could see the sadness taking hold of him. However, being Shay, he quickly recovered and, with a forced smile, stroked my hand. He thanked me for my honesty and sincerity, and explained that he had once been in a similar situation and understood. He wished us, Razi and me, the best of luck.

As we parted, he said, "Who knows, maybe our paths will cross again in the future?"

*

The weeks after I received that email were the most thrilling and exciting of our relationship. We spoke a lot about our own future and the future of both our families together, and agreed it was time to give Itay a brother or sister. My feeling was that this time Razi had genuinely chosen to be with me. Despite the pressure at the startup company, we met frequently, much more than we ever had before. Our meetings oozed with love and dripped with hormonal activity, and when Razi had to go away on business trips, I'd join him for the weekends, so we were able to go on enjoying that wonderful sense of togetherness.

At last, I was able to take him to meet my parents, and they, to be honest, admired him very much. My brothers were taken by his charm, as had happened with Anna, who had grudgingly been willing to give him the benefit of the doubt and stopped talking against him behind his back.

It all happened so quickly, and I was more than a little surprised when, a mere month after we had gotten back together, while we were visiting Rome, Razi knelt before me like a real gentleman, and presented me with a dia-mond ring that looked like it had been carefully selected.

We held the wedding at the Dan Hotel. It was a classi-cally modest event, and the first time our two families had met. This included Razi's brother, Ronen, the professor, and his wife Niva, who had returned to Israel from the US.

My parents were beaming with happiness. They danced and celebrated with us all through the ceremony. I could not really say the same about Razi's parents, but at least they were polite enough to force a smile and offer their congratulations. Razi's youngest daughter, Gaya, did not attend the wedding, but Oren, his eldest, did, and he seemed to be genuinely happy for his father.

After the wedding, we went to Switzerland for our honeymoon, to a picturesque, pleasant village somewhere between Zurich and the Alps. We slept in a charming apartment that belonged to friends of Razi's family, but who were currently away on a safari in Africa.

When the plane landed in Switzerland, I gazed happily at the snow-capped Alps. I felt like Heidi — the girl of the Alps, whose adventures I had thought of in my childhood each time I imagined a snowy mountain ridge. But none of the mountains of my imagination looked as enchanting as the ones I now saw in reality.

"You know," Razi said, his tone nostalgic, "I've been here many times with my dad, travelling for business, but this time it's different."

"Why?"

He wrapped his arm around me. "You don't understand how much of a difference it makes to finally be with the woman I love most in the world!" His eyes bathed me with their warmth.

"You make me happy too, Razi," I said. And I meant every word.

Our honeymoon seemed to have been taken out of a Hollywood production. We enjoyed pampering breakfasts under the shadow of the Alps; we toured the most spectacular locations; and in the evenings we dined in fine restaurants and then spent the nights partying in bed.

One night, Razi seemed a little distressed. I sensed he was hesitant about something, and preoccupied. A few minutes later, as he was staring up at the ceiling, he asked me if Olga was still sending me messages.

"No," I answered. "After we parted ways, I told her she had to stop. She apologized and I haven't heard from her since."

"Apologized? Well, I'm really grateful for that..." he said. He turned his gaze to me.

"Razi, what do you want from me? Yes, she finally understood that we weren't together, and that if she sent me another message I'd go to the police. I can only assume she said she was sorry to show me she agreed."

"Oh, all right," he said, cynicism clear in his voice.

"I actually found it very nice."

"You do realize," the way he was speaking had started to make me feel stressful, "that you are my wife, and that she harassed you by sending those messages. And now you are no longer in the picture, God only knows what she's going to do. I'm pretty sure she's still at it with her investigations."

"So why don't you call her and set up a meeting? That way, maybe you two can straighten things out. You still have enough money in the bank to get her off your back."

"And what will I tell the investors? 'Thank you for your money. Instead of developing your technology, I've decided to pay protection to a delirious woman, just so she won't accuse me of being responsible for her husband's suicide'?"

"Razi, if you two really wanted to, I'm sure you could find a way to resolve this disagreement."

"Nickie, why don't you talk to her?"

"What? Why?"

Razi didn't answer.

"A moment ago, you accused me of being in contact with her, so why are you trying to drag me back into this thing again?"

"Because she sent Bondi to talk to Alex, one of my employees. Bondi wanted to see the text messages Giora had sent him in the days before the presentation."

"So? What could she possibly find out?"

"I don't know what she might find out, but it doesn't take much today to turn a prince into a monster. A little fake news on social media and this whole initiative could go to hell."

"I understand."

"Nickie…"

"I'm sorry Razi, I don't want to get involved in your business," I said with finality. "Good night."

Razi was silent. When I woke about two hours later, I saw he was still awake and staring at the ceiling. He noticed I had woken up but said nothing, so I turned my head away from him and went back to sleep.

Chapter 20

When we got home from our honeymoon, an official notice was waiting for me. It informed me that my employment with the company was being terminated after thirteen years. The news did not exactly come as a bolt from the blue. I'd heard talk about downsizing in the company for many months. The rumors had been preceded by the loss of a large tender and the merger of several companies in the field. All had contributed to the firing of senior management members like me.

After long deliberation, and on Razi's advice, I decided not to rush into looking for a new job, and to relax and enjoy a few months of downtime, and try to expand our family. I told Razi, while we were trying to get pregnant, that I wanted to buy an apartment that would be suitable for both of us, and for the needs of our two families.

I had been dreaming about buying an apartment for many years. Over time, I had saved a million shekels. Razi was supposed to contribute his share too, but had no available money. It was all invested in the company. "A company is the best asset we can have," he insisted.

When I suggested we take on a mortgage, he refused. "Why should we pay the banks? I'll take a loan from my father and it will just be deducted from my inheritance," he said. "He gave my brother a loan, too. But we can't ask him now. Only when the company has completed developing the software."

I invested a lot of time searching for suitable properties, and when I sent Razi pictures of apartments, he invariably approved them, telling me, "I trust you." But every time we actually went to see an apartment, he came up with reasons why we shouldn't buy it.

Two months later, I was about to give up, and did not hide my frustration over the fact that he wasn't cooperating, when Razi called, highly excited, and said, "I've spoken to my dad. The people renting his villa in Tzahala are leaving and we can move in there. We wouldn't need to buy an apartment and pay a mortgage."

"I need to think about it."

"He needs an answer, Nicole. If we give up on this, he'll simply look for other tenants."

"All right, let me think about it until tomorrow," I replied.

The fact that he wanted to stay close to Dorit, who came up with countless excuses to keep him near her, raised question marks in Anna's mind. But I told her he just wanted to be close to Oren and Gaya, and that I had to respect that. After all, what really interested me was establishing a warm, loving home for our shared children and the children each of us had from our first marriages.

A month later, we moved into Shraga Zonenberg's villa — and the stress returned in full force.

*

The biggest mistake I made was agreeing to Razi's suggestion that I manage SEG's finances. This happened after Razi fired his company's CFO and suggested I replace him.

SEG's lavish offices were located on the tenth floor of a luxurious building in Herzliya Pituah, the stronghold of Israeli high-tech companies.

Razi was waiting for me in the parking lot when I arrived, and he escorted me up to the office. He introduced me to Adi, the secretary, and showed me the development department. It numbered twelve people. The marketing department consisted of four additional employees. Razi went over the financial data with me and introduced the sales targets to me. When we went out for lunch, I met Alex, the company's development manager.

On our way to the restaurant, Razi told me he had recruited Alex, a former LSB Defense Technologies engineer, about eight months before. He invited him to join the company, and to develop the artificial intelligence in return for a generous equity package.

After lunch, I met with Alex again and he made an excellent impression on me. The development he had planned seemed interesting and promising to me, and when he opened his laptop and showed me some in-depth details, including schedules, I got the impression that his facial expressions demonstrated confidence and a strong belief that he would be able to meet his objectives.

"Great. Looking good," I smiled.

"Yes," Alex agreed.

"Looks like you know what you're doing."

"Obviously, he does," Razi barged into the conversation. "Otherwise, he wouldn't have cost us so much money." He laughed.

"Have you developed similar technology in the past?"

"I've developed artificial intelligence, but not exactly like this one."

"Oh."

"Don't forget that Giora Golan only registered the patent," Alex said.

"What do you mean by that?" I asked.

"That this is merely the conceptual structure. The application itself is much more complicated," he replied.

"And that's what Lock-space is supposed to get?"

"Yes," Razi interrupted again. "They will get everything they were promised, so you have nothing to worry about, Nicole."

Alex, who was about to reply, was suddenly silent. I looked at him and then at Razi and his tense expression. When Razi looked back at me, I had the feeling he had forgotten we were husband and wife, and that maybe he was, in some way, apprehensive of me.

I was silent for a moment, and then said, "Razi, I trust that you all know what you're doing."

"See what a wife I have?" Razi laughed, and Alex smiled politely.

Razi and Alex spoke with each other like two old friends. When I left them on their own, I wondered what the true reason was behind Razi asking me to join the company, and when he had concocted this particular plot.

Chapter 21

"Razi, I don't want to stress you out, but I don't think it's right for me to be working at SEG," I told him after Itay had gone to bed and we were sitting together in the living room. "I don't think marriage and work go together. Perhaps you should look for someone else for the job?"

"I'm fine with the way things are right now," he replied. "You're going to be a part of the company." His wide smile concealed the great tension I sensed he was feeling.

"It isn't healthy, Razi. You have a lot on your mind, and its best that we keep home and business separate."

"Nicole, darling." He took my hand in his and his tone changed, becoming softer. "I'm sorry about what happened yesterday with Alex. I really didn't mean for it to go that way. It was just that you brought up the Lock-space matter to him and he's not very familiar with the details."

"Doesn't he know about the sale?"

"No, and he's not supposed to know. Nobody is supposed to know," he determined vehemently.

"But…"

"Nickie, you have to understand, Alex is merely a company employee. True, he has a lot of privileges within the company, but after what I've been through with Giora, I don't want to rely on anyone anymore, and I certainly don't want any partners."

"Got it," I said and took a sip from my cup of tea.

"Other than you, that is. You're my only partner, both in life and in business."

"All right."

"This is what being a husband and wife is all about." Razi turned his beautiful smile on me.

"Yes, but …"

"Which is why," Razi interrupted, "I need you to find out what Olga knows."

"Razi …"

"You need to understand, Nicole, she's crazy. I've raised millions for this project. I'm building an amazing team, and this messed-up woman could ruin everything for us.

"Razi!" I couldn't help it; I was upset with him.

"I'm begging you. Please help me with this."

"All right," I softened. "I'll try to meet with her. "But I want you to promise me this is the last time you use me to spy on Olga for your benefit."

*

A week later, I went to Haifa to meet Olga. She chose a small café on the outskirts of the city. When I arrived, she was already sitting with a bottle of mineral water and two cookies on a small saucer. Her body was full, her face pale, and her hair cropped and dyed red.

"Pleased to meet you."

"Me too," she said in a Russian accent.

"Finally, we meet face to face." I smiled.

Olga did not react. She scrutinized me closely and did not try to hide it.

"I'll have a latte, please," I told the waitress as Olga took a bite out of one of her cookies.

"I love the Haifa beach. When I was younger, Danny, my ex, had friends here. A couple we used to meet here on Saturdays."

Olga said nothing. I looked at her and was silent as well.

"You ended up marrying him," she said softly, but her tone was tinged with accusation.

"Danny? Yes."

"No, the other one."

"Razi? Yes." I smiled again. "We were married a few months ago."

"Are you pregnant?" she asked, dread in her voice.

Was I? "No, no," I replied quickly. "Look, what do you want from me?" I asked. "I did what you asked me to do. I brought you the SIM card and I heard that Bondi had met one of the employees. My personal affairs are none of your business."

"Yes, they are, because now you're working for the company as its CFO."

"What? How do you know that?" I asked, surprised.

"He ruined my life," she said, pain in her voice. "My husband is gone, and no one can bring him back to me."

"But you saw that Razi and his father had nothing to do with your husband's death," I said, surprised again.

"He should have listened to him," she mused.

"What? Who?"

"Giora…he didn't want to go …"

I suddenly understood, "You're talking about the presentation Razi gave to the Lock-space engineers?"

"Da," she affirmed in Russian.

"The one Giora was supposed to attend with Razi?"

"Da."

"But it's a good deal."

"No," she answered curtly. "It isn't."

"A million dollars," I said.

"That is impossible."

"It is possible. There's a patent," I replied.

"The patent is worthless." She raised her voice. "I know." She bit into her second cookie, then slid a straw into the bottle and drank from it.

"Olga, you need to understand …" I started to explain, but she lashed out at me.

"Read," she said, and took a bundle of pages from a plastic bag. The pages contained photocopies of transcripts of conversations. She handed them to me to read. Olga did not take her eyes off me as I read them.

"Dr. Golan explained to Razi the meaning of having an alternate technology on the satellite?" I asked after reading the pages.

"Da," she replied.

"Because it is an outdated technology, it consumes more storage and data traffic resources."

"Da."

"And could actually damage the satellite after it's been launched. Damage that could result in losses amounting to hundreds of millions," I continued. I looked at her in silence. Why, I wondered, did she care so much about the satellite? What was she hiding?

"Olga, understand, sometimes, when you go to companies like Lock-space to give a presentation, and they ask if the technology really exists, the entrepreneurs or the company's sales representatives don't want to miss out on the deal. So, they say the technology exists and only then rush to develop it because they believe they can. Their primary goal is to close the deal and bring in money, so the company can continue developing the technology. It's a common practice in the startup world."

"Giora objected."

"True, and now it's become more difficult, much more difficult, without him. But in time, they will pull it off."

Olga was silent, looking at me as she sipped her drink through the straw.

"Olga, I understand you feel they weren't being very fair with you with the purchase of the company shares, so perhaps we could ..."

"Five million dollars," she said abruptly and rose to leave.

I sat there for a few more minutes, thinking how I should tell Razi — about the conversation — and about the fact that I now thought he had a mole in his company.

Chapter 22

"I told you, she's insane," Razi said me as we sat in the café. "Five million dollars? For what? Because he jumped off a roof moments before the presentation?"

"Calm down, Razi," I said firmly.

"Or because I've been bringing in engineers to try and crack his stupid patent for a whole year?" he went on as if I had not spoken.

"Razi, show some compassion!"

"Nickie, the woman's crazy. She's the reason he killed himself. She should have been the one jumping off that roof."

"Razi, you need to start thinking clearly. None of this matters."

"What? What doesn't matter?"

"I've been thinking about what she said all the way here, about the patent being worthless, and that you won't be able to develop the technology."

"We have to," he declared vehemently. "No matter what!"

"I know. Which is why you need to come up with a contingency plan, a plan no one else in the company knows about. Because I think someone has been feeding her inside information."

"Hold on!" Razi looked shocked. "How do you know that?"

"Because she knows I'm the new company CFO. Who could have told her that?"

"I don't know," he answered.

"Tell me, when Lock-space paid you a million dollars, did you give them anything in return?"

Razi looked at me for a moment, his expression pensive, as if his mind had drifted into other worlds.

"Razi ..." I tried to draw him back into the conversation.

"You swear you won't tell anyone about this? My dad's the only one who knows."

"I swear."

"Yes, we gave them an alternative technology. One that operates with lower resolution, but without artificial intelligence."

"But that is not the technology you committed to provide when you signed the investment agreement," I said.

"Right. Because we're still working on it, as you know," he said.

"What happens if they launch the satellite with the alternative technology? Could there be any damages?"

"It won't happen," he said firmly. "I'm making sure of that."

"Razi, listen ..." I tried to explain the true meaning of his confession, but he was too agitated. He lifted the carafe on the table, poured water into his glass and emptied it in a single gulp.

When we first met, I thought, *he would always fill my glass before his own.*

I took a deep breath and went on, "You are committed to Lock-space". "So, you need to check if someone else already has this technology, or at least a part of it. Maybe you'll be able to buy it, or at least sign a collaboration agreement," I suggested.

"Good idea," he said, and, for a moment, it looked as if he was seriously considering the idea.

"And you know what else she knows?"

"What?"

"That I … that we … are pregnant."

"What?"

"Yes. She asked if I was expecting. So, after she left, I just had to go to the pharmacy and buy a pregnancy test. I went into the café restroom — and couldn't believe my eyes. It was positive. The test was positive."

"You're joking." Razi looked confused. "Is she a witch or something?"

"No need to exaggerate. She must have thought we wouldn't want to wait too long after the wedding. But what does it matter, we're pregnant! We got a wonderful present today!" I said, my eyes shining.

Razi made an effort to smile, but it was clear that he was distressed by this latest turn of events. Myself, I had no dreams of changing the world, and I felt I was the happiest person on the face of the Earth.

*

Over the course of the next few months, Razi became evermore frantic and restless, spending most of his time travelling abroad. The official aim of these frequent trips abroad was to search for additional investors and close additional deals for the artificial intelligence technology. Razi and I were the only ones who were in on the secret, the only ones who knew the objective had changed.

Razi hired the services of a Taiwanese agent, Dr. Joana Chan, a greatly admired figure in the world of satellite technology. He claimed she was a first-class professional in the field of space cameras, and that as long as he was able to make her enthusiastic about the project, she would help us find complementary technology that we could purchase or use.

"I have no doubt she can help us reach our objective," he declared with utter confidence.

Of course, I had started to wonder why Razi travelled abroad so frequently and was present at all her appointments. Couldn't Dr. Chan meet people on her own? Or perhaps he didn't fully trust her. Maybe she demanded he join her for the meetings?

Before one of his departures, I could no longer hold back and cynically asked Razi the real purpose of all the frequent trips,

"Have you fallen in love with the Far East?" I asked tartly. "Why do you need to fly out there so often and, incidentally, abandon the management of the company? The CEO is supposed to be running the company, isn't he?"

His reply was swift and almost overly glib, as if he had been practicing it. "Because together, we're a great team. She knows how to recognize technologies that are suitable for our needs, but when it comes to presentations and negotiations, I trust no one but myself. I'm the only one who knows how to close the deals we need. I'm the only one people believe, and that's why she needs me by her side." He smiled, and I thought I saw cunning behind it.

"Well, if you're a man of such high caliber, I'm sure you've noticed the black jeep with the tinted windows that's been patrolling the area every few days, right?"

"You know how many black jeeps there are in this neighborhood? People shut themselves in their black vehicles and the only time you see their faces is at the local supermarket," he replied.

"You can't really do that either, because they send their hired help." I said this with an edge of cynicism that was intended to draw Razi's attention to the fact that not only was he unfamiliar with the reality of the neighborhood he lived in, but that he did not belong to it either.

"They're called 'au pairs,'" Razi smiled. "And we're going to have one too, pretty soon."

"Are you sure we're not being followed?" I asked, just to be sure.

"Nicole, this isn't some Hollywood movie. What makes you think anyone would take that sort of interest in us? We're private people. You mustn't be paranoid, all right?"

"I don't know," I answered. I could feel the apprehensive expression on my face.

"It must be the private security company that's been making the rounds in this neighborhood for years," he said when he saw that I refused to settle down. "You should feel much safer when they're around instead of worrying over nothing."

"But I'm telling you, there's nothing on the jeep to indicate they're from a security company," I insisted.

"Stop worrying, Nicole," he repeated offhandedly, already thinking about something else. "Next time you see that jeep, maybe you should just ask them what they're doing here." He shrugged and smiled a tired half-smile, as if dismissing the subject and his poor joke, and shut himself in the study.

Chapter 23

In the seventh month of my pregnancy, I stopped going in to the company offices. I wanted to ease some of the pressure I felt I was under, which was why I worked on my office tasks from home. Then, one day, Razi arrived home carrying a leather briefcase and looking upset.

"What's happened?"

"I've run out of luck," he said flatly.

Trepidation flooded through me. "What happened?" I asked. "Tell me."

He opened the briefcase and took out a letter. "Lockspace has sent me an official letter," he said, "telling me they're preparing to launch a satellite."

"All right." That didn't sound so bad to me. I needed to understand why he was behaving so dramatically.

"You know what this means?" Razi's eyes seemed a little unfocused and his voice was no more than a whisper. There was no doubt he was very concerned about something.

"No," I replied, feeling the first wriggling worms of worry myself.

"That we have a year, a year and a half at most, to come up with the technology we told them we already have."

"Okay," I said slowly. "How are things going with Joana?"

"We've met with several companies from Europe and the US, but none of them is even close to having the required level of completed technology we need. And that's why we're putting more effort into the Far East. It looks like there are more options there."

"Hold on, Razi." I wanted to explain to him what the delay in finding the right technology actually meant.

"What?"

"Surely you know a letter like this from Lock-space is binding for our company. According to the agreement we have with them, the board of directors must be notified and an urgent board meeting has to be scheduled."

"No way!" he erupted loudly. 'There's no need to make things more difficult and put even more pressure on me."

"You have to."

"Nickie, nobody knows about this letter, except you and me."

"Razi, I'm the company's CFO. It's my professional duty. If we don't call that board meeting, we'll be in trouble," I explained.

"Let me think about it," he said.

*

Next morning, Shraga arrived at our house. Itay had already gone to school, and while I made different salads, sliced some salmon and prepared some omelets, Razi set the table.

When Shraga walked in — with little, almost dainty, steps, he examined the house in a way intended to remind us he was the landlord. Eventually, he sat down; his expression blank, unreadable.

"Dad! How nice of you to come at such short notice," Razi said.

"How would you like your eggs?" I asked, the frying pan in my hand.

"Scrambled," Razi said.

"Vegetable omelet. No oil," Shraga said shortly. He did not take his eyes off his son.

"Listen, Dad," said Razi. "As you know, since the incident with Giora the company has been investing a fortune in development."

"How much?"

"How much what?"

"How much have you burned so far?"

I looked at Razi as he replied, "Five million dollars."

"And how much is left?" asked Shraga.

"Enough to last us a year or so," Razi replied with some hesitation.

"And how much time will the development take?" Shraga was relentless with his questions.

"At least a year. But you know what's it like with development. It could take longer."

"So, in six months you'll need to raise more funds, and that technology had better be ready; otherwise, you won't get a dime and the business, our business, will close. But I assume you both already know that, so what did you call me here for?"

"We received a letter from Lock-space," Razi said.

"What do they want?"

"They've given us official notice to prepare for a launch."

"When?" asked Shraga.

"A year, a year and a half at most," Razi replied.

"So, this puts us in a marginal position. What do you need? More engineers? Well? You have the money, don't you?"

"This letter…" Razi stammered. "We have to notify the board of directors about it."

"No!" Shraga determined vehemently. "That would only make things more complicated — they might contact Lock-space directly."

"What are we going to do, then?"

"Just deal with developing the technology," Shraga replied. "Forget about the formalities for the moment"

"Hold on," I said from the kitchen. "The agreement with Lock-space explicitly requires us to notify the board of directors. We can't just ignore that."

"Nicole," Shraga looked at me condescendingly, as if silently saying *who are you to defy or disagree with me?*'. Then he said, his voice taking on a commanding tone, "Leave the frying pan for a moment, you're seven months pregnant for God's sake. Come in here and sit with us."

I did as he asked and sat down.

"Listen, you wanted to marry him, didn't you?" he said looking at Razi.

"Yes, but ..." I wanted to make it clear that Razi had wanted to get married too, even more than me, or at least that was what he had said when we met, but I didn't want to increase the tension in the room, so I said no more.

Shraga said, "And you wanted to be the company's CFO ..."

"No, I didn't." I corrected him. "Razi asked me to join the company and apply my skills to help him."

I wanted him to get his facts straight, but Shraga refused to listen to the truth and just carried on, "So now I'm asking you to show loyalty to his family."

"Excuse me, Shraga, but we're talking about my professional integrity here."

"All right." He looked at his watch. "I'm going to be late for my bridge tournament." He rose decisively from his chair, effectively dismissing me, making the point that he didn't think there was any point in arguing with me.

As Razi accompanied him to the door, I could hardly move because of the intensity of emotions rushing through my mind and heart, even more so because my husband had sat there like a little boy without coming to my defense.

"Do you fully understand the implications of this?" I asked Razi as he came back into the kitchen smiling.

"Which aspect do I not understand?" he asked in an amused tone, apparently entertained by the exchange I'd had with his father.

"That the technology Lock-space is relying on to launch their satellite, the technology you have promised to deliver to them, doesn't actually exist. All you've done is wander off to raise more funds!"

"Nickie, Nickie. Listen to me. My dad just asked me not to tell you this, but because you're a partner, it's important to me that you know."

"Know what?"

"The technology already exists and has been implemented in countries Israel does not have trade relations with. Joana and my dad are taking care of it."

"Razi, you have until after my maternity leave, six months at the most, to secure the technology for Lock-space's launch. Otherwise, professional etiquette will require me to call a board of directors meeting and report all this."

"All right, all right," he said, his impatient tone clearly inviting me to stop discussing the matter.

Chapter 24

In the last few weeks before the birth, Razi went on taking his frequent business trips abroad. I wanted him to stay in Israel just in case, but even when he was at home, he preferred to shut himself in the study for hours on end. I barely managed to draw him out for family dinners, and even then, he sat silent and withdrawn.

Other than Adi and Alex, no one in the company noticed the change in Razi. This was because, as a result of the frequent trips he took overseas, he was rarely in the company offices. Alex and Adi were apprehensive about asking him what had caused the change in him in front of other company employees, so as not to put them, or Razi, in an uncomfortable position. On the occasions when they could no longer contain themselves and tried to find out why he was being so silent and withdrawn, Razi would simply smile winningly and say, "This is what I look like when inspiration strikes. Soon, I'll be able to tell you about another project that will change the world."

When I heard about this from Adi, I suggested, for the first time, that Razi should sell the company.

We were both sitting at home, I on a physio ball, and Razi in an armchair in the living room. I laid out the plan I had devised for him. The intellectual property could be worth quite a bit, I told him. What money was left in the company could be returned to the investors, and to Lock-space to compensate for cancelling the deal. And, most importantly, it would allow us to lead a peaceful life without any of our current concerns.

Razi dismissed my proposal, brushing me off as he claimed I knew nothing about ingenious inventions that are ahead of their time. Then he subsided into his withdrawn attitude. Despite the tensions that had gradually seeped into our relationship, Razi did not sink into melancholy. Away from home, he travelled alone and met with Joana Chan at various destinations. The two visited any international exhibition that might, potentially, display the right technology, and approached unknown companies to check purchase options.

Time and again he returned home, his face ashen, and without any genuinely good news, although he still wrote optimistic reports to me and the employees after each appointment, claiming, *'They really love us here and are very excited by our technology and development ideas'*. But his reports did not match reality, because no one demonstrated any interest in investing or cooperating with the project. And then, one day he called sounding different.

"Nickie, are you sitting down?"

"What else could I be doing in the forty-first week of my pregnancy?" I retorted, unable to hide my frustration over the fact that the fetus still remained a guest in my belly, even though the estimated due date had already come and gone.

"We did it, Nickie!" His voice was hoarse and his excitement crackled over the line. "Nicole, you will never believe this — our lives are about to change."

"What's happened?" I struggled to subdue my burning curiosity and spoke with restraint.

"We're in Rome now. Yesterday, we visited the offices of a startup company called AI Software, which is developing exactly what we need, a technology that is able to produce a higher quality image with minimal information resources. It's a technological innovation called 'compressed sampling.'"

"All right, and is it applicable for satellites?" I tried to focus the conversation in a practical direction without sounding too enthusiastic.

"Yes, it's a little different from our patent. The cameras have been developed to take photographs from space with very high resolution. They are installed on satellites and can recognize, decipher and mark actual changes in the field between the current photograph and the previous one," Razi explained.

"Sounds good, and how much do they want?" I was asking as the company's CFO.

"We can't afford to purchase the company for what they're asking — ten million dollars, so I suggested that we use their technology under license and pay them half-a-million dollars for the first year. Should we find the technology is suitable for our needs, we will sign a similar long-term agreement. And they agreed."

I said nothing. My belief, my trust in the whole project

had been waning, and now, suddenly, this new deal ... I didn't know what to say.

There were a few moments of silence between us and then Razi asked, "Well, what do you think?"

"I ... It's really hard for me to answer that question, Razi ... It sounds good, even very good," I replied hesitantly. I had heard too many overly-optimistic reports that had, eventually, proven to be false dawns.

"Nicole, darling," he said quietly, "I know the last few weeks have been hard on you. I just want you to know, none of this would have happened without your faith and support."

"Oh Razi." My voice broke with emotion. "I'm touched."

"I've missed you so much, I'll be flying back tonight if I can get a flight."

"I'll be waiting," I answered, wondering how it was that he always seemed to say the right thing at the right time. The man certainly had razor-sharp senses.

When Razi arrived home, he was beaming with happiness. He brought gifts for Itay, Oren and Gaya. He promised to give me my present only after the children had gone to sleep.

Later, when the house was quiet and we were in bed, he surprised me with a stunning present, a gold necklace with a purple-blue sapphire pendant encircled by a twinkling cluster of diamonds.

"Thank you, my love. This is enchanting." I hugged him. "I'm proud of you."

"You are the enchanting one, my Nicole," he whispered in my ear. "I want you to remember, every time you wear this pendant, just how much I adore you."

As he was making this emotional declaration of love, he gently slid aside the straps of the nightgown I was wearing, secured the pendant around my bared neck and, from there, moved his attention to my breasts. I shuddered with pleasure as we drifted into love-making — the likes of which we had not enjoyed for a very long time. It was the kind of passionate lovemaking that reminded me of the early days in our relationship.

Next morning, a Friday, Razi stayed in bed, while I prepared a sandwich for Itay's school lunch. As I was moving through the living room, my feet got tangled in the pants Razi had dropped on his way to the bedroom. I cursed at him under my breath, bent down to pick up the pants, and put them on the armrest of a chair. As I did so, a calling card fell out of one of the pockets. I picked it up and looked at it as I went on to the kitchen. I examined the card curiously. It read: *Roma Luka-De Papa*, and underneath, in smaller letters in both English and Italian: *Chef De Luka's Restaurant at the Eden Hotel in Rome*.

The card looked brand new. The name of the restaurant was picked out in gold lettering, which glittered in the morning light seeping through the kitchen window. A telephone number had been written in ink on the other side of the card, apparently with a fountain pen as the numbers were slightly smeared. A name was written beside the number: *Shiraz Jasmine Pahlavi*.

I felt an inexplicable need to find out just who this Shiraz was. After Itay had gone to school, I sat in front of the computer. I Googled the name and discovered Shiraz was an American woman, a space scientist of Iranian descent. Until recently, she had been working for NASA, but had defected to the Iranian side to help them develop their nuclear program.

*

In the time I had before Razi woke up, I couldn't stop wondering what it was, exactly, I was supposed to understand from that restaurant card. What was Razi really doing in Rome, and what was his connection with the Iranian scientist? Who were the people he met and what was their connection to the AI Software company? The questions whirled around in my mind and gave me no rest.

Time after time, I went to the bedroom to wake my husband, who was sleeping on his back in our wide bed, his hands spread out to the sides, like a man who has nothing to hide. But each time, I changed my mind and retreated from the room at the very last moment.

Finally, I went back to the kitchen and dialed the number on the card. My hands were trembling. A metallic voice answered in English. It asked me to enter a secret code so the call could be connected. I didn't have the code. I slammed the receiver down and felt utter desperation.

It was at that moment that Razi walked into the

kitchen, hair tousled, still drowsy, and looking like he was floating on cloud nine. He crossed the room and put his arms around me, kissing me and whispering that he had slept like a baby.

I tried to hug him back. I decided, on the spur of the moment, to act as if I didn't know anything about anyone called Shiraz Jasmine Pahlavi, and to try and repress my new and disturbing doubts. But I guess I wasn't much good as an actress because Razi recoiled. He leaned back, looked into my face and said, "You're angry again? What's happened now?"

"Nothing. And I'm not angry," I muttered, as I tried to hide the incriminating business card in my clenched fist. But Razi wouldn't let go. He reached to take my hand and saw I was trying to hide something in it.

"What's this, a surprise?" he asked, and forced my hand open. The now-creased business card was exposed in all its glory. Razi snatched it from my hand, his eyes blazing with sudden anger.

"It's a surprise all right," I lashed out at him. "Who, exactly, is 'Shiraz'?"

"How do you know about Shiraz?" he asked in surprise.

My heart felt like it was being squeezed in a giant fist. "Just turn the card over," I spat, "and you'll understand. I can't believe you're in contact with Iranian spies!"

"Shh ... lower your voice. We don't want the neighbors to hear us," he whispered. "Look, I'll explain everything to you. I never met with any spy. Come on, let's make some coffee and talk out in the garden."

Razi went outside and sat on one of the outdoor chairs. I followed. "I understand why you're nervous, Nicole," he said, "but this really isn't what you think."

I looked at him steadily even though I felt as if my heart were about to break. "Razi," I said, "I need you to tell me the truth — *the whole truth*," I emphasized.

Razi sighed and said, "All right, I know who Shiraz is, but Joana Chan was the one who initiated contact with her. Shiraz is only the mediator in our deal with AI Software. And she's being paid a commission for doing so."

"And what's her connection with the company?"

He hesitated for a long moment, and then said, "AI Software is an Italian company, but its owner was originally from Iran."

"Are you insane?" I whispered. "You'll end up in jail and ruin our lives."

"Nicole, I am merely buying the technology. What do I care who I'm buying it from?"

"Come on, Razi. Are you really that naive? Don't you know there are sanctions in place right now, and Israelis aren't allowed to make deals with Iranians? Maybe this whole thing is a set-up?"

"Oh, come on..." Razi confidently dismissed my words.

"You know what? Remember that black jeep we keep

seeing, roaming around outside our house? When did they first show up?"

"I don't know and I don't care," he replied.

I ignored him and went on. "I'll tell you when," I said. "It was when you decided to hire Joana's services." Another thought occurred to me. "What if they have something to do with the Mossad?"

"Since when have you become so paranoid? Is it the pregnancy, too many hormones putting crazy ideas in your head?"

I decided not to react to that comment. "Razi, I'm asking you to reconsider."

"Nicole ..."

"You'll go to prison," I said. I felt a sudden urgent restlessness. My body began to move on its own. I had to stand up, I knew I couldn't possibly continue sitting discussing something so potentially ruinous. I said, suddenly, shockingly, "I quit."

"Nicole," Razi grabbed at my hand, holding it tightly in both of his. "All right," he said reluctantly, "let me check it out. Meanwhile, don't talk about this with anyone before I talk to Joana."

"Cancel the deal," I said emphatically. "I can't believe you kept this hidden from me! Don't you trust me? Why did you ask me to become the company CFO — just to cover your ass?"

I turned abruptly and went back inside the house. I could feel the tears coming and I refused to let him see them.

A few days later, Razi told me he had fired Joana Chan. Whatever the connection was, I didn't see any more suspicious vehicles outside our house.

Chapter 25

It was a happy day when my second son and Razi's third child was born. Matan was a charming, comfortable, beautiful, smiling baby. Everyone was immediately captivated by his easy-going personality. We decided to hold a small circumcision ceremony, and wait until he was a little older and stronger before throwing a larger party for the whole family.

Oren and Gaya started visiting us, and competed with Itay for the new baby's attention.

Two months after the birth, when I was feeling more comfortable in jeans, we made plans to celebrate the event in a small banquet hall, inviting our families and close friends to join us. But then, two weeks before the party, Razi came home after visiting his parents with a concerned expression on his face. It was already past eleven at night.

"You took your time," I remarked offhandedly, then, seeing his worried expression, "And why the long face?"

"I'm sorry…" he said. "It's my dad."

"What happened?"

"He doesn't want us to have the party in a banqueting hall."

"I don't get it…" I said. I was genuinely puzzled.

"He said we already celebrated with our first children, and we don't need to have a party for each new child."

"What?! Razi, everything's arranged. I've paid the banqueting hall and sent out the invitations."

"My dad says he'll reimburse us."

"It's not about the money. Why do something like that? ... And it's too late, anyway..."

I looked at poor Razi's tortured face. He looked like he was pleading with me to save him. "Nicole, I think we need to cancel this party for Matan."

I sat down. I had to — my legs were shaking with anger. I put my hands on my knees, trying to hold my legs steady. I said forcefully, "I will never let go of something my son deserves to have. *Our* son. Razi, what is wrong with you?"

"What? Why? What does this have to do with me?"

"Tell me," I raised my voice, "doesn't it bother you that your snobbish parents go to Dorit's every week to visit their grandchildren there, and have only been here once to see Matan since he was born?"

"Nicole ..."

"No, Razi. What's bothering them, the fact that I'm working with you? That we had Matan together? What does their behavior mean? Are you completely spineless?" I was furious with him, and I let it show.

"Nicole, I told you, I know my dad. He won't ever forgive me for divorcing Dorit for you."

"For me? You were separated long before we met, at least that's what you told me. But what does that have to do with me? You had other intimate relationships Dorit knew about," I reminded him. "Your family acts like ostriches, burying their heads in the sand. They're behavior is … is just surreal. They refuse to look the truth in the eye, and they try to whitewash reality."

"I'm sorry," he said. He came towards me. "We'll celebrate Matan's birth with your family. They love him and don't have any resentments about my divorce from Dorit." He wrapped his arms around me in a warm embrace.

I felt like my head was about to explode with the thoughts that tumbled through my mind. I was confused. I tried to say something, but instead I pulled away from Razi and went to sit on the sofa, a feeling of desperation threatening to drown me. All I wanted, at that moment, was to close my eyes and sleep because of the physical and mental exhaustion that suddenly overtook me.

"You're tired, let's go to bed." Razi pulled me gently up from the sofa. "It's late and I'm sure you have a busy day ahead of you tomorrow."

"That's true," I agreed and followed him to the bedroom. In the bedroom, Razi hugged me, then gently pushed me away and looked at me for a long moment, as if trying to etch my face into his memory.

"Good night and sweet dreams," he said, and headed off to the study.

"Yeah, sure," I snorted to myself as I brushed my teeth. "Who could possibly have sweet dreams after a bombshell like that?"

What would I tell all the people I'd already invited? I

would have to cancel the banqueting hall, and apologize to the caterers. My concerns and anxieties were growing by the minute and, as I dragged myself to the shower, I couldn't help wondering if all this was an omen, a sign of what was coming. I had to take a headache pill to quiet the reverberating echoes of all these disturbing thoughts. My mind was still seething as I climbed into bed. Eventually, the headache pill did what it was supposed to. My headache eased and I fell asleep.

I started awake an hour later. The doorbell was ringing. At first, I simply tried to go back to sleep, but the doorbell sounded again. I got up quickly and rushed to the door before the children woke up.

"Who is it?" I asked in a loud whisper.

"It's me, Shraga. Open up, please." My father-in-law's voice carried clearly from beyond the closed door.

I opened the door, wondering what on Earth could have made him come to our house so late at night.

"What's the matter?"

"We need to talk," Shraga answered dramatically.

"All right, come inside. Can I offer you something hot to drink?"

"No, I'm fine," he replied.

"All right," I was sorry, now, that I hadn't worn a normal pair of pajamas instead of the long, faded t-shirt I had thrown on before falling asleep.

"Razi tells me you want to hold a banquet hall party for your son?" Shraga said as he walked into the living room and sat on the edge of the armchair.

"Yes, I thought it would make the families happy," I explained, and hated the note of apology I heard in my voice.

"You're right." He smiled. "You have to understand that we're very fond of holding celebrations for our grandchildren, but at this stage, such a large-scale event would offend Dorit and her children, and we don't want to hurt their feelings. Do you understand that, Nicole?"

I just nodded, too stunned, too confused to speak.

"So, I asked Razi if you would stage a smaller event, just you and your nuclear family."

"Hold on," I said. "Perhaps we should just invite Dorit as well? After all, their divorce was consensual." Perhaps it was because I was still a little groggy from sleep, but I couldn't seem to shrug off the feeling of confusion.

"I've considered that, too. But she was hurt by the divorce, even though, as you say, everything was consensual, which is why it would be best to postpone the celebrations for the moment."

"I understand."

"Let's get to the point then. Please sit down, Nicole." It wasn't a request.

I resented his tone. I hesitated, but dropped onto the sofa when he gave me an angry stare.

"When Razi came to us and told us he couldn't live without you," Shraga said in a businesslike tone, "we decided, Aliza and I, to agree to his request to marry you and bring you into SEG."

I nodded. There was nothing else I could to do in that surreal, late-night, unexpected conversation.

"And that is why we want to make your end of the deal perfectly clear right from the start," Shraga proclaimed. "Hold your end of the deal up, and you could live happily with Razi till the end of time. But, should you, God forbid, fail to uphold your end of the bargain, the end of your personal time will come much sooner than you think."

"What?" I nearly screamed in my amazement. Shraga was talking like some kind of threatening mobster. "I don't understand what you're talking about. Nor why you're threatening me."

"I'm not threatening, I'm just trying to explain what you can and can't do," Shraga said in a pleasant tone. He turned to look at me. "And I'm taking the time to discuss this with you now because you have already done some things you most definitely shouldn't have. Maybe because no one was there to guide you. My visit here tonight is to make sure you understand, so you won't repeat the same mistakes. We want to make everything absolutely clear from the start!"

"What 'things' are you talking about?" I asked, my concern growing.

"Don't play coy with me," Shraga said coldly.

For a moment I was too stunned to respond. Then I felt the blood rushing to my head. I lunged to my feet, rage constricting my throat. "Shraga! I'd throw anyone else out of my house for talking to me like this. Do yourself a favor and leave, right now! Before I wake Razi, who's sleeping after working all night. Or do you want to hurt your son, too? Or should I just call the police and tell them you're threatening me?"

"Nicole, I know about the SIM card you stole from Razi, so I think you'd better sit back down," Shraga said. He did not appear at all bothered by my threats. "We don't want Razi to be woken by your shouting. I know you were spying on him."

"You're right. But it was only so you could complete the fundraising," I lowered my voice, despite the fact that my anger was intensifying with every passing minute.

"And I know you want him to sell the company, which would mean we would lose all of our investment."

I said nothing and looked into his narrowed eyes.

"So, now I'm going to *make* you understand." A silver pistol suddenly appeared in Shraga's hand. He pointed it straight at me. "I want to see Matan."

"What?" I screamed in sudden horror as he rose and marched towards my baby son's room. "Razi, get up, your father has a gun!"

Chapter 26

Shraga didn't stop. I was overwhelmed with consuming, maddening fear and ran after him, screaming at the top of my lungs, "Razi, wake up! Matan ..."

"Nicole." A voice was calling my name. "Nickie, Nickie, wake up!" Strong hands took hold of my shoulders and shook me. I tried to push the hands away, but then I realized it was Razi's voice. "Nickie, wake up, please. You've been screaming in your sleep. Whatever it is, it's only a dream!"

I woke with a start. I sat up in bed, still gripped with the horror of the so very real dream. Razi sat up as well, his arms around me.

"It's all right, it was only a nightmare" Razi pressed me to him. His voice was soft, soothing. "Don't worry, my beauty, everything is fine. What were you dreaming about?" His concern was turning to curiosity. "You screamed my name so many times."

"Actually, I ... don't remember." I feigned a smile. "Let's go back to sleep, we'll talk about it in the morning," I urged.

"All right." Razi lay back in bed and was asleep in seconds. I wasn't. I had a hard time getting back to sleep. The harsh events of the nightmare had been very real and had shaken me badly. I could not ignore the burden of the dream's symbolic significance.

I remembered Freud's assertion that dreams were actually messages from the subconscious mind. Messages that the conscious mind might find difficult to cope with, so it represses them. The message sent by my subconscious seemed very clear and simple: I was on my own in this conflict with Razi's parents.

I had always dreamed that Matan would grow up with Itay and his half-brother and sister in the same way I had been raised with my own siblings, but as far as Shraga was concerned, our son was not the equal of Oren and Gaya, Razi's children by his first wife.

Even if the events in the dream had been far-fetched, and there was no existential peril over my son's head because of the connection with the Zonenberg family, I realized that didn't mean he couldn't get emotionally hurt.

Finally, I fell asleep with a heavy heart and an uncomfortable feeling that swelled into a consuming melancholy come morning, when I saw Razi wearing an elegant suit and perfuming himself with his Chanel cologne without taking the slightest interest in what had happened to me during the night. He was completely focused on himself, and treated me as if I was nothing more than thin air.

*

Razi arrived home that evening, his mind occupied by the developing business, as usual.

I took a good look at him as he entered the living room and thought to myself that when you live with a man, you sometimes forget just how handsome and attractive he is. As I looked at him, I thought how he must have had many women in his life.

I poured two glasses of Cabernet, one for him, one for myself.

"What are we celebrating?" Razi asked when he saw me with the glasses.

"Our relationship."

Razi looked at me, his eyes sparkling.

"I had a nightmare last night, remember?" I reminded him.

"Yes, I vaguely remember something," he replied, apparently uninterested in what the dream had been about, but I pressed on relentlessly. "It was about your father."

"Really? Well, you're not the only woman dreaming about him!" He flashed me a devilish smile.

"Razi, tell me, why did you fall in love with me?"

"What? What kind of question is that?"

"I'm serious, there are so many women out there. So why me? And why did you come back after we separated?"

"Nickie, I think you just don't get it. I know it's a stressful time, and you may be getting the impression that I'm not investing enough in our relationship ..."

"But," I interrupted Razi, "we also don't have sex any-more, and I feel that something has died between us."

"You silly girl. You have to understand that stress at work reduces a man's libido, it's a well-known fact, I haven't invented it or anything. Plus, I think I have some prostate problems," he said, and then added, "I keep thinking back to our first date at 'Le Corton', you were so beautiful and elegant. I just knew you were going to be my woman." his voice was suddenly tinged with a dream-like tone, and his eyes closed for a moment.

I took his hands in mine and whispered softly, "Can you tell me about your relationship with Dorit?"

"Nicole, I've already told you about it a million times." He sighed and took a sip of wine, as if trying to draw some strength from it.

"I'm not the first woman you had an affair with while you were married to Dorit, right?"

"What does it matter? I'm with you now, aren't I?"

"It's important to me," I replied.

"Are you sure you want to hear all the gossip? It could take a while." Razi smiled and took another sip of wine.

"I insist on hearing it," I said, and immediately added, "I'm not in a hurry to go anywhere." I made myself com-fortable on the sofa in front of him and waited for his confession.

"All right." Razi reached for the bottle of wine and replenished both glasses. He took a deep breath and began. "So, I'll start by telling you how I got married in the first place. You know I met Dorit in high school and we were an item then, mainly because she was a special kind of girl. There was something dark and strange about her that I found attractive as a teenager. When I joined the army, we had to separate and didn't really keep in touch. After I finished the army, I went to study in the US. One day, she showed up at my apartment and told me she was on a trip and that my parents had given her my address. To be honest, I was a little shocked when she just showed up out of the blue, but I made her welcome and she stayed much longer than a visiting tourist normally would. Then, one night, she literally forced her way into my bed, and that was how it all really began."

"In the years before she turned up again, an American family, distant friends of my parents, 'adopted' me. I had a lot of fun with them. I felt right at home and was very attached to the father of the family. He was the exact opposite of my own father, a warm, outspoken man I could talk to about anything under the sun. Then, one day, with no warning, he committed suicide. He left a letter in which he confessed his true sexual orientation and the secret affairs he'd had with young men. The guilt he felt eventually became too much. He said he couldn't go on lying and deceiving his family and close friends, so he decided to end his life."

I wanted to interrupt Razi. I wanted to ask if he too had had a homosexual relationship with the man, but I hesitated to interrupt his flow and decided to let him go on telling his story. I assumed that if he had been involved sexually with a man, he would have told me, or at least I hoped he would have.

"Of course, the man's family was devastated and fell apart. I was left there on my own. And it was then that Dorit came, and, to be honest, molded herself to the condition I was in. Carefully, almost unnoticed, she found a place in my heart and settled there. She took care of me, fussed over me and made me feel at home again. In the end, we decided to go back to Israel and get married, and then return to the States. When we arrived in Israel, the day before the wedding, we had an argument, a bad one, and I realized I was about to perform the most reckless act of my life — marrying a woman I didn't love. I nearly cancelled the wedding, honestly, but I felt uncomfortable about all the guests that had been invited and, more importantly couldn't handle the thought of the shame I'd bring to my parents. They had already invited all the extended family and friends and were really looking forward to me getting married."

"Are you serious?" I finally interrupted him, too shocked not to. "You married her just because you felt uncomfortable about cancelling the wedding?"

"Something like that." He shifted in his chair in mental discomfort. "Why are you so surprised? You have no idea how many people get married just because they don't want to insult anyone."

I said nothing. I thought people like that could only exist in his parents' hypocritical world, but I obviously could not afford to tell him that as he was finally opening his heart to me.

"In fact," he went on, "when we went back to the States after the wedding, we had some decent times together. Being far away from the poisonous influence of her mother was good for her."

"Yes," I nodded and sipped my wine. I could understand that.

"To make a long story short, our time together in America was actually quite good. It was a time when romance and wild sex had taken over American society and Dorit played along with me. We took part in orgies and swinger parties, and even spiced up our adventures with cocaine to maximize the sheer pleasure of it all."

I barged in to voice my surprise. "What? I never would have guessed you'd be into kinky sex; you look like such a nerd!" I blurted out." I thought for a moment and then added, "Just so you know, there's no chance I'd ever cooperate with something like that." Then something else occurred to me and I asked, "Was it a one-time curiosity — part of being young and stupid — or is that who you really are?"

Razi didn't answer the question and simply picked up the story where he had left off, but there was a naughty twinkle in his eyes that left me wondering.

"When we eventually came back to live here in Israel, especially after Oren was born, things really went downhill. She dedicated her all to the child, and wasn't interested in anything else anymore. She let herself go, didn't want to work, and was so bored that she started complaining about everything. I became a little desperate. She was taking all the joy from my life, sucking it out of me. I thought then about getting a divorce, but I was also thinking about establishing SEG at the time, and I didn't want to get into any kind of confrontation with her at such a sensitive stage."

'It sounds like living in a prison,' I thought to myself, but said nothing.

"And then I met Natasha," Razi said after a long silence. I realized he was confessing to an extra-marital affair. "She was like a breath of fresh air on an arid summer day. She was young, but amazingly ambitious. A surgeon, an insanely motivated careerist, and she was very intelligent, educated and cultured."

"You sound like a dating profile!" I couldn't help it, I burst out laughing. "All right, I get that she was cool and intelligent, but did you genuinely love her or were you just missing some sexual thrills?" I asked. "Because this 'affair' doesn't really sit well with all the remorse you say, at every opportunity, you feel about the damage you've caused your older children." I knew I was challenging him. "And if your feelings were genuine, why did you let her go?"

"Because she didn't want to get involved with my parents. She realized they would do anything to make me stay with Dorit," he said. "I actually met Natasha through my parents. They helped her family after they immigrated to Israel. They introduced Natasha to the topmost surgeons and, very quickly, she secured an internship in the Ichilov Hospital surgical department. It wasn't long after that she received an offer from Rambam Hospital and started working there. When my father discovered our affair, he threatened her and she backed down immediately."

"She backed down from the love you shared?" I examined his face in search of some hint of yearning or regret he might feel over breaking up with that beautiful doctor, but I saw nothing, Razi seemed cool and calculated. I felt as if I was speaking to a robot, rather than a human being talking about someone he had sincerely loved.

He shrugged. "I understood her. She was afraid." He looked up at me. But what does it matter? In the end, my parents weren't able to stop me from divorcing Dorit, so I could live with you. Which goes to show that everything that happened before was for the best. You are much more suitable for me in every possible respect."

I was utterly confused. I found myself wondering if what he was saying was the truth, or whether he was merely trying to flatter me.

"Natasha is a workaholic. It's in her blood. She's absolutely focused on achieving success, and she's given up on the idea of having children, despite the fact that she's been married now for quite some time."

"There are couples out there that choose not to have children." I found myself defending her, then I asked suspiciously, "How do you know all this? Are you still in contact with her?"

"No. My parents are in contact with hers. They hear

stories about her all the time," he said. "She's their only daughter, and they're very proud of her."

"I don't understand why your parents insisted you live for so long with a woman you don't love." I refused to back down. "I think it's strange that you were able to live without love, in a 'mechanical' relationship. I'm just not familiar with that sort of thing. Until a moment ago, I was sure couples only married for love," I said naively.

"You are my salvation." Razi lifted my chin gently and looked deeply into my eyes. "Sometimes you have to go through all sorts of things to find what's really right for you."

I looked back at him. His eyes expressed honesty, openness. I could see love there, and I felt safe again.

"Razi, you have to talk to your parents and sort their heads out, once and for all!" I was furious. "They need to understand that what happened between you and Dorit was diametrically opposed to what your ex-wife says. Before I met you, I was already a successful CFO on a top salary, and you wooed me like crazy. It wasn't the other way around!"

"Nicole." Razi took me into his warm embrace. "What do you care what my parents think? The main thing is that you and I both know your true, invaluable worth to me, and how much I'm in love with you."

"That is hardly enough." I resisted again, refusing to settle down. "Dorit not only slanders me to them, but is inciting them to turn our children into second class grandchildren! Besides, how would you feel if my parents harbored feelings like that about you? Wouldn't you expect me to put them in their place?"

Razi said nothing for a long moment. He looked upset. And that, too, annoyed me. I smiled sarcastically. I didn't need him to reply to my question to know the answer. He would have refused to see my parents until I'd taken care of the problem and come out in his defense, as any wife or husband would do.

"You're right," he said finally, at last being honest. "I would have expected you to do that, but you can't compare my parents to yours, and certainly you can't compare the relationship you have with them to the one I have with my parents. Your parents are much more open and welcoming and never condescend, which is something you really can't say about my dad. You know how he never listens to anything I have to say and criticizes everything I do. Just look at how he takes every opportunity to belittle me instead of being happy about the fact that I've established a successful company with my own two hands."

I said nothing.

"I'll show them yet, you'll see!" His protestation was as sudden as it was angry. "I'll lead SEG to meteoric success and make them eat their hearts out."

"Matan, our sweet son, hasn't done anything wrong or harmed anyone. Why should he be treated any differently from your other children?"

"You're right."

"I can't allow your father to be the one making our decisions for us," I went on.

"All right." Razi agreed with me.

"So, I'm still holding the celebration. It's the right thing to do. I'll just invite my side of the family to our house, and we'll have a respectable party for Matan."

"All right, my beauty," Razi said, and he kissed me.

*

All that week I was busy, enthusiastically arranging the party for Matan. I believed that when Razi told his family just how successful the dinner party was, they would soften up and want to be a part of our future family events.

I assumed Razi shared my feelings and avoided helping me simply because he had increased the pace of the development at work. He wanted to prove that my suggestion to sell the company, and return the money to Lock-space, was unnecessary. Even on the day of the party, Razi hardly helped me with any preparations, even though I tried to get hold of him on the phone numerous times. It was only about noon that he finally answered me.

"I know you're busy, but the party's tonight and I can hardly stand on my feet anymore. Could you come home a little earlier today? We have to arrange the table, and I need your help with lots of other things."

He promised he'd try, but only arrived home at about six, an hour and a half before my family was scheduled to arrive. Under the circumstances, I didn't exactly greet him with a smile, but I also didn't make a big drama out of it, either. I wanted the evening to go well — and peacefully. That was why, when I learned he wanted to go and shower before doing anything else, I went into the bedroom and asked him to help me set the table first.

"Give me a few minutes," he grunted. "I'm sweating like a horse and I really need to shower."

"But they'll be coming soon," I said.

Suddenly, for no apparent reason, my husband's temper flared. "Enough! I'm sick and tired of you acting like you're some kind of boss and trying to run everything," he snapped.

"Shh... don't yell, you'll wake Matan," I scolded him, my voice low and intense. Our son was sleeping in a cradle in our bedroom. I didn't realize I was only further fueling Razi's anger.

"What do I care!" he screamed and started pulling all my clothes out of the closet and tossing them on the bedroom floor like a man possessed. "Why does it upset you so much that I want my company to be successful? Do you think I'm out there having fun at the beach? I'm out there working!"

"Razi, what are you talking about?" I stared at him, amazed. "When have I ever stopped you from working?"

"You can't stand the fact that I'm on the verge of being successful, can you?" He went on hurling my clothes onto the floor, an expression of utter disgust making his handsome face ugly. "Why else would you 'order' me to be here at noon? Tell me that? You think I don't know it's all because you just want to prove you were right?"

"Of course not!" I muttered, stunned by his ranting. And then I heard Matan start to cry loudly. "I just wanted you to help me for an hour or two before our guests arrive." I spoke quietly as I crossed the room to Matan's cradle. I bent and picked him up, nestling him in my arms. I was hoping Razi would realize just how much his behavior was scaring the baby, but he didn't seem to care and just went on screaming and hurling my clothes around.

"Liar! You want me to have nothing left in this world. You took away my family, now you're planning to take over my company."

Matan looked frightened. I hugged him, trying to comfort him. I looked squarely at Razi. Inside I was furious, but I said as calmly as I could, "From this moment on, I'm no longer a part of your company. I wish you the best of luck." I walked out of the room, out of the house, and into the garden. I sat on the garden bench and gently rocked Matan, soothing him and myself.

It was a quarter to seven already. I still hadn't set the table, and obviously didn't now have the time to shower and get ready. I was about to go back inside, pick up the phone and tell my parents and the rest of the family that the party was cancelled, but before I could, Razi came out and said, "I've extended the table. Come back inside and set it. Your parents must already be on their way here."

The party somehow went well, but I was still scarred by what had happened just before it. I found it hard to understand how Razi could have exploded in such vicious anger an hour before dinner, then act, all through it, as though nothing had happened. In fact, he took over the party and was the star of the evening.

After the surreal dinner was over, Razi started begging me to come back to the company. I knew that Razi needed my support to get through the stressful period he was experiencing, but after his outburst in our bedroom, I vehemently refused.

"I really don't get you," he grunted as I was placing the plates in the dishwasher. "We're husband and wife, after all. Why don't you trust me? I only need a bit more time to get the technology sorted. You don't understand how complicated it is. Every time we take care of one problem, Alex shows up in my office with a desperate face and tells me about a new bug in the system. And what do you do, instead of helping me? You threaten to call a board meeting and urge me to sell the company. What do you want? For me to lose everything I've built? Once the technology is fully developed, everything will turn around, you'll see, and we'll be living like kings. I need you to support me instead of constantly making things more difficult for me. You will only gain by that."

"You've been saying that for more than a year," I replied.

"Right, and I took your advice and tried to purchase an alternative technology, didn't I?"

"Let me sleep on it," I said. I was exhausted. "I'll make a decision tomorrow morning."

I barely slept that night. I considered and then

reconsidered the risks, weighing them against the chance that Razi's plan, and his new technology, might actually work. I found myself hoping the latter wouldn't simply add funds to his family's coffers, but would also bring tranquility to our relationship. In the end, though I still wasn't at all sure it was the right thing to do, I made my decision as the cool light of dawn crept into our bedroom. Later, when we sat down to have breakfast, I said, "All right, I'll come back to the company."

Razi looked genuinely happy, but his face immediately clouded over with worry.

"What's wrong?" I asked. "I said I trust you."

"Right," he said hesitantly, "but there's one small problem."

"Which is?"

"My dad won't have you sitting on the board of directors."

For a moment, I hesitated, anger welling up again, but then I saw the tortured look in his eyes as he said, "Nicole, I didn't want to argue with him. Please understand."

"If I agree to this, it will only be if you agree to take responsibility. Promise me that if the development is unsuccessful, you'll summon the board of directors and inform Lock-space in good time. I don't want to get into trouble with them. Are we clear?"

Razi looked into my eyes, as if trying to demonstrate honesty and integrity. Then he said, "I promise."

I expected Razi to keep his word.

Chapter 27

When Matan was eight months old, I discovered I was pregnant again. My happiness knew no bounds. That I was about to become the mother of three children before I turned thirty-five filled me with great happiness.

When I left the gynecologist, who had been delighted to give me the happy news, I wanted to call Razi and share my happiness with him, but I thought it would be more appropriate to tell him about it over a romantic dinner. Itay was supposed to be sleeping at his father's place that day, and I didn't have too much trouble finding a babysitter for Matan. Then I called Razi to tell him I had made reservations for us at our favorite restaurant 'Le Corton'.

"Excellent!" His reaction was enthusiastic. "I've got a long day at the office today. It'll be great to eat out."

*

"How is it that you always seem able to read my mind, Nicole?" Razi was literally beaming when we sat down in the restaurant. "I feel like we're more than a married couple — we're two parts that form a single whole."

"I feel the same way," I answered excitedly, but stopped

myself. I wanted to tell him about the pregnancy only after we had clinked champagne glasses.

"What are we celebrating this time?" he asked when I ordered a bottle of Veuve Clicquot. "Don't tell me I've forgotten your birthday."

"No." I smiled mysteriously.

"What, then? You've received an offer to serve as a venture capital firm's CEO and can help me with a couple of extra million?" he guessed, an amused expression on his face.

"Something even better." I kept my poker-face as the waiter ceremoniously opened the champagne and poured it, with a flourish, into our glasses.

"Cheers!" I clinked my glass with his and waited until the waiter had walked away. "Here's to our baby!"

"What?" Razi looked stunned. "You're pregnant again?"

"You're very perceptive," I joked, "which is why I can't drink too much champagne, but I trust you to finish the bottle on your own, being so excited and everything."

Razi looked confused and emptied his glass in a single gulp. "I ... I don't know what to say," he finally managed. "I promised to ..."

Something suddenly changed, I felt it, it was almost physical. Razi almost instantly became silent and withdrawn. His eyes nervously flicked around, avoiding mine, before they settled on his glass for a moment. Then he said quietly, "I want us to leave."

I was dumbstruck. I couldn't understand what had

just happened. I caught the waiter's eye and asked him to bring the check. I paid and rose from my seat. Razi followed me as we made for the door.

When we left the restaurant, Razi maintained his silence, wrapping it around himself like a dark cloak.

"What happened in there, Razi?" I had to make him talk, about anything, just as long as I wouldn't have to start wallowing in the muddy pool of suspicion that deepened in my heart by the moment. As he got into the car, I suddenly felt reluctant to get in myself, but couldn't think of anything to say to him.

"Razi! Talk to me. What did you promise? And to whom?" I hissed the words quietly once we were in the car.

"This isn't right," was all he said, gruffly. He started the car and we moved off. "Understand," he stammered, "my children have been having a hard time accepting the fact that we've started a new family as it is. They feel like they're being pushed aside, and my ex-wife is nipping at them day and night."

"Why is she interfering?"

"It isn't her."

"Then who is it?" I felt righteous anger filling me.

"I can't believe this, Nicole. This isn't the time," Razi was suddenly depressed and helpless. "You know that Lock-space has announced a launch date, don't you?"

"No, I didn't know there was a date already, but what does your business have to do with expanding our family?"

"You're killing us, Nicole," he said. "Why, Nicole? Don't you think I should have been party to the decision to bring another child into the world?"

"Are you serious?" I felt the tears choking in my throat, so I spoke as quickly as I could. "You knew I wanted to have children as quickly as possible. True, it's happened sooner than I expected. And, true, this is an unexpected pregnancy. But what do you suggest I do, have an abortion? Have you no shame? How can you act now, like...I don't know..." I stopped talking as I stifled a sob.

Suddenly the car in front of us stopped short, brake lights glowing red. Razi, instead of slowing down, gunned the accelerator, then the brakes, then the accelerator again, and then the brakes, the car lurching madly.

Panic flooded through me. "What are you doing?" I screamed as we narrowly missed colliding with the other car. Razi swerved wildly into the other lane, and we nearly crashed into a truck that had suddenly appeared in front of us. Razi swerved again — another near miss. The vehicles around us erupted, hysterically honking their horns. But even all this chaos did not make Razi slow down. On the contrary. He accelerated even more, driving like a madman, jerking the wheel right and left, slaloming his way through the other cars as if he were in a race to Hell.

"Razi, slow down! You'll kill us both!" I screamed, fear exploding through me. But my husband was like a man possessed, and didn't even seem to hear me. His glazed eyes stared fixedly forward through the windshield and he kept stamping harder and harder on the gas pedal.

"Razi, you're insane!" This time I screamed at the top of my lungs, convinced that unless I could somehow stop his mad charge, we would both soon be dead. "Stop driving like a psychopath, do you want to make our children orphans?" A strange, even devilish, smile twisted his lips as our car swerved past another truck at a frightening speed.

"Stop!" I screamed again, helplessly. For a second, I even thought about opening the door and jumping out of the car. But as quickly as the thought occurred, I realized that at the speed we were now travelling, it would mean certain death. The only hope I had was to go on trying to calm him down.

The cars around us were hooting ceaselessly, drivers shouting and pointing at their heads, wagging their fingers to indicate how crazy Razi was being, driving so recklessly. "You're putting the lives of all the drivers round us at risk, not to mention the woman next to you." I yelled. It had no effect on him. Nothing I said, it seemed, could prevent him from continuing with the insanity of the moment. Then I thought of something else. "Razi," I shouted over the roar of the straining engine, "I'm calling your son."

Razi had a soft spot for his eldest son, and I knew he wouldn't want me to tell him about his father's aggressive and wild behavior. I waved the cellphone in front of him to show I meant what I said. It worked. His foot eased off the gas pedal and the car slowed until, at last, our speed was below the speed limit.

The surge of relief made me feel suddenly weak, but not for long. Razi screamed at me so loudly he made my ears ache. "Who the hell do you think you are to call my son? You dumb idiot!"

"But Razi..." I wanted to explain that he had overdone it, gone too far with his wild temper. "Didn't you see what happened back there? The car in front of us, the driver, took a wrong turn and just wanted to correct his mistake. The intersection was very confusing, and mistakes happen. Don't you ever make mistakes?"

"Oh, I make mistakes all the time," he bellowed, "and my biggest mistake was marrying you!"

Much to my horror, he accelerated again, then, just as suddenly, swerved onto the side of the road, stopped the car outside the locked gate in front of the electric power plant, and turned off the headlights.

"What are you doing now?" I yelled, hearing the terror in my own voice. But Razi said nothing. His hands gripped the steering wheel so tightly his knuckles were white, and his head hung down as he breathed deeply, as if he was trying to calm himself. "Don't you know how dangerous it is to stop by the side of a main highway? Especially at night, when it's dark!" I shouted.

"What am I doing?" he murmured. He lifted his head and turned towards me. His face was contorted in a smile that spoke only of evil and madness. I felt a shudder run down my spine. It almost seemed as though he was in the throes of some kind of psychotic fit. As I watched, speechless, his face contorted and turned crimson, the veins in his neck standing out like small ropes.

"You'll understand what I'm doing, as soon as I undo the biggest mistake of my life!"

Chapter 28

I quickly unfastened my seatbelt and reached for the door handle, intending to jump out of the car, but Razi was too quick. He lunged over and grabbed me with both hands.

"Let go of me!" I screamed.

His face changed without warning. Instead of the evil smile, he looked stunned, just for a moment, then he burst into harsh laughter that sounded too loud in the now quiet confines of the car. He said, "I was just messing with you, Nicole. What, were you really scared? You know I'd never do anything to hurt you."

"Are you out of your mind?", I stammered. My knees were shaking, my heart pounding. I continued to tremble uncontrollably in the aftermath of the abject fear I had felt. "You were driving like a maniac. You nearly killed us both on the highway. What the hell is wrong with you?!" Now it was my turn to shout.

"I nearly killed all *three* of us, you meant to say." Razi put his arms around me. "I'm sorry I scared you. I really didn't mean to." His voice sounded mechanical. Devoid of any emotion.

I summoned all my strength and said, "Okay, all right," but my skin crawled in his stifling embrace. "Let's just go home."

Razi smiled automatically, started the engine, turned the car around, and drove back onto the highway.

It was only when we were safely back at home that I allowed the tears to come. And they came in a downpour.

"Nicole." Razi held my hand in his as I sat shaking on the living room sofa. "I'm so sorry. Please stop crying. You're breaking my heart."

"*I'm* breaking *your* heart?" I cried, defiance and outrage making my voice louder than it should have been and breaking my resolve to "play it cool". I snatched my hand away from his. "Aren't you ashamed? Do you even have a heart? What do you think happened to mine when you told me you didn't want our new baby and reacted like a madman?"

"You're right." To his credit, he did sound ashamed. "My dad is very sensitive about his grandchildren."

"You think that gives you the right to add insult to injury? Yes, you left your children so you could live with me, but it was your choice, and we can't live in the constant shadow of that 'original sin'. I want a normal life, Razi! How do you think it feels when…when I, so excited and filled with joy, give you news that's supposed to make you happy…and you…"

I struggled for words, afraid I would begin crying again. "Don't you get it? Are you really that selfish and cruel? This is all just too painful!"

"I'm sorry, Nicole. You're right, and I'm an idiot," he said. "It's my father…he thought we should slow down until they grow up. But you're right, I should never have promised him — -"

"What?" I muttered. "What exactly did you promise him?"

He shook his head and ignored my question. "I really am happy we're going to have another child, honestly. I reacted in an irrational and genuinely stupid way. Please forgive me. Let's go back to the restaurant and start over, forget all this unpleasantness."

I was happy that Razi had calmed down, but the fact that his fits seemed to be gradually becoming more psychotic and uncontrollable, and his mood swings so severe and unpredictable, terrified me.

I wondered, although this did not seem realistic or in line with Razi's character, whether he may have felt pressured to act like 'one of the gang' on his trips abroad, especially to the Far East, and if he had possibly experimented with hard drugs. Maybe, I thought, whatever he had taken had literally fried his brain, and incurred irreversible damage. I immediately suppressed the thought, ashamed to have even imagined something like that about my husband.

We didn't go back to the restaurant. I went to bed and lay there, through the night, listening to Razi's quiet snoring and wondering what I should do next.

In the morning, eyes gritty from lack of sleep, I knew I simply had to talk to someone I could trust. So, I met with my friend, Anna.

For the first time, I told someone other than my

husband about the strange dream I had had about Razi's father. And then I told her about Razi's insanely wild behavior on the road last night.

"Nicole." There was real concern in her voice. It was the first time I had ever heard her genuinely worried. Her face was pale. She grabbed my hand with both of hers, holding it tightly as she looked directly into my eyes. "You need to take some drastic action about this. The way he's been acting is absolutely insane, and extremely dangerous! What if he does something like that again? He could easily lose control and everything would end badly."

"I've thought of that." I shuddered at the memory of that wild ride in the darkness. "I don't know what do to."

"Do you still love him?" she asked.

"Oh Anna. It feels like our love has somehow become a dangerous liability." I sighed. "There isn't a single dull moment. I feel like I'm living in someone else's delusion."

"Then you have no choice. For your own sake, and your children's, you have to divorce him." Her tone was flat, dreary. "I know it won't be easy, mainly because of the children, but you're putting them at risk as well if you go on living with him in the same house."

"I'm pregnant again," I told Anna flatly. "Anna, it isn't that simple, I'm afraid if I divorce him, when he's in such an unstable condition, everything will fall apart and it will start a war with him and his family. God only knows where that might end. And then there's this new pregnancy …"

Obviously very concerned, Anna pleaded with me:

"Take care of yourself, and do me a favor, stay alert!" She hugged me hard and said, "I'm really worried about you, Nicole." Then she had to go, already late for an appointment she had scheduled.

*

Razi went out of his way trying to please and appease me after the rage-filled incidents, and did his best to restrain himself, if only to get me to forgive him.

When the time came for the ultrasound scan, which could determine the baby's sex, I found it hard to contain my excitement. Having two boys already, I was really hoping to have a girl this time, although I knew I would be happy either way. "So long as he's healthy," I kept saying, just as my mother always had.

"You're going to have a daughter!" the gynecologist announced and my heart leaped with joy. Razi looked happy too, but I noticed he wasn't in any hurry to call his family when we returned home.

I tried to ignore the fact that he didn't seem too thrilled that he would soon have a new baby daughter, but I hoped that when she was finally born, everyone, including Razi, would be happy. Despite the fact that my pregnancy was already visible, my 'bump' growing daily, Oren and Gaya did not say a word about it, though they continued to come to our house to play with little Matan. Itay liked them, not because they had a shared brother whom they all liked and played with, but because they were close to his age and, occasionally, they spent time together at mutual social events. All through the months of that pregnancy, our house was full of the noise and happy sound of children, just as I had always dreamed it would be.

*

In the months leading up to the birth of Shiri, our little daughter, Razi was hardly ever at home. He spent most of his time abroad, flying to the Far East for business, or at least that was what he said. He always came back from those business trips with presents for the children and expensive gifts for me, beautiful jewelry he knew I loved. I guessed it was all to make up for his feelings of guilt. Bringing presents home for us was his way of buying some peace and quiet, and it also meant he was able to stay away from home without us complaining. The children bragged to their friends that their father, an important businessman, often traveled abroad, and brought amazing presents back for them.

*

Luckily, Razi was in the country on the Saturday when I started to suffer severe abdominal pains. Early in the morning, when I called the hospital maternity ward to ask what the pains might mean, the nurse had told me,

"You're going into labor, my dear. You should get to the hospital as soon as you can."

I immediately called Razi's brother, who lived nearby, and asked him to come over and stay with Matan. Razi drove to the hospital like a race car driver, taking turns and dodging yellow lights like a real professional. Whenever we approached a red light, I felt a huge surge of pressure — a combination of contraction, fear and adrenalin. We arrived at the hospital, were quickly taken into a delivery room, and Shiri, our daughter, was born within fifteen minutes.

Two days later, I was home with Shiri. Matan was a little intimidated at first, he was still just a fifteen-month-old toddler, and his new sister's miniature size scared him and made him cry. As we now had two babies in the house, plus Itay part of the time, we decided to hire a daily child-minder to come and care for the children.

Two or three days passed and I noticed, much to my surprise, that Oren and Gaya had stopped coming over to our house.

Chapter 29

One Thursday, Razi came home earlier than usual, waving a letter nervously in his hand. "See what my witch of an ex-wife has sent me," he said. He gave the sheet of paper to me. "I couldn't possibly stay in the office after this!"

"Can you warm up a bottle?" I asked Razi, and sat down to read the letter. Although I had already guessed what it said, if only because Razi had called his ex-wife a 'witch' before handing it to me, I was still shocked when I actually read it.

Razi's ex-wife had written a letter that simply oozed with poison and evil. She called me 'the thief', and accused me of breaking up her marriage to Razi because, she wrote, I wanted to get my hands on Razi's, and his family's, money.

'The only reason I have put up with all this until now was because our children seemed to like Matan,' she had written, *'but now they've realized they have been naive and that Nicole has fooled us all. She has been plotting to have more and more children so she can steal as large a chunk as possible from the family property that should go to our children. Because they now realize this, they are no longer interested in visiting your house, or having meals with your other family. From now on, you will be able to see the children only at my house. And you should be*

thankful even for that because I had to persuade them to see you at all. They are very angry that you have allowed this greedy woman to deceive you and steal you away from us.'

'I have spoken to your parents, and with your brother and sister-in-law, and they have all agreed that family dinners will be held only at our place from now on, so that the children will be able to rehabilitate their sense of family. You are welcome to attend these dinners on your own! My heart is breaking over the fact that I am being forced to write a letter like this to you, but I have no choice. I'll do anything to protect the emotional and mental wellbeing of our children, the children you have neglected!'

I dropped the letter as if the mere act of touching it could poison me. Then I gave Razi a stunned look as he stood by the kitchen counter drinking a glass of water.

"I can't believe that your children don't want to come to our house on their own account," I finally said. "She must have poisoned them against us."

"I don't think so," he replied gloomily. "It's hard on her, too. I need to support everyone so that we can all be happy. Nicole, try to understand, please. It wouldn't hurt you to show a little compassion."

I felt a quick flash of anger that, once again, I should be the one asked to be sympathetic. I quickly suppressed it and asked, "So, what do you plan to do? They're teenagers! Talk to them. Explain your side of the story."

"It won't do any good," Razi said stubbornly. "I think I'd better agree to her request for the next month or so, until I can calm things down. Then we can go on with our lives without her interfering with us."

"Razi, this isn't a request," I said as patiently as I could. "It's an ultimatum. Don't you get it? If you give in to her on this, it won't stop at Friday night dinners. Next thing she'll ask for is that you sleep over there to look after the children while she goes off on holidays abroad. And if you don't agree, she won't let you see them at all!"

"So, what are you suggesting?" He stared at me. His expression was one of defeat.

"That you talk to the children. Act as if nothing has happened and invite them to come over here for dinner tomorrow evening."

Razi looked like a man whose whole world had been shattered. He placed the glass on the table and sat by the telephone. I held my breath and waited. I wanted to hear the conversation, but then I heard Matan crying. I walked quickly to the children's room and saw that Shiri was still asleep. I picked up Matan, and returned to the kitchen. I fed him as I listened to Razi's nervous conversation with his ex.

"I said I wanted to talk to *them*, not to you!" I was pleased. Razi was being assertive, determined. "Let me talk to Oren, please. All right, with Gaya, then. What do you mean they don't want to talk to me? Tell them I want to talk to them right now!" He said nothing for a long moment as his face changed. Crimson moved up from his collar until his face was bright red. Finally, he said, "All right. Goodbye!" and slammed the phone down angrily.

"She says they don't want to talk to me," he muttered disappointedly. "I can't believe she's managed to poison them against me so thoroughly."

"Baby, it'll pass." I tried my best to comfort him. "They'll miss you soon enough. Isn't that right, sweetie?" I stroked Matan's head as he sucked comfortably on his bottle, completely unaware, in his innocence, that such an intense conversation had taken place because of Shiri's arrival in the world. The advent of Matan and Shiri into our lives had worked on Razi like a charm. Every time he saw me with our children, especially Matan, Razi would just sit and stare at us, utterly enchanted and seemingly unable to move.

"I can't wait," Razi said, to my surprise, and started measuring the kitchen tiles with nervous footsteps. "I have to talk to them. I have no choice. I'll go to dinner at the witch's house tomorrow night."

"Are you serious?" I was amazed. "What about us? You're going to leave us here to eat on our own on a Friday evening?"

"It's not that big a deal." He looked surprised. "You can just go to your parents."

"But we had dinner with them last Friday," I reminded him. "And they know that this week we're supposed to be having dinner with your family. I don't want to upset them by telling them about your ex-wife's nasty manipulations."

"Don't talk about her like that," Razi said sharply. "She's just a miserable woman. You have no idea what sort of life she had before she married me. She grew up with a mother who was completely out of her mind and used to roam the neighborhood, knocking on doors and begging for scraps of food."

"I remember, you told me all that." I felt sorry for Razi's ex-wife's mother, but then I remembered it was the future of our own family we were discussing, so I said, "With all due respect to her past misery, it doesn't give Dorit the right to break up our family!"

"What do you want me to do, then?" His voice rose. "You want me to disown my own children, is that what you want?"

"Stop shouting, you're scaring Matan." I pressed the baby to my chest as he burst into tears. I hoped Shiri wouldn't wake up from all the noise.

"Matan isn't the only thing that's important in this world!' I could see Razi was working himself up into one of his rages. I started to close down, remembering how my dad always comforted me when I told him about the conflict between the two families.

"Have some patience," he would say, "Razi's older children will grow up, raise families of their own, and will stop being influenced by their mother."

I said to Razi, "All right, you go and have dinner with them tomorrow. But just this once."

Razi went outside to sit in the garden and calm down. A short while later, still agitated, he came back into the kitchen, picked up his briefcase, which was packed with documents, and said, "I'm going to my parents. I'll be sleeping at their place tonight." He left the house, slamming the door behind him.

I watched through the kitchen window as he went to his jeep, opened the back door and put the briefcase on the back seat. Then he opened the driver's door, hesitated, turned, and saw me looking at him. He looked back, and suddenly slammed the car door, and walked briskly back to the house.

"Nicole, we need to talk," he said as he came into the kitchen.

"All right," I said. "As long as you keep your voice down." We walked through to the lounge and I and sat on the sofa in front of him.

"You can't tell anyone else about what you're going to hear from me now. My father's worried that I've told you too much as it is."

"Too much? What is it you weren't supposed to tell me?" I said angrily. "We're husband and wife, aren't we? Didn't you promise me there would be no secrets between us?"

"The company's not in good shape. All the money we had has been spent developing this new technology," he said quietly. "I have to raise more money; otherwise, everything will have been for nothing."

"I know."

"Have you seen the latest financial reports? The company's expenses have exceeded our initial budgetary plans by thirty-four percent. That means the company will have to raise at least another twenty-three million dollars to finish developing the software."

"Then maybe you should replace the development team?" I suggested.

Razi answered quickly, his tone patient. "I wish it was that easy; Alex is manipulating me."

"What? I had no idea ..."

"I'll find a solution, don't worry. Once I raise the money, everything will sort itself out."

"What about looking for additional partners?" I asked.

"That would considerably dilute our holdings, and we could lose control of the company," Razi replied.

"But what would happen with Lock-space?"

"My dad and I have decided to go all the way."

"What do you mean?"

"No one needs to know what's happening in our company other than us."

"Why are you telling me all this?"

"I'm merely informing you," Razi said a little stiffly.

"You're informing me, but you won't allow me to report it, as my job requires me to. So, how does this work exactly?" I suddenly understood that I was about to get into deep trouble because of the Zonenberg family. I didn't bother to hide it, saying, "Wait, now I understand everything. You're doing all this so you'll have someone to blame if it all goes wrong. Once it was Dr. Golan, and now it's me."

Razi looked at me in silence. I could see he hadn't expected me to react as I had.

"I'm going to summon a board meeting. You can explain everything to them," I said. I stood up.

My husband stared at me, obviously surprised and dismayed. "Who do you think you are, telling me you're going to call a board meeting?" he hissed. "You're just jealous! You don't want me to be successful, that's obvious!"

"I joined the company as a CFO because I trusted you and I wanted to help you. I've been trying to stay calm, despite the constant insults you've thrown at me. You cheated Lock-space, and then made me an accomplice because you wanted a scapegoat in case your deceit was ever exposed. And now you have the nerve to come in here and tell me fairy stories?" I tried to calm down, but simply couldn't. "Don't you think you've crossed a line? Do you think you're dealing with some kind of an idiot?"

"You'll get nothing from my work with your defeatist attitude," he grumbled. "I'm making superhuman efforts to take care of our children's future — and you're standing in my way." He paused for a moment, then continued, "I don't know what's happened to you, or when you lost your trust in me."

"Don't you understand, Razi, I've never been interested in any of this? I didn't marry you for money, and I didn't join the company because of the new technology. I joined it because of you, to help you. I sacrificed a successful career and left my labor market for your private company."

Razi went on as if he hadn't heard a word I'd said. "I've

thought of everything," he said, his voice icy. "And I've decided that unless you fall in line with me, you won't be able to stay in the company."

"You're going to go to jail and mess up our lives," I said. I suddenly felt completely empty and disheartened.

'You're the one who's messing everything up," he yelled at me.

"I want a divorce." I said. "I'm not willing to risk my integrity and reputation for your sake."

"That's never going to happen," he replied vehemently. "So, forget about it!"

"Go to hell," I shouted at him. I snatched up my cell-phone and ran to our children's bedroom. I made sure the children hadn't been wakened by our shouting, and thought how lucky it was that Itay was sleeping at his father's house. I shut myself in the room and called Anna. When she answered, I spoke to her in hushed tones. I thought Razi had almost crossed a red line into violent behavior during that argument, and I was afraid things might go from bad to worse.

Razi's screaming voice, accompanied by the sound of things being thrown and smashed and broken, went on outside the room, further fueling my fears.

When Anna heard my brief version of the events of the last few hours, she suggested I go to her place imme-diately and wait there until Razi left. I accepted her offer, but then a heavy silence settled on the house. When I cautiously unlocked the door and left the room, I found Razi gone. Walking through the house, I discovered the laptop I had received from work, the one that contained all my personal information, was also gone.

Despite my worries about the computer, I felt relieved for a moment. The possibility that Razi would stay away from the house, even if just for a few days, until I figured out what to do next, seemed like a very good thing, a relief.

I went into the kitchen and found that Razi had smashed many valuable objects during his insane fit of rage. I was amazed to discover among the broken fragments, parts of the priceless Rosenthal porcelain set we had received as a wedding present. Razi knew how precious that set had been to me.

I photographed the fragments, one photo after another, then swept them away with tears in my eyes.

Why had I agreed to join the company? I knew that going to work there would soil our relationship and disrupt our family. The company had always been a sensitive issue, but I had never imagined Razi would go as far as he had to be successful, even hiding the technology's failures and oversights, and endangering the funds and reputation of his business partners. Even being prepared to let Lock-space launch the satellite with erroneous software that could cause hundreds of millions of dollars in damages did not seem to disturb him.

The following morning, a messenger arrived with a large envelope and had me sign for it. I sat on the living room sofa, sipped my chamomile tea, tore the envelope open, and looked at the letter. I sat and stared at it for long minutes, finding it hard to believe it was real. My entire body started to tremble with anger, frustration and helplessness.

I had never been in a situation where someone had put a 'freeze' on my bank account. Indeed, no one had ever had any reason to take any such action against me. I had always been meticulously careful in paying all my bills and taxes on time, even the few parking tickets I had received over the years.

Cold sweat beaded my forehead, as I called my bank only to hear the assistant bank manager tell me, sympathetically, that a freeze had indeed been imposed on my personal bank account.

"Unless you take care of this quickly," she said, "you will have to return your credit cards and checkbooks."

The letter also included a notice of immediate termination of my employment. I wondered when Razi had had the time to plan all this. It appeared the Zonenberg family lawyers worked at the most unconventional hours; there was no other way to explain the fact that a mere few hours after my argument with Razi, I received an envelope containing such dramatic documents.

I was waiting for Itay in the living room when he came home from school. I knew that I couldn't hide all of the damage Razi had done in the house, and that I'd have to explain what had happened. This was the second time a man he was attached to had left our home, and I was afraid this might adversely affect his future relationships.

"Sometimes people experience different moods, some

of them extreme," I explained to Itay. "And what happened yesterday was one of those times. Razi and I had a little argument. And sometimes, after an argument, a person might need some time on their own to calm down. It's happened to me in the past, and will probably happen to you too one day. There's no reason to worry. I'm sure Razi will come home soon and apologize." I was trying to tell Itay some of what had happened without telling him everything, and that was the gentlest way I could think of.

"Mom, you're always going to stay with me, right? No matter what happens."

"Of course," I said. I was suddenly filled with sadness and sorrow for what was happening to him … to us … and hugged him. I knew Razi's fits of rage had become too extreme; normal people didn't get so violently angry. I knew it was unhealthy for children to be raised in such a charged atmosphere. I was torn between my concern for Itay's emotions and the anger I felt at Razi; an anger made even worse by the fact that I couldn't understand the real reason for his abrupt departure. I couldn't understand why he was so afraid of telling the truth.

My next telephone call was to Nitai, my lawyer.

"I'm sorry, Nicole, but this letter is a declaration of war," he said emphatically. "As they say in French, *a la guerre comme a la guerre*, you need to do whatever it takes. Go to the police," he suggested. "File a complaint of assault against Razi. Together with that, we'll file a request with the court this very day, asking for a restraining order for as much time as possible. Then we can devise our strategy and move forward."

The word 'assault' echoed in my head. I wanted to expel that word from inside me, deny it, spit it out. I went out into the garden, and sat on the bench taking in some welcome fresh air. Then, with disquiet in my heart, I walked back to the living room. Nitai was still on the phone, still insistent. "You said he deliberately drove recklessly on the highway, and that he smashed things in the house. That is violence any way you look at it. You have to go to the police."

But this was Razi we were talking about, for God's sake. He was my man! How had we reached a situation where I had become a victim of violence? I just couldn't understand it. I told Itay and the babysitter I was going out. I needed to clear my mind, and try and make an intelligent decision, I drove out to the neighborhood country club and sat where we had first met. I wanted to remember that first look between us; the first smile that I had found so attractive and that had invited me to be close to him.

'I'm not going to fight him,' I thought to myself. *'I didn't fight for what was due to me when I divorced Danny, and I'm not going to fight Razi either. Certainly not while we have two small children.'*

I called Razi and told him, "We need to talk."

"You're not coming back to the company," he said immediately.

"That's all right. I would prefer we stop working together."

"And I'm not going to remove the freeze from your bank account. Next, you're going to be faced with a lawsuit from the company for breaching your fiduciary duty."

"Razi, you're hurting Matan and Shiri, they're both still babies."

"You're at it again?" he said angrily. "Using my own children against me? You manipulator. I divorced Dorit for your sake and you ruined my life!"

The tone and style of his words both insulted and surprised me. I could hardly believe he was acting with such coldness, as if I was a complete stranger to him.

"Razi, you're twisting everything up." I made my tone as serene and calm as I could, despite his insults. "What is it, Razi? Is this related to the technology? To your ex-wife? Why do we need wars, lawyers and bank freezes? Can't you see we'll both lose this way?"

"Why? Just because! You should ask yourself why!" His voice rose in outrage. "You are ungrateful and greedy, that's why! And I'm never coming back to you after you threw me out of the house with nothing but my underwear."

"I never threw you out of the house, you left ..."

"Don't wait for me, it's over between us," he said, and disconnected the call. Shocked, unable to even move, I just stared at the phone.

Chapter 30

That night, I needed sleeping pills to fall asleep. One thing I had determined was that I would show no sign of weakness. Razi had chosen this path, and I had no choice but to react — and in full force.

In the morning I checked my cellphone. There were no messages from Razi.

I called Eilam, my younger brother, who lived nearby. I had to unburden myself and consult with someone close. Someone who could tell me how to tell my parents about what had happened, and my decision to go all the way and get a divorce, to escape the insanity of the Zonenberg family.

My parents were old and not in good health, and I was afraid such bad news might harm their health even further. When my brother came over and I had told him my side of the story, he told me, to my amazement, that he too had had a violent episode involving Razi. It had happened when I had first introduced Razi to the family. He had made such a good impression that my brother took him on as a business partner. However, their partnership had ended very quickly and amicably, or at least that was what I had thought. Now, Eilam told me that a vocal argument had developed between them, one that quickly led to blows being exchanged, or, to be more precise, to blows that Razi had dealt my brother. Only my brother's wish to keep the peace in the family had made him hide the entire affair from me. It explained why my brother and his family had recently been avoiding family gatherings that we attended.

"God," I muttered. I was embarrassed and felt my stress levels rising again. "I'm so sorry for having introduced this violent creature into our lives."

"Don't be sorry, Nickie." Eilam hugged me. "You have two wonderful children by him. Now you have to take care of their future."

"The situation has become even more complicated," I said, and I told him about Razi's deal with Lock-space.

"What? Is he insane?"

"He sold them technology that doesn't exist."

"What?"

"And it turns out the launch date for the Lock-space satellite is very soon."

"He'll go to prison, and you along with him — you're the company's CFO. You'll never find another job in the field," Eilam said.

"I know."

Eilam shifted in his seat uncomfortably. As a little girl, I had always laughed at him when he was busy thinking. His body would sway as if he was dancing in a daze.

"So, what should I do? Just sit and wait?"

"Are you crazy! Of course not. If he wants to go to prison, so be it, but you have to clear your name."

"How?"

"Can you contact Lock-space and tell them what's going on?"

"It's not that simple. I am contractually obligated to be loyal to the company. I should be safe as long as I don't actually violate that contract. If I somehow thwart the deal, I would be hit with a lawsuit that would ruin me."

"Then you don't have a choice; you have to summon the board of directors."

"He's going to go crazy," I replied. I felt suddenly hopeless. "I'm in a bind here."

Real concern showed in my brother's eyes. "Just make sure he doesn't come back home," he said.

*

The next morning, I met my lawyer, Nitai, in his office.

"I've managed to cancel the foreclosure order," he said, "so you don't have to worry about that anymore."

'At last!' I thought, *'Some good news.'*

"I think the worst is behind us now," he said. "Now that Razi has been served with a restraining order, he'll never dare come back to your home."

"I'm not sure this is where the story ends," I said. "I have a feeling I'm in over my head with him."

"Why is that?"

"We live in a rented apartment that belongs to his father. I'm working for his company in a position that makes me the easiest target if they need a scapegoat. It's like being the finance minister for a corrupt government," I said.

"Are you sure there's no chance the two of you will be able to patch things up?" he asked.

I shook my head. "I'm afraid not. Razi's behavior has been gradually getting stranger and stranger. His fits of anger have become harsh and violent. In the past, they used to be brief and he would quickly apologize and then act as if nothing had happened. But lately, they last longer, and after each fit, he goes quiet, becomes withdrawn. He just sits on the living room sofa holding his head in his hands. He looks so depressed and preoccupied that when my mother last saw him, she said, 'Poor Razi, he's been working too hard. I can see he's exhausted by all these frequent trips to far-off destinations. I just hope he won't collapse altogether.'"

Then I added, "As far as I'm concerned, our relationship has become destructive, not to mention the fact that we ... we ... don't have intimate relations anymore, and there's not even a hint of the passion we had at the beginning of our relationship. I'm also afraid for our children. They've seen how he's been behaving and they could be in danger too."

"You do understand that instituting any kind of legal process against the Zonenberg family could prove to be difficult in the extreme, both financially and emotionally?"

"I have no choice, and I'm not afraid of it," I said defiantly. "The truth will triumph!" I declared.

When I got home, I prepared the letter I intended to

send to the board of directors. I labored over it for a long time; I wanted it to be right in every sense. I sent a copy to my attorney, Nitai, so he could go over it and rephrase the legal passages. We were under no illusions. We knew if it wasn't absolutely correct, legally and factually, it could be used against me in the future. After Nitai had edited the letter, he told me, "Send the letter to Razi and see what his reaction is before you send it to the rest of the board members."

I did as he suggested and waited nervously for Razi's response. I paced the house restlessly, until the phone rang and Razi's number was visible on the screen.

"Nicole!" he shouted, rage in his voice. "What the hell is this letter I've had from your lawyer? Have you gone crazy?"

I let him finish and then said calmly, "Copies of that letter are going to be sent to all board members in one hour. The only way you can stop it is by sending me a letter, properly written and signed, confirming that I had nothing to do with your personal or company failures."

He laughed without humor. "I've got news for you, Nicole. The letter has already been sent to the board members."

"What?"

"I sent it myself," he said.

"Why?"

"To show them why the company needs to file a lawsuit against you immediately. Nicole, this attempt to blackmail me won't work. This letter will cost you a lot of money."

"Razi…"

He disconnected the call. I dialed his number, but the call was forwarded straight to voicemail.

Half an hour later, Shraga Zonenberg called me.

"Nicole?"

"Yes."

"I need you to vacate the house by the end of the week. You've got four days," he said laconically.

"All right," I answered coolly. I was not too upset. It was in keeping with the way the Zonenbergs operated and I had been expecting the call. I had already made arrangements.

I walked through the rooms in the house and thought about how the dream had blown up in my face. All I had wanted was love, a warm and happy home, and lots of children. Now I was left with nothing but my children. I had listened to and suffered Razi's anger without fighting back for too long. As I walked, I allowed my own anger to take root. It was in those minutes that I chose to fight, and I started planning the moves that would see me emerge from this whirlwind of trouble as a new and stronger woman. I decided that from that moment on, I would manage this breakup with Razi as a businesswoman, not as his wife.

Before I did anything else, I wanted to talk to someone who was familiar with the Zonenberg family, someone who could give me some guidance about how to handle them and their devious ways. I could think of no one better than Olga, the late scientist's wife, who had also suffered at the hands of that family.

I called her.

"Olga?"

"Da."

As soon as I heard her voice, the dam broke and the tears began to flow. I cried a deep well of anger, mainly over the humiliation I had been subjected to, over the fact that my dream of a blissful life was gone, destroyed by Razi and his lies. I cried for Shiri and Matan having been born into this kind of reality, and I cried because I had been foolish enough to fall in love with a man who had cheated and deceived me, from the moment I had met him.

"Nicole, calm down," she said firmly.

"All right. Sorry. I'm all right now." I said between sobs. "I just had to let my feelings out, but that's it now. It's over. I won't be shedding any more tears over Razi Zonenberg!"

"What is over?"

"Razi is. No more Razi. It's over. Even though he's still the father of Matan and Shiri, the baby I recently gave birth to," I muttered.

"It's about time," she said, and I could hear the relief in her voice. "So, at last you're ready?" she asked.

"For what?"

"For getting what we deserve."

"What do we deserve?"

"The Lock-space launch is going to happen in one month," she said confidently, demonstrating her familiarity with everything that had been going on in the company.

"I know," I said, "but how do you know that?"

She laughed shortly. "I have been constantly monitoring Razi and his family. What, you thought I'd let it all go?"

"And will they manage to have the new technology ready in time?" I asked. I was intrigued and wanted Olga to tell me more. I was thinking she might know things I was not aware of.

"That depends," she answered briefly.

"Depends on what?" I was still trying to understand.

"On us," Olga replied in a satisfied tone.

"I think we should meet," I said. "So I can tell you about everything that's been going on lately."

Olga agreed immediately.

*

The following day, Olga and I met in a small café not far from her house. I told her everything that had been happening from my point of view, and she told me she wanted to recruit me to help her in her mission. She said that Alex was now working with her. He had met with Razi and, per her request, had recorded the meeting.

"That recorded conversation could help us with Razi and his family, if and when we get to that stage," she said.

Chapter 31

Before she played the recording for me, Olga told me how Alex had called Razi and told him he needed to meet and speak with him urgently. Razi had rejected his request, claiming he was too busy. But when Alex had insisted, and said that the meeting had to do with the development of the technology and the satellite launch, Razi had quickly agreed.

From what Alex told Olga, the meeting had started with Razi sitting patronizingly behind his gleaming executive desk, staring at his computer screen, and only occasionally throwing a glance at Alex, in an attempt to avoid meeting his eyes.

Alex, for his part, told Razi about everything that had been bothering him.

"Now, listen to the recording," Olga said. She pressed the 'play' button on the recording device and I heard Alex's voice speaking in quiet, measured tones.

"You know that Dr. Golan was my lecturer at the university? Well, when I finished my studies, he took me on as an intern and we worked together for two years to finish his patent."

"I didn't know. But why is that important now, Alex?" asked Razi.

"He taught me everything," Alex continued. "And

when I finished my internship, he recruited me to LSB Defense Technologies. He was so happy when you invited him to become a partner in the company. He thought he'd finally be able to utilize what he had been working on for years."

"The patent doesn't work," said Razi.

"It does," Alex said firmly.

"You've been telling me that for several months," Razi said, "and I want to believe you, but you keep getting into trouble with all these bugs. How long have you been working with me? A year? A year and a half?"

"Something like that."

"Do you have any idea how much money I've invested? Millions. I gave you a full team, I tried to find you similar technologies, in fact I've done everything I could possibly do, but you still haven't been able to produce a finished product."

Alex said nothing for a moment. I imagined how Razi must have been looking at him helplessly, his face tortured, realizing he had been trapped.

Olga paused the recording for a moment and said, "That was when Alex realized he had to take advantage of the moment, and carry out our plan."

She pressed the 'play' button again. Razi was speaking.

"Do you know a launch date has been set already? That Lock-space's engineers have sent us a list of questions? It won't be long before they realize they have the wrong technology, that our software doesn't work. And that, Alex, puts me in a world of trouble,"

Alex said nothing. He simply allowed Razi to go on talking in the hope that he might let slip more secrets he had been hiding.

"Tell me, what do you need, more money for development? More engineers? Change your entire team? For God's sake Alex, I'm depending on you."

"Razi," I'm leaving," Alex said assertively.

"What?"

"I'm sorry," Alex replied, his tone more relaxed.

"Have you gone crazy?" Razi almost shrieked the words so loudly that I imagined the whole office must have heard him.

Adi, the secretary, must have called to ask if everything was all right, because I heard the telephone ringing and then Razi was shouting, "Not now, Adi, not now!"

Then Alex said, "This is Golan's patent, he's the one who should have been here. I can't do this to him!"

"He killed himself!" Razi lost his what little had remained of his temper.

"You took it from him," Alex said flatly, then added, "I think you should talk to Nicole." I heard the door opening and slamming. Alex had left the room.

*

I had been home for a few hours after my meeting with Olga when Razi called me. I didn't answer at first, but he kept calling and calling. Eventually, I answered.

"Yes, Razi."

"You backstabbing traitor! What's your connection to Alex?"

"Oh, we're longtime friends," I said, smiling.

"Longtime friends? You barely spoke to each other when you worked here! Now you're suddenly longtime friends?"

"Some friendships develop out of a mutual interest. You should know that better than anyone."

"Nicole, he's left the company. Do you realize what you've done?"

"He's gone because staying didn't feel right to him. Because he's finally realized who, what, you really are!"

"It's because of you! You tried to come between me and the board of directors, and now you've turned my development manager against me. Do you realize we won't have any technology for the Lock-space launch without him? Do you understand what that means? Do you want to ruin me completely?" The last sentence came out in a pleading whine. It was the first time I had ever heard him talk like that.

"What goes around comes around," I said. "And nothing lasts forever." I was adding fuel to the fire. There was a silence between us for a long moment, then I said, "We need to talk. Be here at noon." And I hung up.

When I told Nitai, my lawyer, I had told Razi to meet me at home, he said I'd be better off meeting him in a public place. Razi could be dangerous if he 'blew a fuse', and I shouldn't take any unnecessary risks. I agreed and called Razi back.

A few hours later, we sat in the neighborhood café where we had gone the first time we met. Razi looked as if he hadn't slept for a week. As soon as he sat down, another woman joined us. Razi looked up in surprise.

The woman looked directly at Razi. "Do you know who I am?" she asked him. He didn't recognize her.

"No," he said.

'Had Olga really changed so much, in such a short period of time?' I wondered, my heart wrenching for her pain and loss.

"Would you like a glass of water?" I asked Razi.

"No," he said again, still looking at the woman with the red-dyed hair.

"Perhaps you should ask your father. He knows me. He knew me well enough to come to my house the day after the *Shiva* and steal my husband's stocks," she told him.

"Olga Golan," he said, obviously startled.

"Olga Golan," she agreed grimly.

"What are you doing here? I'm here to discuss intimate matters with my wife. Why have you joined us?"

Olga and I were sitting next to each other, facing Razi on the other side of the table. Razi and Olga were staring into each other's eyes. I felt the moment was right, that this was the opportunity to finally tell him what was in my heart.

"Razi," I said, jerking his attention from Olga back to me. "I loved you, and you took advantage of me. Now, I understand that I was simply the excuse you needed to convince your parents you wanted to divorce Dorit. You wooed me partly because of that, and partly because of Olga. You arranged for me to become your personal CFO. You thought I'd do anything for you, even if it meant risking my professional license, thus providing you with a scapegoat you could accuse of negligence if, and when, things went wrong."

His face hardened. "None of this will help you, Nicole. It's over between us. The lawsuit against you is on its way." Even now he couldn't stop threatening me.

I tapped my cellphone screen and said, "I want to read you the email I've prepared with the advice of my lawyer. An email I am about to send to Lock-space. I'm asking them to make the proper examinations to ensure they're getting what they paid for."

Razi's face darkened even more. "Don't you dare," he said, threat in his voice.

"So, you would prefer to provide them with technology that doesn't work?"

"If Alex hadn't left the company, the bug in the code would have been corrected," he said.

"Alex won't be coming back to work," Olga said. She looked at him and I could see the contempt in her eyes. "But the corrected code is right here." She took a USB flash drive from her purse and waved it at Razi, a triumphant smile on her face.

"What? How?" Razi muttered. I watched as different emotions chased one another across his face. Anger, fear, and finally, alarm, as he realized that this time the tables had been properly turned, and that now he was utterly dependent on the scientist's wife.

"Did Alex tell you about the relationship he had with Giora?" Olga asked, and added, "He's a good guy, Alex, he's got decent values."

Understanding dawned on Razi's face, "So, all those development bugs were because of you? This past year, all that money spent for nothing..." he looked at her and was silent.

"It was my money, my husband's," Olga said coolly, her face set in absolute determination. Her whole body started trembling, as if all the long months of anger, frustration and grief had been stored in her body, and only now was she releasing them after her long war with the Zonenberg family. A war during which she had also been searching for the real reason behind her husband's death.

"I'll destroy you," Razi's features were contorted with rage. He stood suddenly, his chair clattering back noisily. Despite the red heat in his face, he had the cold look of a killer.

"You see?" I was alarmed, but I tried to keep calm and talk logically. "It's exactly because of this kind of outburst that Lock-space should know there's a bug in the system, one that you can't find a solution for without the code Olga has, and without Alex. I suggest you calm down. You and your family have gotten too used to being able to patronize and manage everyone, but now you need to ask yourself what you can possibly do in this situation.

You're down and Olga's up." I looked up at him with more equanimity than I felt. "So, you'd better come to your senses," I finished.

"Nicole," he said to me urgently. "It's all because of her, don't you see?" Razi blurted out in desperation, "I told you she was crazy from the very first moment."

This was his way of trying to weasel out of a situation he couldn't control, by putting the blame on Olga.

"Razi, do you want to realize your dream? Do you want the technology for Lock-space?"

Razi was silent as he thought about my words. Then he realized he was cornered and didn't have too many choices left.

"I assume that's a yes, then," I said. "Come to Attorney Yaakobi's office tomorrow to sign the paperwork for Olga's compensation."

He still didn't say anything.

"Bring your family lawyer too. You're going to need him."

"Why?"

"Because there's another condition to all this. We, you and I, are going to get divorced in a dignified, respectable way. A way that will guarantee our children's financial future."

Razi said nothing more. He simply turned and stalked out of the café.

When he had gone, Olga stood up and said, "You won't ever regret doing this. Trust me, most of Razi's business trips abroad, especially to the Far East, have been fake.

He has dark sides and many secrets. He never abandoned his … adventures from the time he lived in America. On the contrary, in the past, he managed to drag Dorit into going along with what he wanted to do, and even now, he still does what he wants, but he's been including the flavors of the Orient."

She, too, left the café, leaving me sitting alone at the table.

*

The following day, fashionably late as usual, dressed in a business suit and wearing a tough, uncompromising expression, I arrived in Attorney Yaakobi's office.

Nitai, my attorney, was with me, along with Attorney Shimshoni, who specialized in family law. Razi and Shraga arrived with their lawyers, who were known as the best in their field. As befitted the Zonenberg family, who regularly bullied and silenced people by intimidation, they hired the most expensive lawyers in the country to scare off anyone who dared to oppose them.

The office secretary led us all into the lavish conference room that had a magnificent view of the Tel Aviv beach.

Attorney Yaakobi, who was representing Olga, sat at the head of the table while I, Olga, and my lawyers, sat on one side, the Zonenbergs and their attorneys on the other.

"From this moment on, I will be managing this meeting," Attorney Yaakobi intoned. "No one will interrupt while someone else is speaking. I demand that this meeting, despite the emotional baggage carried by each of the parties, be conducted matter-of-factly, so we won't need to prolong it beyond the allotted time." Attorney Yaakobi spoke in a sonorous, assertive voice. He looked pointedly around the table, almost daring anyone to contradict him. Satisfied, he started reading the main points he'd prepared for discussion off the screen hanging on the wall.

When he had finished laying out the meeting's objectives, he added, "This meeting will be terminated once the guiding principles of the detailed agreement have been agreed upon and signed. The final agreement document will be handed to you in one week," he said, turning his eyes to the Zonenberg family's attorneys.

Olga and I both felt confident and calm. We realized that now, all the trump cards were finally in our hands, and the Zonenbergs had nothing much left to mislead and intimidate us with.

Though Olga and I felt self-assured, the atmosphere in the room was tense and rife with anger, and hostile looks, like malevolent lasers, were constantly directed at us from the Zonenberg family.

When Attorney Yaakobi presented our demands, Razi interrupted rudely. He said, "I'm not interested in divorcing Nicole. I love my family. All I want is for Nicole to agree to the separation of our shared reports to the tax authorities."

When I heard Razi's new and illogical request, I immediately replied, "The only chance you have of going on hiding the double, triple, and perhaps even quadruple, lives you've been living, is to grant me an uncontested divorce and make me your ex-wife. I refuse your demand." I was still calm and unruffled, and I felt only uncompromising anger at Razi's words.

"The question here isn't whether or not you are interested in divorcing Nicole, Razi," Attorney Yaakobi said to clarify, beyond doubt, that we weren't there to settle everything, but to reach a signed agreement that would be acceptable to all parties. "We will, however, leave this meeting with a divorce agreement that will be admissible in a court of law. An agreement that will not give you the option of refusing to giving Nicole a divorce," he added emphatically.

When Attorney Yaakobi had finished presenting the data in our possession, and the principles Olga and I were not willing to compromise on, a long silence settled on the conference room.

"I want a few moments to consult with my attorneys," Shraga said eventually and received Attorney Yaakobi's consent.

Shraga and Razi left the room for a brief consultation with their lawyers that lasted longer than it was reasonable to expect.

The rest of us, left in the conference room, used the time to stretch our legs or make personal, unrelated telephone calls. I needed the break to gather my strength for what I knew would be a harsh continuation of the meeting — and to make sure I gained my objective.

At the end of the recess, Razi, Shraga and their lawyers filed back into the room without even glancing at Olga or me. Razi and Shraga let their attorneys speak and sum up their offer. First, they tried to dissuade us from tying the divorce agreement to the other issues discussed in the meeting, claiming the future of our small children shouldn't be decided in a business meeting, and that we should give this crucial decision the proper attention it required in a separate session.

"No chance!" I and Attorney Yaakobi said together.

The meeting ended satisfactorily for both Olga and I, with all the guiding principles of the agreement signed by the relevant parties.

Additionally, Olga had put another condition in the agreement, that of the guaranteed future employment of Alex, and his financial security within SEG, both in the near future and after the company was sold or additional investors added.

Attorney Yaakobi insisted the transfer of the code in Olga's possession to SEG would only go ahead after Razi and Shraga had transferred fifteen percent of the company's stock to Olga. This transfer was in addition to the monetary compensation she was demanding, and would allow her to supervise their integrity, become a board member, and, in the future, influence the company's conduct.

It took about a month to finalize all the agreements.

*

When the detailed divorce agreement was ready, Attorney Shimshoni summoned me to his office to sign it.

"Nicole," he intoned gravely, "your future and the future of your children are anchored to the agreement you're about to sign. It's important for me to review the agreements reached after much strenuous effort. In the agreement, it has been determined that you and your children will continue to reside in Shraga's house in Tzahala without paying rent until Shiri turns twenty-one. After that, the house will be registered in the children's names."

"Additionally," Attorney Shimshoni continued, "it has been agreed that Razi will pay you a monthly alimony of ten thousand N.I.S., and will also share additional expenses related to the raising of the children, so that the lifestyle you've been accustomed to will not be harmed. Is everything thus far clear and acceptable to you? And will you sign this agreement and set out on a new path?" he asked, meeting my eyes and, holding a pen out to me.

"Of course," I answered, and smiled, for the first time in a long time. I felt an immense sense of relief as I took the pen from him and signed, in his presence, both the agreement and the statement in which I declared I willingly accepted all their terms and conditions. I thanked Attorney Shimshoni and shook his hand.

Despite the long and wearying journey that I had taken with Razi, I now felt more optimistic, full of hope and stronger than ever before.

I walked out of Attorney Shimshoni's office, and into a new life.

Acknowledgements

I wish to thank **Orly Krauss-Weiner**, for the literary adaptation and perfect collaboration, for the support, contribution and patience with which she guided my first steps into the world of writing.

My heartfelt thanks to literary editor, **Amnon Jackont**, for his insightful and important comments, both practical and logical, which significantly contributed to the coherent construction of the plot.

To **Hila Harpak**, copyeditor and second literary editor, for her thoroughness and professionalism.

Many thanks to translator **Yaron Regev**, who I nicknamed "Bionic Eyes", because of his perceptiveness and phenomenal sense of logic.

Yaron was responsible for the book's English translation and also contributed greatly to the Hebrew edition with his insightful and perceptive remarks.

My grateful acknowledgments to **Lidor Greenberg** for his quick responsiveness, patience and attentiveness that led to designing the book's cover in a way that best relayed the book's message.

I would like to thank **'Niv Books' and staff**, and his unflagging attentiveness.

And most of all, I wish to thank **my courageous and supportive children,** who patiently accompanied me on the way to the completion and publication of this book.

Finally, my thanks go out to you —
the readers.

Yours,
Rachel

Manufactured by Amazon.ca
Bolton, ON

14031668R00178